THE TORCHING

THE TORCHING

Olivia Callahan Suspense

Kerry Peresta

First published by Level Best Books 2023

First edition

ISBN: 978-1-68512-323-9

Cover art by Level Best Designs

This book was professionally typeset on Reedsy.
Find out more at reedsy.com

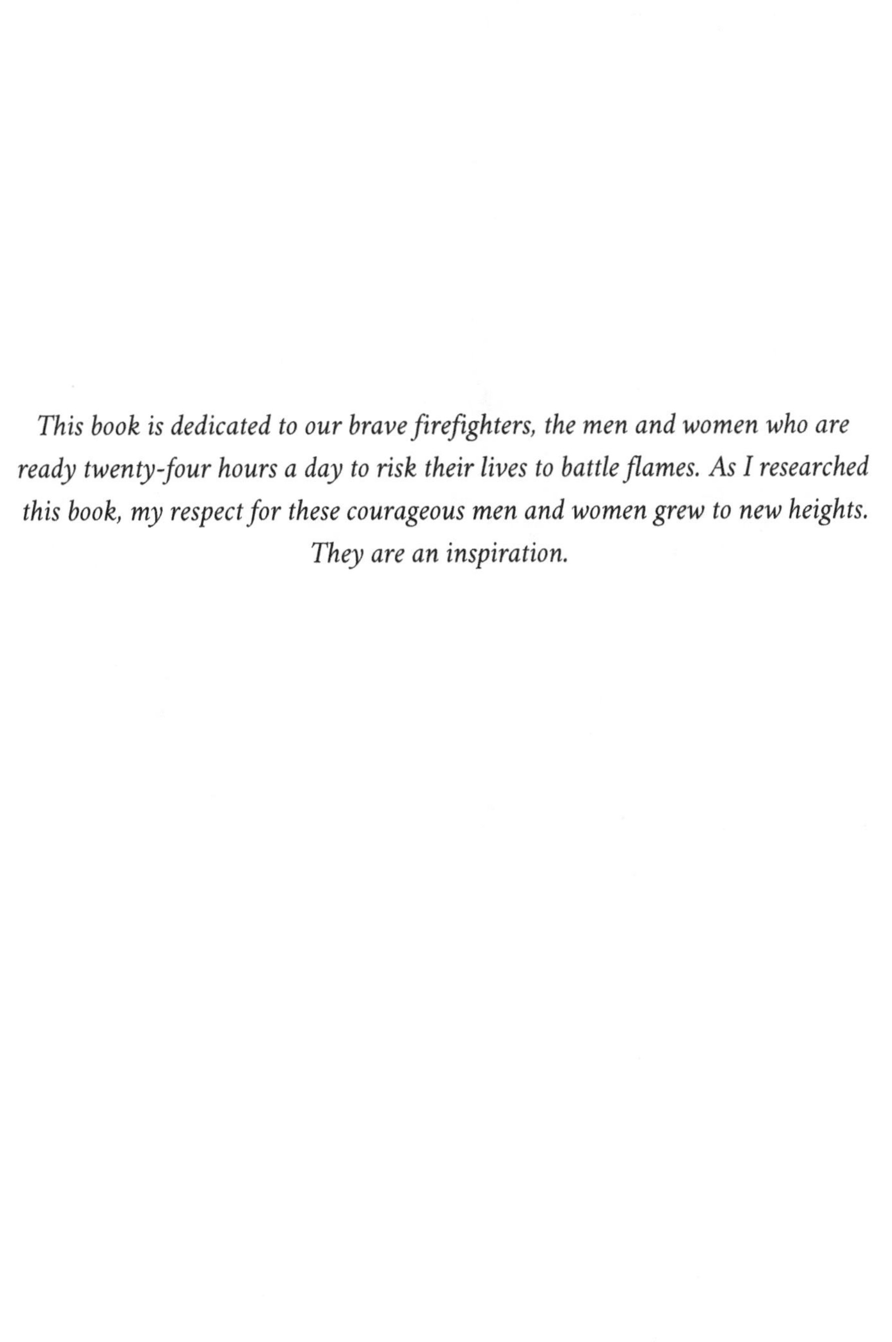

This book is dedicated to our brave firefighters, the men and women who are ready twenty-four hours a day to risk their lives to battle flames. As I researched this book, my respect for these courageous men and women grew to new heights. They are an inspiration.

"The weakest of all things is a virtue
that has not been tested in the fire."

—Mark Twain

Praise for The Torching

"Thumbs up for Kerry Peresta's *The Torching*. I love a good character-driven suspense novel, and Peresta gives us an engaging, multi-layered protagonist in Olivia Callahan. Then she tosses in an arsonist! She had me at the first match strike."—Tracy Clark, author of the Cass Raines Chicago Mystery series and the Det. Harriet Foster series and winner of the 2020 and 2022 Sue Grafton Memorial Award.

"Where there is smoke, there's fire and more for Olivia Callahan. A cold case tests what she knows about her family and mentor. An arsonist is on the loose, leaving calling cards. This is a slow burn of a mystery with several explosive endings. *The Torching* is a book you won't soon forget."—Gabriel Valjan, Agatha and Anthony-nominated author of the Shane Cleary Mystery series

"A contentious election, a crazed arsonist, and long buried family secrets, combine to give newly minted PI Olivia Callahan all she can handle. Loaded with twists and turns, Kerry Peresta's *The Torching* is an unforgettable read!"— Bruce Robert Coffin, award-winning author of the Detective Byron mysteries

"Kerry Peresta has done it again, giving us Olivia Callahan, a complex heroine, who is strong, yet vulnerable, clear-headed one moment, lost in the terrifying fog of traumatic brain injury the next. In *The Torching,* we get to ride along as Olivia battles to rebuild, literally and figuratively, her life and her home, while her murky past continues to throw shadows over her present and future. Tightly written, this one's a heart-pounding page-turner from beginning to end."—Annette Dashofy, award-winning and *USA Today* bestselling author of the Zoe Chambers and Detective Honeywell mystery series

Prologue

February 1979

The smell of the greasy, stench-ridden corridor behind a block of local restaurants made him want to puke.

He ran his hands through his blond, thinning hair and wiped the sweat off his forehead. God, it was hot. He stared at the older man beside him, chain-smoking cigarettes and staring at the ground. An 'untenable situation' that needed resolving, he'd insisted.

Now, here he stood in this godforsaken alley in the middle of the night.

Metal dumpsters piled high with rotting food and leftovers lined the backs of brick buildings. A trio of raccoons picked their way across the asphalt and hoisted themselves inside. Bats performed aerial acrobatics in the dim glow of the single streetlight at the end of the block. Two fat rats scuttled around the dumpsters, enjoying their nightly smorgasbord. The men hid in the dark, careful to avoid the halo emanating from the streetlight. Three stories above, shirts and pants on a clothesline strung between the two buildings flapped in the breeze.

The older man threw down the cigarette and ground it beneath his heel. He stared up into the night sky. "Someone forgot to take in the laundry."

The younger man frowned. "Why'd you need me to come?"

"Wanna make sure I get my money's worth. It's *your* guy."

"I don't know if he's reliable or not. Why do you think?" He jammed his hands in his pockets, pulled his coat collar tighter around his ears. "Cold for February, I'll say that."

"Got a bad feeling about this," the younger man grumbled as he watched a giant cockroach dart across his shoe. "You talked to him, right? Settled on a price? Listen, all I did was give you a name. I didn't need to watch."

"We're in this together, bud." The older man squinted at the back of the building. "It's almost time. The kitchen closes in a few minutes."

Five minutes later, a metal door squealed open. Light from inside the restaurant kitchen split the night. The smell of hot grease floated outside. A man's shadow fell across the steps leading down to the asphalt. He wiped his hands on a white apron before he trotted down the steps, walked around, and leaned against the wall. He pulled a pack of cigarettes out of his pocket and lit it. Took a deep drag. Tilted his head with a contented sigh.

The two men edged further into the blackness, crouching between the dumpsters, anticipating the fateful event scheduled in this rat-infested back street. At the sound of crisp footsteps striding down the alley, the older man chuckled softly.

"He's right on time."

The younger man had trouble controlling the tremble of his hands. He stuck them under his armpits and peered through the shadows to watch the man emerge. He only knew this man through whispers and insinuation.

The footfalls drew closer. The man wore a winter beanie, a black sweatshirt, and jeans. He bounced a crowbar against the side of his leg as he walked. His knuckledusters glinted in the sparse light.

The younger man's eyes bulged. "Knuckles? He's not planning to kill the guy, is he?"

"I told him to make sure he was breathing when he was done. I don't want to *murder* anybody. I only want him to back the hell off. Find another place to live. Maybe another country."

The younger man adjusted his squatting position between the dumpsters. His breath fogged the frigid night air.

"Get a grip on yourself," the older man said.

The kitchen employee casually ran his eyes up and down the crowbar guy as he walked through the alley. "What's up, man? You got a flat tire?"

Without a word, the crowbar guy pulled the ski mask half of the beanie over his face, walked straight toward him, lifted the crowbar, and brought it down on the employee's skull, who dropped like a stone. Cringing and helpless on the ground, the employee's fingers scraped the asphalt as he tried to drag himself away. Blood dripped from his head. His muted cries sputtered into full-fledged howls. Another swing of the crowbar—right across his face—silenced him.

The older man smiled. "There goes his nose."

The younger man cowered between the dumpsters, eyes closed, hands over his ears.

Another crack of bone split the night. An awful groan erupted from the kitchen employee's throat.

"Yessireebob. I believe I got my money's worth. Son, I want to shake your hand." He shoved out his palm.

The younger man stared at it in horror. "I didn't need to see this!" He jumped up. "Let's get out of here!"

The older man swung his arm across the younger man's chest as a blockade. "Let's wait until it's finished."

Five black-clad souls sauntered down the alley. They spotted the crowbar guy, who jerked his chin in the direction of his victim.

The rest of the beatdown was eerily silent except for shoes thudding against flesh and muffled cursing. When they finished, crowbar guy walked to a dumpster and got rid of the crowbar and beanie. He slid off the brass knuckles and put them in his pocket before he threw a lighted pack of matches into the dumpster. When flames appeared, he jerked a thumb toward the street. The group strolled to the end of the alley nice and easy, then split up.

The victim lay on the ground in a pool of blood, an unrecognizable heap of torn flesh, and twisted limbs. The older man crept toward the victim. Placed two fingers on the kitchen employee's neck. "He has a pulse. Let's go," he told his reluctant accomplice.

The dumpster fire exploded. The acrid smell of scorched food and commercial waste permeated the alley.

Sirens screamed. A couple of patrol vehicles rounded the corner.

The men bolted down the block and disappeared into the night.

Chapter One

May 12, 2022

Forty-three years later

"Can't believe we did it, Olivia."

I laughed. "Did what? Survive raising girls?"

Callie waved her hand. "You know what I mean. They're high school graduates. It's been a long road."

"Thank God they're going to the same university. I hope your kid is less adventurous than mine."

Callie grinned. "I don't think you have anything to worry about. Anyway, we always have the option to drag them back home if it doesn't work out."

"I'd rather avoid that option," I replied.

The satisfying notes of the traditional "Pomp and Circumstance" drifted through the air.

My dear friend and I locked eyes.

"I'm sorry your ex couldn't be here to watch his daughter graduate," I patted her shoulder as tears slid down her face.

The royal-blue-gowned students in rows of three abreast strode from the gym onto the grassy field.

Callie slapped the tears off her cheeks. "One of these days, I'll have a decent marriage, and Amy will have a decent stepdad." She jumped to her feet. "There's Amy. Hi, sweetheart," she called.

I made a little tent with my hand and squinted into the afternoon sun. When I found my daughter, Lilly, I started my phone's video function. In the background of the frame, a firetruck screamed out of the station.

"Graham was a good dad, he was just...somewhat addicted to bimbos." I closed out the video and sat down. The two hundred or so graduating seniors took their seats in front of a portable stage.

Callie watched her daughter with laser focus. "At least Monty's out of your life. Isn't his prison sentence now like...what, another twenty years or something? *My* ex-husband sits on my doorstep, upset and weird and demanding that I come back." She grunted. "As if that'll ever happen."

The blare of fire engines tapered off.

"Monty's waiting to see if the prosecutors are going to bother with the accessory charge. He's sitting in the same cell. I'd think they'd at least tack on another ten years, or move him to max security. So far, it's not even made it to court."

A woman with hair coiled into a bird's nest on top of her head glared at us. I adjusted my tush on the cold, metal bleachers and lowered my voice.

"Graham's ego took a hit when you hired me to investigate his...uhh... indiscretions. It'll take time for him to recover. He'll get over it, Callie."

She craned her neck in the direction of the vanishing sirens.

"This must be the third fire in the last month. Have people given up on fire safety? It's not rocket science. Maybe it's an insurance scam."

"I try to avoid the news. For obvious reasons," I replied.

"Whatever," Callie said, returning her attention to the stage. "Even if you don't like being *in* the news, it doesn't mean you have to get off the planet."

I opened my mouth in preparation to fire back that she'd not been the one on the front page of the local paper for weeks, but a silver-haired man in navy slacks and a white shirt walked onto the stage. He and the principal stepped away from the mic to talk.

A hush blanketed the field. My daughter twisted toward me from her chair on the football field. She rounded her eyes, lifted her hands.

My left shoulder blade started to throb, which was *not* a good sign.

I sighed and waited for the shoe to drop. Because, according to Lilly's face, a shoe was definitely dropping.

Callie frowned. "Isn't that the Fire Chief?"

"I don't know, but Lilly's worried."

After another five minutes, the uniformed man tapped the mic to make sure it was live. Each tap rocketed around us like gunfire.

He cleared his throat.

"We've been notified that the fire we've been summoned to is the home of one of our graduating seniors."

I held my breath.

His raspy voice boomed across the field. "Lillian Callahan? Are your parents here?"

My brain lagged a fair amount before the words penetrated.

I jumped to my feet on rubbery legs, slung my purse over my shoulder, and pushed past all the knees in my row. Lilly popped up from her seat and ran, one hand pressed onto the square brim of her cap and her graduation robe flapping open. We met in between the stage and the fifty-yard line and hung onto each other.

Chapter Two

Smoke assailed us halfway up my long, winding driveway. A dingy, gray film coated my windshield. I jabbed the brake to slow down, but my trembling foot slipped off the brake. Lilly gave me a look that broke my heart.

The surging, ballooning smoke hurled itself at us like angry fog. Visibility fell to near zero the longer I drove. I slowed to a crawl. We inched along the lane until the strobing white-and-red lights cut through the smoke. I counted two fire engines and one black SUV on the lane as I approached. A couple of firefighters raced into my house. My door lay on the porch in three pieces, and an axe was propped against the wall. Each firefighter wore oxygen tanks attached to large, anteater-shaped masks. With their cumbersome, reflective-striped protective gear and masks, they looked more suited to step on the moon than inside my beloved Maryland farmhouse.

I brought my car to a shuddering halt.

We stepped out. I put my arm around Lilly.

Vaporous clouds of smoke cloaked my house. A couple of firefighters worked with giant, yellow firehoses. The men had divided themselves into teams, and the muted shouts told me some of them were behind the house. Flames leapt toward the sky from the backside of the roof. I counted six firefighters working on the house that I could see—plus the ones in the back. Tears trickled down my cheeks, and a terrifying thought struck—what about my cat?

"Lilly," I said, my voice shaky, "Where was Riot when you last saw him?"

Lily's face went white. "Mom…"

I grabbed her by the shoulders. "No, no...Riot's smart. He will have found safety. I'll find him. Stay here."

I ran across the yard to a woman dressed in navy slacks and a white shirt with metal glinting on the front and official-looking patches on the arms. "I'm the owner," I yelled over the whump of igniting flames, batting my way through smoke.

She shook my hand and identified herself as the public information officer. "Sorry to meet under these circumstances, but glad you were out of the home. We have it controlled. The team inside is checking to make sure it is contained. As far as we can tell, the seat of the fire is in the attic. Give us thirty minutes, okay? But, ma'am, I'll need you to stay back. Our investigator will be here soon. She'll let you know when it's safe to go inside.

"My cat's in there," I cried. "Can you have someone look for him?"

She spoke into a radio.

The smoke started to let up. Three hoses trained on the roof gushed out torrents of water. The huge flames stretching into the sky began to shrink. Radio chatter stuttered around the space. The firefighters stayed in constant contact, radios slung across their chests with a strap that held a mic.

These guys would not know where to look for Riot.

With an apologetic glance at Lilly, I skirted the trucks, avoided the PIO, and dashed across the yard, up the front porch stairs, and into the house.

"MOM," Lilly wailed through the billowy smoke.

Coughing, I ran inside. "Riot," I screamed. "Riot, I'm here, buddy."

I looked behind the couch. Underneath the dining room table. On top of his cat tree. Underneath the wingback chair. He wasn't in any of his favorite spots. I plowed through the murkiness and melting sheetrock.

A bullhorn blared, "Ma'am. We need you to exit the building." "Now!"

My throat was closing. My eyes stung like crazy. I needed to find him and get the heck out.

I scrambled into the kitchen and opened the lower cupboards, then the uppers. Searched the seats of the barstools, underneath the kitchen table. My heart thrashed like a wrecking ball in my chest. "Riot? I'm here, boy. Come on out," I begged. A timid sound reached my ears. I waited. I heard it again, louder.

A shaggy, orange head appeared on top of the cabinets. I climbed up, grabbed him, and raced out the back door. The backyard firefighter team made group gestures that I interpreted as 'get the hell out of here and let us do our job, ma'am'.

I zigzagged through the first responder obstacle course to my car, blinded by the strobing lights. Lilly spurted fresh tears and held out her arms for Riot. We watched in silence as the flames soared into the sky. After a while, we heard less commotion from the firefighters, and the smoke around us grew white and wispy.

A red-faced PIO barreled toward me. "I need you to stay out of the house until our investigator has completed the investigation."

I wiped my sooty hands on my pants. "Your guys wouldn't have found my cat. Riot would have been scared to death by the way they look. I didn't have a choice."

She told me the fire investigator had arrived, and under no circumstances was I to enter the home without her permission.

Lilly held Riot tight against her chest.

"Thought you hated this cat," I joked.

"Whatever, Mom," she said.

A small, thickset woman with short hair approached.

"Mrs. Callahan?"

"It's Ms. I'm the owner."

"Good news, Ms. Callahan. The rear quadrant of the roof and attic sustained most of the damage. The firefighters are checking the ceiling of the second floor now for hot spots. I think you got lucky."

"It didn't spread?"

She smiled her assurances. "They're going to clean up here and have a final look around. They'll let me know when it's safe to go in." She stuck out a hand. "I'm Tasha Jackson, fire investigator. I work with these goofballs." She grinned.

I shook her hand.

In the background, firefighters wrapped hoses. A couple of them worked the hydrant. Another walked the perimeter of my home. Instead of the burble of radios, most of them had ditched the headgear. A man got out of the black SUV and strode toward the PIO. After a few minutes of speaking with her, he approached me. He introduced himself as the Battalion Chief, told me he was sorry the fire had interrupted such an important occasion, and if there was anything they could do...to call the PIO. She wiggled her fingers at me, then went to talk to the camera crews and TV reporters that had crashed the scene. His expression somber, the Battalion Chief handed me his business card.

"If you need them, Red Cross services are available for three nights at a local motel, and $600 gift cards for each displaced person. Please contact your insurance company immediately, they'll do their own investigation."

I gave him a blank look and took his card.

"Our investigator will talk about next steps, and ask you some questions to complete her report. Please remember not to go inside the area of damage alone, Ms. Callahan. Do you have somewhere to stay?"

With a sigh, I glanced over my shoulder toward my compact office on the corner of Worthington Avenue and my property. I could stay in the office guest bedroom, and Lilly could stay at my neighbor's house. "Yeah. We do. Is the...do you think the bedrooms in my house are okay? Can we get some clothes?"

He yelled a couple of names and asked them to check. They walked toward my house. The porch that stretched across the front of my house looked as if someone couldn't decide whether to drown it or blow it up.

The public information officer waved off the reporters as she walked in my direction. One of the firefighters stared at me so long it became uncomfortable. I groaned. Was he one of them? A cult fan of the 'Mercy's Miracle' persona? Why had I thought it was a good idea to write a book? After the publisher's marketing department flew me all over the country for publicity events, the book hit the bestseller list and stayed there. The story of my survival and struggle to re-create my life had developed a rabid following.

I gave the firefighter a hard stare. He dropped his gaze. Reporters screamed questions at me from a distance. The PIO did her best to keep them under control.

I longed for a normal life.

My mind flew back. I closed my eyes, remembering.

The first few days, waking up in the hospital panicked and breathless and unable to move; the second week, when I'd begun to see flickers of light, the third week, when my fingers twitched and hope sprang to life. Neurology interns stealing in and out of my room at odd hours to see the 'miracle' restoration. I remembered my daughters' first visits and the terrified looks on their faces when they realized I didn't remember them. The fourth and fifth weeks, when physical therapists did everything they could to help restore my mobility and speech.

I could still visualize the reporters closing in on me. Waving their microphones in my face before I could even form a coherent sentence. I remembered watching my mom herding my daughters to my room on the fifth floor of the hospital, and the television crews that formed a tight knot around them as they made their way to the entrance of the hospital.

My youngest daughter had burst into my hospital room with an excited smile. "Reporters are dying to talk to you, Mom! Get ready."

I rubbed my eyes and sighed.

Reporters were a plague to be avoided now.

"Olivia? Are you okay?" The PIO looked at me in concern.

I blinked. "Sorry. Yeah. I'm okay."

She held out her cell. "Create contact info for me?"

I entered my number, and my neighbor Callie's, for good measure. The two firefighters that had inspected the bedrooms returned with a thumbs-up. "Bedrooms look good. Stairs are intact."

The PIO smiled at me, tilted her head toward the reporters. "I didn't realize you were *that* Olivia Callahan."

I attempted a smile. She was trying to be nice. She had no idea that I hated the notoriety.

She handed me her card. "If you need *anything*. I mean it." She left.

Lilly put her hand on my shoulder. "Mom? Everybody's leaving. Now what?"

I squeezed my eyes shut. How do I accept this new reality? With reluctance, I opened one eye, then the other.

My beloved front porch was a nightmare zone. Half the roof had caved in, and water dripped from the eaves. It felt like a huge loss. I crossed my arms, thinking.

Though I had few memories of my marriage, I'd been told that my ex, Monty, and I had resurfaced the floor and hand-painted the ceiling. We'd hung the porch swing together. We'd enjoyed swapping stories on the porch we'd designed together. My gaze swept across the front yard and the flowering bushes that I'd planted a decade ago. Some of them were blooming. I smiled. If my flower bushes could continue, oblivious to the destruction…then so could I.

The roar of a fire engine's pulling away jerked me from the ruminations.

With a shaky breath, I told Lilly, "I'm not sure what happens next. We can't stay here for a while, honey. It'll be a few weeks. I'm thinking Callie's for now."

As another fire engine backed out, the arson investigator arched her eyebrows expectantly. "You ready?"

I hooked a thumb at the exiting vehicles. "I was told I can't stay here tonight, so…."

"Yes. It'll be a while before you can move back in. We will do a preliminary report tonight, a more thorough one in the morning. I heard the upstairs is messy, but intact. I can gather you and your daughter some clothes, but you may end up buying new stuff. Smoke's hard to get out."

I gulped in a breath.

Tasha patted me on the shoulder, her spiky, blond tufts somewhat wilted by the smoke still drifting through the air.

Lilly stared at the house. Riot struggled to get out of her arms. She buried her face in his fur. My heart ached for her.

Poor kid hadn't even gotten to graduate with her class, and she'd just been displaced. What must she be feeling? Her phone kept lighting up with texts.

I'd make it up to her, somehow.

I breathed hard in an effort to avoid a full-on sloppy cry.

"How long do you think it'll be before we can get back in?"

Tasha considered the house and crossed her arms. "Procedure dictates I'm first on scene for an Origin and Cause Report. I'll scout around and rule out stuff like electrical, appliance, typical accidental stuff. Lightning in the area. Power outages. That type of thing. I need to go through my checklist of routine questions with you. If it looks accidental, you'll be back in sooner, and it depends on what your insurance company finds, too. Have you contacted them yet? In the meantime, I have an extensive list of agencies you can contact for clean-up and water damage. We need to get that roof patched asap. I have an emergency number you can call. If I find evidence of arson, the police may make this a crime scene. If that happens, their investigators are usually in and out in a day or two. But first things first. Let's get my questions over with. Ready?"

My inner thoughts went wild.

Was I ready?

No! I don't want to rehash the carnage of my labor of love for more than fifteen years. I can't do this. Every board, every window, every door, was painted, sanded, and restored by my ex-husband and me—solid proof that once upon a time, my life worked. I don't want to answer questions about something else in my life that has been reduced to ashes! Memories. My marriage. My identity. All stolen. I thought it was turning around. I had hope. Is my future destined for the ash heap, too?

Tasha's smile was warm as she waited. I liked her. Equal parts compassion and professional.

"We can do it at my office," I said. "It's down there."

She nodded. "I saw it when I drove up. Let's go. It won't take long."

Chapter Three

After a disastrous night of tossing and turning, dreadful nightmares, and crushing heart palpitations, I finally gave up on sleep. Could I not accomplish the simplest thing…like getting my daughter through her high school graduation…without a crisis intervening?

Running my hands through my hair, I trudged from my bed to the small guest bath in the back half of my office and brushed my teeth, rinsed my face, and stared numbly into the mirror over the sink. My eyes were blood-red, the result of a hysterical crying jag that had occurred after I'd gotten everyone settled down except me. We'd stuffed a bunch of clothes in Callie's washer and called Lilly's older sister Serena in her dorm in Richmond to tell her the news. The three of us had a proper meltdown at Callie's kitchen table, but I kept my true emotions in check in order to convey strength to the girls and Callie. It was fine, everything would be fine, don't worry. It'll be okay.

It was what they needed to hear.

The minute I'd gotten Lilly and Riot settled at Callie's, reassured Callie a hundred times that I'd be fine at the office, and no, I didn't need her to sleep on the couch so I could use her bedroom…I drove to the office. The hushed solitude of the office when I opened the door, the ticking of the wall clock in reception, the shadows down the long hallway that led to the guest bedroom all served to intensify the enormity of my loss. An assault on my house felt less like a violation and more like the dark hand of fate.

I'd fallen apart. Dropped to my knees, thrown out my hands, sobbed a broken prayer. I did my best to be both mom and dad to my daughters since their dad was in prison. But it was never, ever, good enough. My pity party had lasted long into the night. I'd finally taken a shower and tried to sleep.

With the rising of the sun, I pushed aside the self-pity. I didn't have the luxury of sinking into hopelessness. People depended on me. *I* depended on me.

With a frown, I stalked from the bathroom, found some clothes that weren't too smoky, and threw them on.

The front door lock rattled with the key, then opened. A masculine voice called out. "Olivia?"

I rubbed my forehead. Had I forgotten to call Tom? "I'm in the breakroom, Tom." My words came out crackly. I coughed.

He walked into the narrow breakroom that held a fridge, small stove, sink, and tiny sitting space. His face pinched with worry, he fisted his hands on his hips. "Are you okay?"

I stirred cream into my coffee. "News travels fast."

He dropped into one of the chairs nestled underneath a bistro table. "How's the house?"

I shrugged. "It just happened last night. I have no details at all. The investigators are supposed to…." I blinked back tears. "They're supposed to let me know when."

I tried to avoid his gaze. If I felt the full brunt of his concern, I'd be a wallowing, sobbing mess. This much damage to my house was like losing a limb. Two limbs, maybe. I stroked my coffee mug with my thumb.

His gnarled, knotted hand covered mine. "Girl. You know I'm here for you. What can I do? Have they told you what they think might've happened?"

I slapped my hair off my cheeks and tried to wind it into a knot. It wouldn't stay. I let it fall to my shoulders. "It started in the attic. The fire investigator, her name's Tasha, she came right away. It was manageable, they said. I don't know the extent of the damage, but I can't go in. They need to do an investigation first. I was warned to keep out."

Tom's eyebrows drew together. His eyes twinkled. "Is it a crime scene yet?"

"Don't think so. Why?"

He made tut-tut sounds and shook his head. "Thought I taught you better than that."

"But..."

"Don't you want to have a look?"

"Well, yeah, but—"

He glanced at his watch. "It's barely eight. When do you think they'll be there this morning?"

I shrugged. "Tom. It just happened. I know...nothing."

He gave me a look. "What do we do for a living?"

I was quiet and stared at my hands. The zest for my eminent career path had been quenched with every surge of those fire hoses. With each crack of another stud consumed by flames. With every cloud of smoke that clogged my throat as I watched my beloved home burn. And that awful smell. Would it stay with me?

"I'm gonna take a look," Tom said. "You coming?"

I felt a stirring in my chest. With both my hands, I wiped my face. "Okay," I whispered.

We walked the half mile to my house. The birds sang, the mature trees alongside my lane stretched long boughs across that blocked out much of the sun. Squirrels and rabbits scurried out of the way and into the brush. Such a gorgeous, sunny day, and I couldn't muster a smile.

It didn't seem possible that life cruised along undisturbed as I muddled through, carried along on the compassionate concern of Tom Stark, my mentor, friend, and now...my mom's voice rang through my mind: *Sometimes we need to let someone else carry us, honey.* I glanced at Tom. Now, he was that someone. At my core, I felt homeless. It wasn't a good feeling.

When we arrived, I stared at the ground rather than the desecration.

"Not so bad," Tom remarked. "Let's walk around back, then go inside."

I followed him around to the back yard, glancing over my shoulder, hoping the investigators wouldn't show up and freak out on us, arrest us, or whatever it is that they do in these situations. However...Tom had forty years' experience covering his tracks. He'd know how to be discreet.

He pulled on nitrile gloves, and gave me a pair. "I came prepared," he smiled, testing the back doorknob. It opened. "Didn't even lock it." He rolled his eyes. "Life in a small town." He handed me some booties, pulled on his own pair. "Let's do it. When are the restoration folks comin'?"

My lips quivered. I followed him in.

"They can't get in until the investigation's done."

"Well, we'll see if we can expedite that." He winked. "I have connections."

My eyes roved the kitchen. Sagging ceilings, sheetrock pulling away from the walls, white-gunk footprints all over the place. I covered my nose. Three inches of soot covered the kitchen counters.

"Can't stay long. The smoke's embedded. Toxic. Maybe fifteen minutes or so, then we'll leave. He stood very still, calm and stoic, surveying the kitchen. "Looks good. Fixable. Water and smoke damage in here, mostly. Down here, it's cosmetic. Won't take long to get it squared away."

His footsteps cautiously outside all the steps left by the firefighters, he peered into the other rooms, and paused at the den. "Come on into the doorway. Watch where you step."

I took his place in the doorway. Tom moved a pace or two back. "Study the bookcases and end tables. All the doo-dads and such. Anything missin'?"

My heart thudding so hard I could feel it in my throat, I looked around the room. The ceiling drooped in the middle as if it were pregnant, and white, sticky sheetrock footprints tracked in two directions. Every surface and piece of furniture looked as though it had been flocked like Christmas trees, except instead of white flocking, it was gray. My vision blurred. I had the sensation of sinking in quicksand. Tom's voice penetrated my brain. "Olivia. Focus. You're okay. We'll be done in a few minutes." He patted my shoulder.

I rotated my neck. Beetled my forehead. Scanned each surface. My gaze stalled on the middle shelf of a bookcase—the place of honor for photos I wanted to showcase. The 8x10 of Hunter and I in the Shenandoahs was gone. Had I moved it? No. A sheaf of soot covered the shelf as if it had never been there at all. I turned to Tom. "A framed photo of Hunter and me. It's gone."

He stared at my face a few beats, cataloging that piece of information in his well-ordered mind. "Let's move upstairs. Didn't you say it started in the attic?"

I followed him up the stairs, a tough task as the sloppy, white footprints covered almost every inch. We skirted them the best we could and arrived at the pull-down for the attic. The stairs had been left down.

"Eight minutes," Tom said. "Follow me up." He gripped the support rod, gingerly testing the stairs, then disappeared into the attic. I sucked in a breath and followed him.

The carnage was unbelievable.

Three inches of soot covered the flooring, and black, scorched insulation with a pink underbelly hung from the ceiling and the walls. The back half of the attic was solid black. Pieces of shutters and roofing lay on what was left of the attic flooring. A quarter of my roof was gone, much of it incinerated, and the rest in sad pieces in the backyard. I pictured the flames leaping high into the sky yesterday afternoon. Had it been an accident? Or had someone set the fire on purpose, knowing we'd be at Lilly's graduation?

The unscathed side of the attic held wilted, smoke-damaged boxes of photos and paraphernalia that Monty had put up here years ago. I hadn't even been up here but one or two times since the divorce.

Tom carefully navigated the plywood flooring in his booties and squatted down at the far end, where the roof had burned completely through. The morning sun's gentle rays crept through shingle debris and scorched roofing, and fried electrical wires. "Look here. You can barely make it out, but it's a paint thinner can. You ever keep paint thinner up here?"

I shook my head. "Monty kept all the paint stuff in the garage."

"These little fluffs? This bucket? You remember any of this?"

"No, but I'm never up here. This was Monty's thing. He'd store stuff here."

Tom scanned the space. Smiled. "I can tell. That OCD sumbitch did all that. I bet they're alphabetized." He waved his hand at all the neatly organized boxes in rows. "Now look at this pile over here, they threw stuff around to make a big, clear area for the accelerant. Whoever did this was in a big hurry, or they'd never left the accelerant container up here." He let out a breath as he stood. "This thing was set in the prime spot for fire to get oxygen…I guarantee the investigators will determine that this bucket, the paint thinner, and the residue and fabric were meant to combust. Takes about forty-eight hours, but it's a sure way to start a fire. Plus, did you notice? The photo was removed before the fire started, or there'd be signs that something was there. This is arson, Olivia." He glanced at his watch. "Two minutes."

I took a quick series of photos, then hustled after Tom down the stairs. In the den, I took another series.

We left the same way we came in. We removed the gloves and booties and took our time walking back to the office. My mind cartwheeled through possibilities. Monty? Was he at it again, pulling strings with his buddies on the outside to wreak havoc in my life? Did someone take the framed photograph as a message? Sounds like something Monty would do, but he knew I never wanted any part of a life with him again.

As we walked, Tasha pulled in from the highway and waved at us on her way to my house. "Official fire investigation report coming right up," I told Tom. "After that, my homeowner's insurance. Hopefully, both on the same day."

Tom nodded. "Good deal. The restoration companies need to get in there as soon as possible." We walked into the parking lot of my tidy office space. Above the front door, we'd hung out his sign. 'Stark Investigations'. After we had decided that I would intern with him as an investigative assistant, we agreed to share offices. Tom was winding down his business, anyway, and wanted to get rid of his office rent.

Worked for me.

I plodded after Tom, wishing with all my heart that I was anywhere but in the middle of another mess after a long series of messes.

We entered the back office, which I'd divided into two spaces, one on either side of the room. His dented metal desk and file cabinets against one wall, and my mid-century, sleek, L-shaped desk and low-slung file cabinets on the other. In the center of the room, I'd placed four comfy armchairs around a large, square coffee table.

Our receptionist Sherry burst into reception. “Olivia! Tom! Are you here? Ohmigod, what happened?” I heard her throw down her purse on her desk and race through the breakroom to the office Tom and I shared.

Our little foray back to my house had drained my energy. I stared at Tom with a silent plea to take the wheel. For now.

“Mornin’ Sherry, gal. I’m just findin’ out, too. We snuck in and looked around before all the official stuff started happenin’ All I know is it’s arson,” Tom said, and glanced at me. “I think we need to keep that bit about the missing photo under wraps, Olivia.”

Sherry’s eyes were as big and round as a harvest moon. “What photo?”

“Her and Faraday,” Tom grunted.

Sherry’s palms clapped across her mouth.

I smiled weakly. “Yeah.”

“Monty?”

I shook my head. “Can’t imagine. He’s in enough trouble, right? He’d be an idiot to do something like this.”

“Where are you staying? You can stay at my place? It’s small, but I’ll make room. It’ll be fine, and it’s just a ten-minute drive.”

“Thanks, but staying at the office is a better idea. I want to be close, y’know? Keep an eye on repairs. I can probably get in and have a more thorough look around after all the investigations are done.

“It’ll be a crime scene tomorrow. Locked down,” Tom said.

Sherry slumped into one of the chairs. “I can’t believe this.”

“Me either, Sherry.”

We sat quiet.

Tom got up, walked to his desk, found a few files in his filing cabinet, and threw them on my desk. “Here. Call them and see if they need anything. Tell them we got a special goin’ on.”

“A fire sale?” I suggested.

Sherry frowned at me.

Tom shook his head. “I’m ignoring that. The best way to deal with a problem is...work. It’ll free up your mind from the worry. Don’t do any good to worry, gal.”

My smile was half-hearted, but I picked up the files.

"Listen, I've got some ideas. I'll make some calls. You just get your mind turnin' a different direction for a while. I'll work the fire."

He was right. What could I do? The investigations would have folks tromping in and out, taking photos, dusting for prints, creating a general hubbub. One thing was sure, though…I doubted I could get my mind 'turning in another direction,' as Tom said.

Sherry went to her desk in reception. Tom left to do whatever. I was a lowly assistant at this point, so I had no plans of my own, really, other than try to be a productive human being in spite of the arson case. My life for the next week would consist of calling restoration companies and wrangling with insurance adjusters, and trying to help Lilly adjust.

I drummed my fingers on my desk. Then I smiled.

Though the investigations would create general chaos during the day, everyone would be gone at night.

Except me.

Chapter Four

Detective Hunter Faraday toweled off, thinking about the tasks that lay ahead at Richmond PD. Since he'd been assigned as de facto Homicide Unit lead detective, he'd had to keep regular office hours. He chafed under the restraint, but a promotion to Sergeant meant more money. A lot more. After selecting a pair of khakis and an oxford button-down from a long line of slightly different versions of the same hanging in his closet, he walked into his kitchen to make his usual breakfast. Two eggs, orange juice, and a couple of slices of bacon. Plus an assortment of vitamins.

Passing by an accent table in the hallway of his townhouse, he stopped to consider a framed picture of him and Olivia from one of their treks to the Shenandoah Mountains last fall. He'd gifted her the photo in a frame so they could both enjoy the memory. He reached out with his hand and touched her face, then frowned and continued to the kitchen.

Slamming cabinet doors, searching in vain for a clean frying pan, he cursed. What was it about this woman that put him in a bad mood? All he had to do was think about her, and his good mood sizzled right down the drain. "I started the day with a good attitude," he murmured to himself as he grabbed a used pan off the stove, turned on the faucet, and squirted some soap. He wondered how Olivia was doing. She hadn't texted in weeks, and yeah, they were in an 'off' period, but they kept up with each other anyway. They'd been friends before things had gotten out of hand, and now...again...he wondered if Olivia was right for him. Or any guy, for that matter. Talk about issues.

His cell buzzed. He snatched it, and blasted, "Faraday" into the phone.

The caller paused. "Hunter?"

Oh. It's Shiloh.

"Hey," he said. "Sorry, I'm running late and not in the best mood. I grabbed the phone before I could identify your number."

"Need those reading glasses, huh?" she teased.

Hunter hated it when she did that. Middle-age jokes cut too close as the south side of his forties snuck up on him." What's going on?"

"I'm in town. A two-day seminar. Want to grab lunch? We can talk about homicides and investigation techniques and why I haven't heard from you."

Hunter rubbed his beard stubble and ignored the jab. "Sounds great, but this is a bad day. How about tomorrow?"

They agreed on a place and time.

Hunter rushed out the door and hopped in his Jeep Wrangler Rubicon wondering why he even made the effort to be with Shiloh. Was it fair to her? What is if he was using her to get his mind off Olivia?

After the morning meeting, doling out assignments, and finishing up reports from over the weekend, Hunter leaned back in his chair and stretched. He absolutely despised the duties assigned to his new title of Sergeant and had no idea what to do about it.

He left the office to grab lunch at Harry's.

The mobile delicatessen was an icon in downtown Richmond. An early version of the famous Airstream family of RVs, this one dated to 1958. Hunter had been a customer since he'd joined the police force as a rookie straight out of college in 1997. A dark-haired man with a deep Richmond drawl leaned over the counter. "What'll it be today, Sergeant? Congrats on the promotion, by the way."

Hunter put his hands in his pockets and smiled. The sweltering Virginia sun burned right through his shirt and undershirt. "You know I'm a sucker for the chili dogs with jalapenos. I'll do that. With fries and a diet Coke."

"You got it."

Hunter sat at one of the picnic tables around the RV. As he relished his first bite, his cell vibrated. He stared at the phone with a frown.

After a few more hasty chomps, he accepted Olivia's call but remained quiet. The heat of his offense radiated from him like the scorch of the sun. She hadn't kept in touch, but then again, neither had he.

She spoke first. "I know you're irritated."

In spite of himself, he smiled. The melodic voice would forever charm him out of his bad moods. "How do you know that?"

"Listen, I have something to tell you."

"Here we go." Hunter took a monstrous bite of the dog.

He pictured her mouth. Her eyes dancing. Whatever it was she wanted to tell him, he hoped it involved getting together. "What is it?"

"Hunter, my house caught fire. It started in the attic. We weren't there. Fire department got there fast. Everything's under control."

He blinked. "When?"

"Uh. A few days ago."

As Olivia reiterated what had happened, Hunter's complexion, under the tasteful stubble, mottled. "Let me get this straight. Everyone knows you experienced a *fire*...which, to my mind, is a calamitous event...except me. Why is that? Don't you think I'd be concerned?"

"Hunter," Olivia said, her voice pained, "I couldn't let my family find out from the media, for goodness' sake."

"But it's okay for *me* to find out from the media." Hunter stuffed the rest of the dog in his mouth, thinking how typical this behavior was. If her life rolled along nice and calm, he didn't hear from her for weeks. If she had a crisis, she called. He wasn't sure how he felt about that. Since she'd never known her father, he wondered, sometimes...if she used him as a proxy.

"I don't mean to upset you. I want to keep you in the loop. *My* loop. That should count for something."

Hunter sighed. "Okay. So what happens now? I assume the investigation is completed."

She paused, then burst out with, "All the evidence is at the lab. My investigator tells me they're backed up, so who knows when I'll have an official...whatever. Report."

After a few beats, Hunter smiled. "I see. You waited to tell me so I wouldn't run up there and get involved with the investigation—"

"You would have, and you know it," Olivia interrupted. "You're all buddy-buddy with those guys now...I bet they drive down to Richmond once a month to buy you a beer. You have a new job, and I didn't think you needed the extra stress. I'm fine, Hunter."

"Have they called it?"

After a slight pause, she said, "Probably arson."

Hunter wondered why that cut so deep. When you cared about someone, wasn't it appropriate to reach out when something extraordinary or dangerous happened? For support, if nothing else? He shook his head in frustration. As a cop, he was offended. As a man who'd hoped he and Olivia would be engaged by now, he was just plain pissed.

"You there?"

"I'm here," he said. "But I won't be running up to freakin' Maryland every two seconds. Not anymore. So please, don't factor what *I* think into any more of your decisions about when...or if...to keep me in your *loop.*" With a little flourish of his arm, he pressed the end call button.

Chapter Five

"I can't imagine," Callie said, her ponytail swishing back and forth, "I just can't. After what you've been through."

Her pained expression irritated me. I appreciated the concern and her kind offer to let Lilly and me stay at her house, but once again, I was a 'victim' of something, and it made me angry. I was so over it. *So* done with pathetic, syrupy pity.

I cradled the mug of coffee she'd put in front of me. "We'll survive it, like we always have. Lucky that it started in the attic. What if it had started downstairs?"

My cell vibrated in my pocket. "I asked for a walk-through. This is the investigator."

Callie prattled on. "It's good the investigator is a woman. A woman will be more understanding and aware of…I don't know…what you've been through."

"Have to take this," I told her and walked into the foyer. Tasha and I agreed on a time to inspect my home together, and I returned to the kitchen. "What does being a woman have to do with anything?"

"Olivia. It's not like you're a normal person." She chuckled.

"Which means…?"

"You're Mercy's Miracle now and forever. Amen."

I sighed. "Callie, thousands of assaults happen to women each year. They sustain major injuries like mine, and some lose memories, too. I'm not the only one trying to get my life back. Why can't people get over the whole thing and let me move on? By this time, I'd think you'd understand."

Callie put her hand on my arm. "Honey, I do. Totally. But you have to learn to accept it."

"I don't want to," I grumbled.

"What did the investigator say?"

I made a face. "I think the yellow tape is cleared now, and I'm hoping the restoration people can come today, before the mold and smoke smell are forever imprinted on my frontal lobe. I can't wait to get in there and open all the windows. Tasha and I are going to meet in a couple of days to go through."

"Olivia, I've been thinking, and, well…that fan club so intent on helping you re-discover your past? The Friends of Olivia? The one you swore to stay away from? Shouldn't you check in once in a while…for keep-upsies?"

I plunged both hands in my jeans pockets, a furrow deepening between my eyebrows. "I don't *want* to keep up with that world. I'm trying to live my life." I squinted at her. "Keep-upsies?"

"It's a private group on Facebook. Have you read the comments? Seen the memes?"

"I haven't joined," I confessed.

"I'm a Foofoo now. I joined under a different name to check it out. You should stay informed. Some of it is over-the-top weird."

"You're a what?"

"A Foofoo. Stands for 'Friends of Olivia.' F-O-O."

"You've got to be kidding."

She sighed. "You should check in once in a while."

"And make myself more paranoid than I am? Walk around with pepper spray and a Glock?"

I didn't tell her I already did that, but whatever. My hand drifted to the reassuring grip of the Glock on my belt. I was trying to get used to wearing it more.

"What about the fires?"

"What about them?" I asked.

Callie gave me a quizzical look. "Those Foofoos are a weird bunch. What if—?" She let the question hang in the air.

I snorted. "Since when did a fan club think it would be a cool idea to set the object of their affection...*on fire?*"

Maybe it would be smart to at least check in. "Do you have to join or something?" I asked her.

She nodded. "It's a private group. You have to be approved. You could use a different name, but if someone knows how to track your IP address, well...they'd know it was you."

I scowled. "You think these people are serious, don't you?"

"They think they're helping you...that there's a conspiracy against you, and they are flying a banner to 'protect' you? Help you rediscover your past. It's a mission with them."

My cell rang. "Mom," I told Callie. She gave me a sympathetic look. She knew Mom would be hysterical about what was happening.

"I'll give you some space. I have to do laundry anyway." She left the kitchen.

I coughed into my elbow. Again. The smoke must've lodged in my throat when Tom and I snuck through the house, and now I had a cough that wouldn't let go. I answered and put the phone on speaker.

"Hi, Olivia. How are you holding up? Is there anything I can do? What's that cough...is that from smoke? You weren't in the home when it happened, right? Should you get that seen about?" My mother's voice floated through Callie's kitchen. I'd told Serena to clue in Mom since she and Mom both lived in Richmond now...when the fire happened, I'd been in no shape to handle her over-the-top reaction. I'd needed to process. "I'm okay, Mom. Serena filled you in, right?"

"Yes, but...I should've been there. What a time for me to miss one of the girls' graduations. I had a fever with this virus, but I'm feeling better, and—"

"Mom. Don't come. I repeat. Do. Not. Come. You don't need this insanity, and we are fine. The investigation is ongoing."

"Investigation? What investigation?"

Oops.

I cleared my throat in preparation to sidestep the truth. "It's routine, Mom. An investigator always comes out as soon as possible to determine what happened." I left out the part about Tasha alerting me to keep my eyes wide open—that arsonists like to come back and survey the damage and gloat, and I should watch my back. Also, I didn't share that my house was a crime scene now. One look at the yellow tape and Mom would've turned into a shrieking mama hyena. More so, I mean.

"How long are you out of your house?"

"Haven't gotten that far. The living quarters in the office aren't bad."

"Lilly there, too?"

"Callie is a saint. Lilly and Riot are there as long as they need to be. Amy is ecstatic."

Mom heaved a sigh of relief. "Good neighbors are priceless. Have you and Tom figured out what happened?"

I had to think a minute. Should I tell her that I walk through my property, sit behind a bush, and watch my house a few hours each night? That Tom and I are putting our heads together to figure out why the security cameras at my house were off when the fire occurred? That he has cop-friends scattered throughout Baltimore PD and has arranged to be informed if there's a hit on the prints? That we're doing backgrounds on the firefighters?

Um. No.

"The arson investigators have it, Mom. They're in touch with me."

Mom sucked in a breath. "You're not on your own as a PI yet, are you? Not with the damage to your house and the craziness of the investigation?"

"Not yet, Mom, but soon. I completed the private investigation online courses, and I've finished two years of shadowing Tom. In a few months, I'll have a license. Prepare yourself."

She was quiet.

"I like the work, Mom. It's interesting."

"It may be interesting, but it's also dangerous."

"Tom doesn't take the dangerous assignments."

"How is Tom, anyway? Isn't he getting on up there?"

I thought about that.

"He has good days and bad days. He's like, at least seventy."

"That is *so* old," Sophie's voice was sarcastic. "At sixty-four, I'm not that far away."

"You'll never be old, Mom." I laughed. "How's my favorite neurologist and stepdad?"

"Perfect."

"Tell him I'll stop in for an exam next time I'm down there."

After a pause, she continued. "You know I'm here if you need me. I'll drive up. Are you taking some time off? How is business, anyway? I can't imagine…how you market for that kind of work."

"I think Tom's trying to take easy stuff. Insurance fraud. Some Workers' Comp. Tom says I'm an adrenaline junkie," I babbled, seeking parental approval like a ten-year-old. "Isn't that cool? I don't think I was ever like that before the assault. Was I?"

"No. The opposite. You were cautious and careful."

I sighed. Mom was still getting used to the new Olivia—the daughter who had survived an assault and traumatic brain injury only to discover she couldn't remember a thing and her healing brain had upended her personality. My walk-backs into a convoluted past had been tough. I needed to be patient. The past three years had been difficult for Mom, too.

"I realize this is hard for you, Mom, but Tom's in the process of turning his client list over to me. Not much to market but the name change. It's a built-in client base."

She grunted. "Tom's been doing this so long that his clients are probably dead by now."

"They have family."

After a few beats, Mom said, "My father hired him once. When he was trying to build his investigative business."

My eyes widened. "You never told me that."

"He's a good man, and I trust him. If you're determined to pursue this line of work, he's the one guy I'd trust to show you how to do it."

I smiled. That was something, anyway.

Chapter Six

I opened one eye and reluctantly shook off sleep. Who was knocking on my door so early?

I looked at the clock. Half-past nine. I dragged myself out of bed and decided answering the door in pajama pants and a T-shirt would have to be okay. Scratching my head and yawning, I opened the door.

Tasha.

Of course, it would be the energizer bunny fire-goddess. "Come on in. I'll fix coffee."

I walked into the breakroom, grabbed my stash of French Roast, and poured it into a grinder. Soon, the air was redolent with the rich, dark smell of Espresso beans. I got us a couple of cups. Tasha took hers black.

"Pardon the informal attire," I joked. "So, what's up?"

She pulled her cell phone from a pocket, started scrolling, then pointed it at my face. The images displayed there showed the burnt wall in my attic, smoke stains, and various swirls and spirals. I didn't know the first thing about the science behind fire patterns and smoke directions, but the whole experience could be utilized as a learning experience. Looking at my situation as something I could add to my professional toolbox scraped off some of the evil foreboding oozing into my perimeter.

I focused on the pictures as she enlarged them one after the other. "Arson Unit guys cleared the scene yesterday. See this blackened, paint thinner can? Deliberate. Note the location of the seat of the fire. Again, deliberate." She paused to find another photo. I sipped my coffee, a headache building behind my eyes. It was way too early to do this.

Her words flitted through my mind like moths around a light bulb. My sense was that all these words dovetailing with Tom's suspicions boiled down to one thing...*someone is out to get me.*

Again.

I put my hands over my face.

The words stopped.

I felt the warmth of her hand on my shoulder. "The good news is that your house is in great shape. A clean-up team is already there, so you must've set it up early on? The insurance adjuster has been out, too. Things are rolling along," she reassured me.

I stared at the ceiling, thinking about the last three years. "Do you realize how many times I've dealt with threats? This is like...groundhog day. My whole life. Groundhog day."

"Forensic examination takes time. Your fire is a priority, but the lab is backed up. Try not to jump to conclusions. It may not be what you're thinking."

Yeah, right.

We stared at each other.

With a smile, she rose from her chair and looked at her watch. "You ready to do a walk-through?"

I rode with her to my house, clutching a nervous stomach. She parked in front of my detached garage. We walked into the front yard and stood in front of the house.

She flattened a palm over her eyes and scrutinized the roof. In the fresh morning sunlight, my house didn't look as horrible as I'd feared, but still. Looking at it in the full light of day was like a punch to the gut. I thought about the wonderful—and terrible—memories made on my beloved front porch. Now, the porch and furniture were covered in grime, and the sad-looking, drenched porch would have to be replaced.

I took a moment.

Tasha glanced at me. "The restoration companies work miracles. They're fast, too. All in all, you were lucky."

I stared at the door. The front screen sagged against the exterior of the house, torn from its hinges. The wooden door lay in the yard in jagged pieces. Plastic covered the doorway.

"The guys have to use a halogen tool and an ax to open doors that have deadbolt locks," she offered.

Tasha lifted up a corner of the plastic. I slipped on the booties Tasha had provided and stepped across the threshold. My mouth was dry. Tasha had indicated that the downstairs was fine, but her definition of 'fine' and mine were miles apart. The interior looked even worse than when Tom and I had walked through.

The ceilings sagged all the way to the back of the house. Sheetrock hung at odd angles, and my area rugs were soaked and ruined. Black clots of mold had begun to form. Tasha pointed out the most damaged areas, below the starting point of the fire.

"So this is lucky, huh?" I blinked away tears.

"Many times, there's not much salvageable. In a week, you'll be amazed at the difference."

The furniture, rugs, and curtains were beyond saving. My refinished hardwood floors looked fine, however. Old, solid-wood floors were almost indestructible. A smile tugged at the corners of my mouth. At least the floors wouldn't have to be replaced.

"Do you want to see where it started?" Tasha asked.

Of course, I did. I was curious to see if her findings matched Tom's. We walked upstairs to the far end of the hall. She pulled down the attic stairs. I wondered who had closed the attic and why. It had been open when Tom and I had inspected things, and we'd left it that way. My eyes started to water from the acrid smell.

Tasha powered on her flashlight. "It's dark up here with the electrical eaten through. Watch your step." Industrial fans hummed in strategic points of the attic. Clots of melted insulation swung from the ceiling. The cloying smell of smoke and mold made me dizzy.

"Some of this stuff is salvageable. I can help you bring boxes down if you want."

"That's okay," I muttered as I stared at the wilted, smoky boxes that held photos of my family. I'd not even gone through them yet. Were those memories gone forever? Photos tended to jog my memories, and now...these might fall apart in my hands.

Tasha pointed. "It started here. The arson investigators found a newish, silver bucket that held a cloth that had been saturated in accelerant. "There's a nice, clear area where the bucket would have been placed next to the wall, and the saturated fabric would have ignited. Did you know that accelerant fumes will self-combust? Within twenty-four to thirty-six hours? It gets hot in attics."

"I didn't know that," I lied. Tom would be proud of my poker face.

"I think we covered this in the initial interview...but...you were in a different head space. I'll ask the question again. Do you get along with your ex? After everything that's happened?"

I thought about how to answer. What does 'get along' mean anyway? Does it mean we chat regularly? Does it mean I enjoy being with him? Does it mean we compromise with each other for the sake of the kids? On all counts, the answer was obvious.

"No," I said.

"Took you a while to answer."

I squinted at her. "You read my book, right?"

"Well, yes, but—"

I chuckled. "So, no...we don't get along. It's complicated. He would love to think we *do* get along, however."

She frowned. "Could he have done this?"

"I think Monty is capable of anything."

We were silent a few beats.

She held up a scrap of fabric. "One whiff tells me this is paint thinner. You see paint up here?"

I scanned the space. "Monty didn't keep paint up here."

"Our investigation noted the fact that this attic had been pristine and well-ordered. The arsonist made a big mess in this quadrant, perhaps throwing the light off Monty as a suspect, but we're not sure. Baltimore PD Arson

Unit sent an investigator to have a little chat, and he seemed to have an honest reaction. He was shocked and appeared to know nothing about it." She lifted one shoulder. "Maybe he's a good actor."

I shook my head and stared at the scorched area, the drooping, decrepit roof, the mold, and scorched walls. "I assure you, if he had someone do this, his face would light up like a Christmas tree when he was asked about it. He's not *that* good an actor."

Tasha smiled. "Okay, then."

Chapter Seven

Three weeks passed in a blur of renovation experts, restoration companies, mold remediation, and arson investigation interviews. I'd heard the word 'ongoing' so many times I was sick of it. There was nothing more to be done except wait or hope for a print to pop. Tom worked on transitioning files to me, and I worked on weeding out the ones that no longer needed attention. When Sherry mentioned that we should invest in 'girl time,' I agreed. I was so, so ready for girl talk.

Our Wine, Whine, & Win group had dwindled to Callie, me, and Sherry. We'd founded this group a year into my recovery from the brain injury, with the admonition that we focus on exploring different types of wine, whining about our lives, and wrap it up with a win. Our fourth member, Hannah, had found true love—or so she said—and moved to Florida. We'd sent her off with bundles of gifts, good wishes, and a fair amount of regret. We'd been uncertain about her decision. In the end, even though the romance had been rushed and we'd never met her beloved...it was her life.

We missed her. She'd provided a soft, thoughtful place to land when the inevitable freak-outs erupted over kid problems, divorces, or creepy ex woes. I looked forward to our Wine & Whines, but they felt very different without Hannah.

As I drove to join my friends, I thought about my nightly surveillance of my house and Tom's efforts to get info from his cop buddies. Nothing significant had turned up on my security system or otherwise, and I was doing my best to soldier on. However, I'd refreshed my skills with my Smith & Wesson .38 and now wore it everywhere. I'd stuffed my closet with cute jackets that covered the paddle holster I wore on a belt.

I made a sharp turn into a parking lot right off Main Street in Westminster. I checked my weapon. All safe and sound and buttoned up halfway between my side and the middle of my back. Amazing what wearing a weapon does for one's confidence.

Callie and Sherry waved madly from our favorite table by the plate glass window facing the street.

"We ordered," Sherry said as I approached the table. "I got us a white wine— sauvignon blanc. In honor of your uh…the restoration work on your house." She picked up the bottle. "Freemark Abbey. Napa Valley."

"Perfect, thanks." I poured the wine, thinking about what she'd said. The damage to my house would be repaired, but what about the damage to my soul? Whoever set that fire should prepare for all hell to come down from Tom and me if the cops don't get them first.

We toasted. Callie looked expectantly around the table. "Ready to start? Sherry, want to go first?"

She lifted one shoulder and toothpicked a square of cheese. "I'm trying to get used to my new place. Loving that the divorce is final after all this time. The financial settlement turned out fine, and I don't have to worry about money for a while. Overall, things are pretty boring…" she slid her eyes over to me. "Except for Ms. Adventure, here, with whom I have the pleasure of working. I'm trying to keep her out of trouble."

I frowned. "Not my fault. It comes looking for me."

"Only because you're famous," Callie chimed in.

"Can't help how I look," I said, chewing a fig and following it with a hefty dose of wine.

"Unrecognizability. That's what I want. Is that a word?"

Callie and Sherry smiled. The TBI had left me with curious verbal lapses. They were used to the interesting words that popped out of my mouth. "If not, it should be. It's my photo on the book that's plastered everywhere. If that wasn't happening, then I could get away with—"

"Murder." Callie grinned. "You know. Your new career? Figuring out murders?"

I sighed. "Police detectives figure out murders, Callie. All Tom and I do is gather information that helps with investigations."

Sherry waved one of her hands. "You guys are good as the cops any day."

I chuckled. "Yeah. If only we had years of training in cutting-edge forensic capabilities and access to NCIC. We can get into some databases that the public can't, but we can't go all super-commando, like the FBI."

"I'm in awe," Sherry breathed.

"Not so fun when someone sets your house on fire. Just saying."

A testy silence fluttered across the table.

"Any news with the investigation?" Callie asked.

I rolled my eyes. "Nothing."

Callie cleared her throat. "When is Hunter coming?"

I munched a cracker. "Hunter will not be involved."

Callie looked shocked. "Since when?"

"Since he got all bent out of shape because I didn't tell him soon enough about it, I guess. That was a week ago. I'm leaving it alone. He doesn't need to be here, anyway. Tasha and Baltimore PD are all over it."

Sherry's brow furrowed. "He's been involved in every detail of your life for three years. What happened?"

I groaned. I did not want to talk about Hunter.

"He's still in Richmond, right?" Sherry prodded.

"Yeah, he got a big promotion a few months ago. He's fine."

"He still have dinner once a month with your Mom and Dr. Sturgis?" Callie asked. "And Serena?"

"Yes. Can we stop talking about Hunter, please?"

A silence stretched.

"I miss Hannah," I blurted in a desperate attempt to change the subject.

"You do?" Sherry asked, her pale blue eyes wide. "I thought it was good that she moved, given what happened between you two."

I flapped my hand. "Yeah, but I forgave her. She didn't realize what she was doing."

"Okay," Sherry said, reaching for more wine. "Who can we invite to take her place? It'd be nice to have a woman with a good marriage. You know, for balance."

Callie tapped her chin. "I have an idea."

I winced. "And we all know how those turn out."

She scanned me from top to bottom. "You need a break. It's obvious, and you said yourself that you need to be unrecognizable." Callie gave me a wicked smile. "What better time for a makeover? Besides, I doubt your clothes will be salvageable, anyway. She wrinkled her nose. "Judging by the way those few things the investigator grabbed for you and Lilly turned out."

I frowned. "They can do wonders with smoke damage at the cleaners. Tasha told me sheets, towels, clothes...most can be laundered."

"Yeah, but that's going to take a while. How about I take you shopping? Get you a new look?"

I snorted. "Yeah. *That's* what I need right now. A new look."

A brief silence lingered. My lips pulled into a pout. I looked down at my outfit. "You don't like my look?"

"Oh, gosh...I love your, um, casual look, Olivia. However, you don't need swarms of reporters climbing all over you about this arson situation in *addition* to the Mercy's Miracle persona. Didn't you say that as a private dick or whatever you call it—"

"Investigator," I interrupted.

Sherry laughed.

"Investigator...sorry...that discretion is needed? Olivia Callahan, the miracle that rose from the dead and, for all intents and purposes, *castrated* her former lowlife ex is anything but discreet. Now you want to blend into the background. I can help with that. We'll for sure make it classy, though."

Sherry leaned in, eyes twinkling. "Callie's a haute couture expert."

Callie blushed. Touched her hair. "I don't always wear a ponytail, you know."

"It's true. I have a hard time disappearing. But all the things Tom's teaching me...it just feels right," I muttered. "It *has* to work."

"Let's go into the City, visit some of those cool stores by the Inner Harbor, or even DC. Let's blow it out, so no one recognizes you anymore. The book is a blockbuster, right? You've got the cash...let's spend it."

In the end, and after I'd sucked down another glass of the marvelous white...I agreed.

The following morning, I dragged myself out of bed at seven o'clock, took a shower, and picked out a clean shirt and jeans from the pile of dirty clothes amassing on the floor. A faint knock sounded on the front entrance door, and Callie entered. "Hey! Ready?"

"Define 'ready,'" I growled from the breakroom.

My wardrobe needed updating, sure, but not a complete overhaul. Right? Or did it? Callie operated in two modes—full stop or full steam ahead. No telling what I'd look like when she was done with me.

"Your house doesn't look so terrible," she announced. "The roof's started, and part of the porch is up. I bet it won't take long to get back in there."

"Yeah?"

Callie nodded. "Tasha thinks so, too."

I chuckled. "Of course, you'd pop over to meet Tasha. Why not?"

"That whole 'good neighbor' thing, hon."

"More like 'nosy neighbor' thing, hon," I shot back with a smile.

She wagged her left hand. The huge rock she wore on it twinkled. "Okay, okay, so I do tend to...stick my nose in. But you aren't in your right mind right now, and—"

"Thanks."

"It doesn't hurt to have another person's perspective that's all." She slid her eyes up and down my form. "We're going to fix you up and it'll be *fabulous*."

My smile was about as convincing as a commercial for Depends.

Callie always looked cute. In *my* closet, the choices were Capris, jeans, sweaters, and T-shirts. One or two colorful tops for an evening out. That was it. And now, all my clothes were toast. Literally.

Today, Callie wore big gold hoops in her ears, a fabric headband swept back her lush, dark-blond hair; her makeup and outfit looked perfect, and she'd lost fifteen pounds over the last year. She looked great, and I looked as rumpled and tired as I felt.

We walked out the front door of the office building that sat upon my five-acre slice of Baltimore County in Glyndon, Maryland. On the cement slab that served as a front stoop with two steps down to the compact parking lot lay a large bouquet of daffodils and daisies wrapped in tissue and tied with a yellow ribbon. I picked up the flowers and motioned Callie on ahead. Opened the small envelope. Extracted the card.

"Who's it from?" Callie called out over the roof of her car. "They must've dropped off the flowers after I went in. I didn't see anyone."

I opened the office door, tossed the flowers inside. "Satisfied client," I mumbled as I buckled into her late-model Mercedes E-450 Cabriolet without the least bit of envy.

Well, maybe a little.

The drive to Baltimore's ritzy Inner Harbor was quiet. A soft, jazzy, instrumental played in the background. As I watched the beautiful, rolling hills of northern Maryland slide by, all I could think about were the flowers.

The card had said, 'Love, Foofoo forever.'

Forty minutes later, we pulled into a parking garage five stories high, found a spot on the top, and rode the elevator down.

We headed for the heart of trendy shops and outlet stores that I would not frequent on my own…ever. Callie's taste was way different from mine, plus her bank account was about one hundred times the size of mine. So.

We walked past the actual Harbor itself, crossed the street, took a left. Then Callie, all smug and schmaltzy, propelled me into a salon that LA glitzy didn't even begin to describe.

I felt like a poodle that hadn't been clipped in five years.

"I don't think I can do this, Cal," I said in a small voice.

"Of course, you can. How long has it been since you at least *cut* your hair?"

I twirled one of my over-long locks around my index finger. "Two years?"

With an eye roll that could've sliced through pizza, she pushed me inside. We were brought two glasses of wine and ushered into a male stylist's booth, where I endured some tut-tutting and head-tilting and hard fingers pushing my head this way and that.

I sighed.

He asked if I wanted to keep my color.

"She doesn't," Callie said, breathless with excitement.

"You want me to change my color?"

"O-liv-i-a," Callie drawled, "It's time, don't you think?"

I picked up a chunk of hair and stared into the full-length mirror in front of the stylist's chair. In the harsh, brilliant light of the salon, I had to agree my hair looked more tired brown than glowing auburn. I made a rude noise with my lips and jammed my arms across my chest. "*No.*"

Callie stared at the stylist with a look I didn't understand.

He sprang into action. "This salon is committed...absolutely *committed,* darling, to making you happy." He cocked his head, inspected my hair with narrowed eyes. "Let me show you something."

He produced a book of a thousand gorgeous female heads in varying degrees of geometric, sharp-angled hairstyles. After a few pages, I was hooked. From what I'd patched together of my former life, Monty had never been one to fuss about my clothes, and he'd never been one to throw around compliments. All I'd known was an ultra-casual approach to motherhood and housework. I didn't even wear makeup most of the time, and when I did, just mascara and lip gloss. My caustic, flipped-upside-down personality urged me to get serious about this. Suddenly, I had a visual in my mind of burning all my Capris in my backyard and along with them, all my overlarge, blousy tops in an array of stain-disguising colors.

I pointed at one of the cute styles with bangs. "That one. And I want to go platinum." I needed a drastic change, not a minimal one. The full-on obliteration of my old look would be refreshing. Who the heck did the Friends of Olivia group think they were, anyway, to call themselves my friends? I shuddered at the visual of the creepy flowers, the way my name and photos had been slammed across media platforms for two years. I settled into the chair and drank the rest of my wine. Callie's next step would entail committing to makeup. I'd do that, too. It might not be blending into the background exactly, but no one would recognize 'Mercy's Miracle', anymore.

Except maybe Hunter.

What about *his* reaction?

I rubbed the back of my neck, thinking. Why should I care?

The stylist scurried to my side and began 'stripping' my hair, which sounded alarming, but he assured me it was all part of the process. That it would take a few hours. I leaned back and tried to relax.

Chapter Eight

Before I'd even had a chance to look at myself in the mirror and regret what I'd done, a knock sounded on the front door to my office. I tore through the breakroom and into reception. It was early. Sherry hadn't made it in yet. I jerked open the door.

Tasha.

"Um. Is Olivia here?"

I laughed. "Are you serious?"

She peered at me under hooded eyes. "Olivia?"

"I'll go get her," I said.

She frowned. "Are you her sister?"

"Come on in, Tasha."

"What have you done? "she asked, inspecting me.

"New hair, new makeup, new eyebrows, new clothes." I stuck out my hands. "Look. I even got a stupid manicure."

"What happened to your lips?"

"I got bushwhacked into joining my friend for an impromptu filler session. They're supposed to get less puffy by tomorrow. I'm not sure what to do with them."

"That's freaking hilarious."

"Whatever. I'll start using lipstick more. It'll be fine. They didn't put much in."

"Why would you do that?"

The front door opened, and my daughter walked in. Since my back was to her, she looked right past me. "Is my mom here?"

Tasha grinned. I turned, nice and slow. Stuck my hands out to each side. "Ta-daaaaa!"

Lily's hands flew to her mouth. She started laughing. "You look like Gwen Stefani."

I blinked. Did I? That wouldn't be so bad.

"You mean my hair?"

"I'm imagining you with makeup, and yeah, the hair, too, but you look like you're related to her now."

Lilly stepped over to the breakroom, grabbed a bottle of water from the fridge. "Are you going through a mid-life crisis or something?"

I thought about that. Was I?

"I'm too recognizable. I changed it so I wouldn't get all this whispery attention when I walk into a room."

Lilly laughed. "Oh, yeaahhh," she drawled. "Looking like *that,* you'll get no attention. None."

"Funny. Don't you like it?"

"Would it matter if I didn't?"

I gave her an exaggerated pout with my new lips.

She laughed. "Mom. It looks amazing. It fits the, uh...the new you."

"I'm working into it. You headed to the Y?"

She nodded. "My relief comes mid-afternoon. So I'll be in and out if you need anything."

Sherry walked in and beamed her bright smile at us. "Morning, everyone," she said. Her mouth dropped when she saw me. She just stood there, staring. I desperately wished I'd had time to fix myself up before everyone passed judgment.

"I...I..." Sherry stuttered, her mouth on the floor. "I knew you guys were doing this yesterday, but I never thought it'd be so...drastic."

I smiled. Drastic was what I'd been going for. "So you like it?"

She tilted her head and sat at her desk. "I'll have to get used to it."

I pushed away my hurt feelings. Had I made a mistake? Did I look terrible?

Tasha drew close. "Maybe we should talk in your office?" she whispered.

"Go on in. I'm going to chat with my daughter a sec."

I drew Lilly aside. "Things okay at Callie's?"

She shrugged.

Uh-oh. I knew that shrug. "What's going on?"

"Can I get back into my bedroom? It's been weeks, Mom."

"I repeat...what's—"

Huge sigh. "Amy's mom is having meltdowns. I think her ex is bothering her. I don't want to be around all that."

My PI Spidey senses sprang to life. "Define 'bother.'"

"Miss Callie is crying a lot. And she mumbles to herself."

How clueless of me. Callie had been so intent on helping me that I'd overlooked asking her how *she* was doing. "I'll talk to Callie and see what's going on. But yeah, you should...I mean, *we* should...be able to get in soon.."

Lilly groaned. "But you've had those smoke fan machines going, and the fumigation people have come and gone, right? That's done?"

"There'll be a lot of hammering and a crew going up and down the stairs. Let me think about it. They're working on the roof, too."

"Riot and I need out of there, Mom." On that note, Lilly grabbed her beach bag and her book and flounced to her car to begin another day as a lifeguard at the Y. Her tires crunched as she drove away. I made a note to revisit getting my lane paved. Or hard-packed dirt. Something.

My phone buzzed in my back pocket with a text.

The text from Lilly read: **Date with Bradford tonight. Movie.**

Quick tears puddled in my eyes. In five weeks, I'd be dropping her at college in Richmond. It was some solace that Mom and Gray lived there, and her older sister Serena was in the same dorm. Still.

My baby was growing up.

I walked into my office to join Tasha.

Tasha cleared her throat, handed me a few sheets of paper. "I'm sorry to say we have nothing on the arsonist."

I scanned the report. "Why not?" I barked, irritated that everything had hit me at once this morning. Had I had my coffee? I glared into the breakroom. I think I left my cup untouched in there.

She shrugged. "These guys are hard to pin down. Sometimes it happens.

No prints, no leads, nothing."

"But you had the bucket. The paint thinner can. Surely there were prints, or security cameras at the places where the paint thinner came from? Or the bucket?"

Tasha nodded patiently. "We checked all that, Olivia. I'm so sorry. It's a lot of ground to cover…those paint cans and thinner are all over the place. It would take years to pin it down. The investigation is ongoing, however."

I thought the top of my head was going to explode. I rose from my chair, turned to stand in front of the chair, and stared down at her. She shrank into the chair. "This is ridiculous. You know that someone is probably out there right now wondering when they can do it again, and you guys have nothing? How can I feel safe? There has to be something."

I sank back into my chair and put a palm over my eyes. What next?

"Yo," Tom barked in his characteristic greeting as he entered our shared office. His mouth went slack when he looked at me.

Okay. That's it.

"Look, guys. I haven't even had time to get ready this morning. I need a few minutes. Can you wait?"

Tom sat at his desk.

"Tasha, thanks for the update. Let me know when there's a lead."

She agreed and left.

"I'm not saying a word," Tom said with a grin.

I spun around and walked to the guest bedroom. I needed a shower, fresh makeup, my first cup of coffee. It would be fine. I stalked into my bedroom, tore off my clothes, and turned on the shower. Everything would be *fine.*

Later, I heard Sherry and Tom chat in reception as I put the last touches on my face and pulled on sleek leggings and a red, stretchy top that I'd never have bought myself in a million years, but Callie had insisted. Red was my future, she'd said. I applied red lipstick to my new, poufy lips and walked into the office ready to tackle whatever Tom had for us today…and whatever Sherry could throw at me. Thank God she was organized and efficient. I was not.

All chatter ceased as I left the breakroom with my (finally) first cup of coffee and walked into reception. Tom's face was a study. His light, gray eyes widened. What little hair he tried to coax into submission around the sides of his head had drifted into thready, tangled clumps the color and consistency of dental floss. Why he didn't shave his head made no sense to me.

"Now look here, Olivia," he said once he got his voice back, "What have you gone and done?"

Sherry tittered at that. "Wow. I don't think I've ever seen you with makeup on."

I shrugged. "I had lessons yesterday. I like it."

Tom frowned. "Damn. You stick out like a sore thumb, girl."

"I needed to be less...Olivia Callahan and more 'serious private investigator,' Tom. I'll make it work." I looked at my phone calendar. "We have an appointment. Did Sherry send it?"

Sherry frowned. "Of course I did."

I laughed. "Of course you did. Did you see it, Tom?"

Tom pulled out his cell. "Oh, crap, sorry, been distracted with this health stuff and all those tests."

"Do you need more time off? I can handle things until you feel better."

He shook his head. "I'm okay. Who is it?"

"Looks like...Dylan Palmer." My eyebrows rose. "Isn't he in politics?"

Tom grunted.

"He wants to meet in Pikesville. He's there for a presentation or something. Kelvin's Bakery? Reisterstown Road?"

Tom nodded. "Yeah, Hole in the wall, but that's where he likes to meet. What time?"

"Ten."

"Okay, better get goin'."

I typed a response, included my number, and told Mr. Palmer to text us if he was running late or couldn't show.

"Let's take your car today," Tom said, his comfortable drawl more pronounced than usual.

As we drove off, Tom stared out the window.

"What's going on, Tom? You always drive."

After a pause, Tom said, "You know how old I am, Olivia?"

I pursed my lips, thinking. Did I?

"Around seventy?"

"Almost seventy-six."

"Okay. So?"

"I been playin' this game a long, darn time. Let's see now...."

I waited as he counted the years. Maybe this was a little trip down memory lane. Old people like to do that, right?

"Fifty-six years. Makes me tired thinkin' about it."

"You're as young as you feel, Tom. Age is only a number," I said, making the heinous sin of two clichés in a row.

"Gal, I got this feelin' that you should take the reins. Sooner than later."

Where was this coming from?

His sigh was long and loud. "I got the cancer."

My hands tightened on the steering wheel. I had trouble focusing on the road.

"Wait. Did you get a second opinion? Did you research it? We can figure out options. It'll be okay, I'll get my doctor involved, and we'll find specialists. But first, a second opinion. Okay?"

Tom tossed me a sad smile. "Then what?" he asked, bringing a halt to my dithering. "Will a second opinion make any difference? I've seen all the scans and x-rays, and I've accepted it. Olivia, it's stage four leukemia, and a man my age has little chance of comin' back from that. I need to make the most of the time I've got left. Which means I'd like you to take the lead from here on in."

Anxiety drove a stake through my heart, but I forced myself to be calm. Calm for Tom. *Not worried.* He needed calm, right? Sick people must have calm around them. I would be calm for Tom, come hell or high water. I'd put post-its around my mirror. "Okay," I said.

He ran his hand across the top of his head. "I been thinkin'...I want to go over my files with you. I got repeat clients from thirty years ago, though they're all dyin' off now. But their families need an investigator now and again. I don't have much family besides distant cousins and such, so I want you to have my files. Stark Investigations has had a good run, but it stops now. You better be thinkin' of a name, gal."

I tried hard not to freak out. Sure, Tom had been sick, but... this? This was terrible news. "Do you...have they..." A tear bled from one eye.

"They tell me it could be a week or it could be three months. But three months is about as long as I got, God willin'." Tom looked out the window at the beautiful hills of Maryland horse country. "Sure will miss this. A Maryland summer is somethin' to behold. The fireflies...up in the trees like tiny stars...." His voice trailed away. He looked at me. "I feel good today."

We pulled onto Reisterstown Road and drove down the bustling, busy marketplace that comprised Reisterstown and on into Pikesville. Past Wegman's. Past TJMaxx and various beer joints and Asian restaurants. Past dicey areas that rubbed shoulders with the more manicured communities. Past two- or three-story redbrick buildings from two hundred years ago that abutted newer homes that lacked the historical charm of the old. At ten on the dot, we pulled into the parking lot of a small establishment that boasted three tables in and two out. A couple with a toddler and a dog on a leash stood at the glassed-in counter. Tom waved me to a table to wait on our potential client.

Tom returned with two breakfast wraps and two mugs of coffee. The coffee was good, the breakfast wraps were not. "Why are we here?" I asked, looking around at the small, decrepit space.

"Politician and all. Wants a safe place to talk about something not so legal. Betcha ten bucks."

"You're on," I said. Tom loved to bet on things. It was harmless, and I was happy to humor him. I wouldn't think yet, about moving forward as an investigator without Tom. I couldn't.

A black Lincoln pulled in. A large man with thick, silver hair and hands the size of dinner plates got out of the car. He wore a sport coat and an open-collar shirt. I pointed.

Tom turned around. "Yep. That's him." Tom stood, walked to the door, and opened it.

Dylan smiled at the gesture. "Good morning, Stark."

"Prefer Tom," he said with a slight grimace. I blinked at the exchange. Had these two met before? Tom pulled a chair from one of the other tables and put it at ours. "Not the best accommodations, but *you* picked the place."

Dylan's laughter exploded from deep within his chest.

Heads turned. The toddler hid behind her mother's legs. The dog stood at attention, his ears alert.

Tom had taught me to notice the small things. One thing I'd already noticed was the guy's condescending manner. His mere presence was intimidating. I'd wait to crown him an asshole, but I'd bet twenty bucks he was. I almost said this out loud.

After shaking hands for roughly five long seconds, the men approached the table. Dylan's gaze fell on me. The smile wavered, replaced by a look of...what was it? Darn. I was so tired of my brain playing Scrabble with my mouth. Lust? Disdain? Predator? Thug? I tried to pick out the best words to suit the occasion, but the word 'predator' conjured up images that bothered me. I stood and reached across the table. Dylan gripped my hand and gave it a hard squeeze, then dropped it. I couldn't help but compare the men's pissing contest handshake to Dylan's pathetic 'woman' handshake. Not that he cared, but I did. I sat back down in my chair and crossed my arms. Tom would have to take the lead on this one, because I doubted my ability to control what might come out of my mouth.

Dylan continued to look at me with brown, flat eyes too small for his face. At least he hadn't recognized me. I smiled. Dylan smiled, too. He assumed my smile was for him.

What a creep.

Tom settled in his chair, stuck his long, thin legs out, and crossed them at the ankles. "What's on your mind, Dylan?"

"Keeping my seat as state representative." He grunted. "The primary is the end of July, as I'm sure you know, Tom."

Dylan looked at me. "And you are...Tom's assistant?"

"You might say that," I responded.

He blinked. "Okay. You have a name?"

The ultimate test. To tell him my name is Olivia and not to hear the dreaded, 'oh, you're *that* Olivia.'

"Olivia."

He grinned. His stature reminded me of my ex... broad shoulders, barrel chest. Too tall to fit in a normal chair. A bully.

"Nice to meet you, Olivia."

I returned the smile with one of pure relief. He hadn't recognized me.

Tom threaded his fingers together on the tabletop. "So what do you want, Dylan?"

Tom's bluntness was not lost on me. Something was going on between these two. I draped an arm behind my chair and settled in to watch.

"I'll cut to the chase. It's the ninth hour, and I need intel on my competition. It needs to be quiet. I can't risk any bad press at this point."

"I know how to do my job," Tom muttered.

"I know you do," Dylan added, "but a lot's at stake here. More than you know."

Dylan dug into his sport coat pocket and came up with a couple of pieces of paper, and shoved them at Tom. "Name, home address, social media, email. Family's names. Colleges. I want everything you can find. You have access to that...monitoring system the police have...?"

"A'course. I can get into stuff even the cops can't find." Tom said.

I stared at him, my admiration knowing no bounds. He'd taught me how to use these databases, and he was right. These systems could find almost anything.

Tom chuckled. "Not like this isn't routine, Dylan. We do this all the time."

"If it's not contained, it'll be traced right back to me."

Tom shook his head. "You'll be fine. Discretion is our business." He grazed me with a side look. I could hear his thoughts. *Yeah, except for blondie here. She sticks out like a sore thumb.*

I slid a little lower in my seat. I'd already figured it out. I could be the distraction in the foreground while Tom did his thing in the background.

But Tom was going bye-bye. So now what? I let out a small groan.

"We boring you, sweetie?" Dylan asked.

My eyebrows drew together. I leaned forward. "I have a name."

The big man waved one of his ham hock hands. "Kidding."

Condescension masked as humor. He lost another point.

As an airhead, clueless wife in my former life, I'd learned more than I ever wanted to know about toxic behavior. And Dylan-boy here had better be careful. Tom gave me a look. I nodded once. The men re-focused on each other, agreed on a price, basic timeline, and reporting methodology. We rose together. I resisted pulling aside the tail of my shirt to give him a glimpse of the Smith & Wesson on my belt. This time I kept my hand to myself when the men shook. Dylan gave me a look, then left.

I was sorry I hadn't asked Tom to put down twenty on the guy being an asshole.

Chapter Nine

Hazel laid a ten-dollar bill on the counter at Birdie's Café, received her change, and picked up her sandwich. She hurried outside, up the steps, and into her office next door, trailing clouds of her trademark scent, Chanel Chance.

The morning therapy sessions passed in a flurry of note-taking and hysterics. Two boxes of tissues by noon must be a record. She thought about her first afternoon session as she munched her chicken salad sandwich. Olivia Callahan. Their client-patient relationship had weathered many storms during the past three years, but Olivia hadn't bailed on therapy. Hazel felt proud that she had been the singular one who'd been able to pry open the shell of this abandoned, abused woman who'd become a shining beacon for female victims of assault. Lately, though, she'd become concerned. Her professional boundaries with Olivia were slipping. It was hard to keep one's emotional distance from a client that she enjoyed so much.

Hazel crumpled the lunch leavings into a paper towel and dropped them in the trash, refreshed her lipstick, and pulled out a bottle of water. Her mind straggled back to her new friend, Pete. The disorienting sense that she was about to fall off a cliff plagued her, but how long had it been since a man had given her this much attention? It was fun. That's all. She was determined to enjoy it without unrealistic expectations.

Olivia knocked on her office door and entered.

Hazel's eyebrows rose at the bright-white hair and full makeup.

"Sorry it's been a while," Olivia self-consciously twirled a strand of her hair.

"This is better than that six-month break you took a year ago. I've been looking forward to this. You've changed things up I see," she said with a smile.

"Callie talked me into this. I'm still getting used to it. What do you think?"

Hazel cocked her head and smiled. "It's what you think that matters."

Olivia wrinkled her nose. "I hate it when you say that."

"I know you do." The women laughed. An old joke.

Hazel invited her client into the counseling area of the spacious room, which held a twelve-by-sixteen patterned area rug, an upholstered couch, matching armchairs, side tables, and her therapist's chair. Olivia plopped onto the couch, and Hazel sat in her chair, an end table between them. Hazel leaned in. "So. Catch me up."

Olivia took a deep breath. "Crazy stuff. I know you heard about the fire. Thanks again for reaching out."

"Of course. How's that going?"

"Almost ready to move back in. The fire restoration companies are phenomenal. Lilly is climbing the walls at my next-door neighbor's. The attic and roof are in the final stages of repair, but we don't mind a little noise. We're ready to sleep in our own beds."

Hazel nodded. "I assume the neighbor you're talking about is Callie?"

"Yes." Olivia chuckled. "She does factor in once in a while in our sessions, doesn't she? You must feel like you know her." Olivia heaved out a sigh and stretched her arms across the back of the couch. "I've given them every scrap of information I can remember. The Fire Department investigator has attached herself to me. She funnels information. She's not supposed to, but she does."

Hazel scribbled in her notebook before continuing. "I assume Hunter's come in to support you?"

Olivia started twisting her hands together, a gesture Hazel recognized as tension.

"We're not seeing each other right now."

Silence blanketed the room.

After long seconds, Olivia groaned. "What is it with that man, Hazel? I can't do life with him and don't seem to be able to do it without him, either."

"Why do you think that is?"

Olivia glowered. "I repeat: I hate when you do that."

Hazel put her pad and pen aside, folded her hands in her lap, and said nothing.

"I think…I think *I love him*. Okay, I said it."

"This is a big realization. How are you feeling about it?"

Olivia's cinnamon eyes widened. "Do you think it's been there, and I've avoided the truth?"

"It's hard to be objective about ourselves, Olivia. We can be right in the middle of something and blind to the dangers…or delights of…" her voice trailed away. She stared at the brick wall behind Olivia's chair. *Was Pete a hidden delight in her own life? Or a danger?*

"What? Dangers or delights of what?"

Hazel shook the images of Pete away. "You've been hot and cold with Hunter the past two years. From what you've shared in our sessions, I have a feeling he's in love with you, too. You guys have to figure out what to do with those feelings."

"He's putting pressure on me. Did I tell you he proposed last year? It was too much. I couldn't handle it. I don't blame him if he moves on."

"Me either," Hazel agreed.

Olivia gaped. "You aren't supposed to say things like that."

"Sorry. I'm too comfortable with you. I admit it. I take it back."

"You can't take it back."

Hazel laughed.

"Besides," Olivia said, "I have more urgent things on my mind."

"Being…" Hazel prompted.

"Tom has cancer."

Hazel put a hand to her cheek. "Oh, no."

"Stage Four Leukemia. And he wants to focus on transitioning the business over to me."

"Please tell him I'm thinking of him, okay? That's awful news."

"It *is* awful, and I don't know what I'm going to do without him. What I know about being an investigator, I owe to him."

The women sat in symbiotic silence for a few seconds.

"How long?" Hazel asked.

"Three months at most, he told me."

The older woman blew out a long, sad breath. "Life comes to an end sooner than we think."

Olivia squinted at her. "Aren't you and Tom around the same age?"

"Haven't told you yet, not telling you now."

Olivia laughed. "I can google it, you know."

"I hired someone to scrub my presence a while back. Except for the innocuous bits. I'm getting ready to retire, too, you know."

"About time," Olivia quipped.

"We really do know each other too well."

"We should trash the therapy and be friends."

She shrugged. "Professional ethics say to refrain from close friendships with clients. It's too emotionally complex, and the regulations are to wait a couple of years before even trying. I'd be useless as a therapist if we became close friends, and given all that I know about your life, I think you'd be uncomfortable. Our relationship isn't a level playing field. You can understand that, right?"

Olivia rolled her eyes. "Okay. Let's hold off on being friends. Whatever."

Hazel pulled her pad back into her lap. "Let's talk about the white elephant in the room." She eyeballed the top of Olivia's head.

Olivia laughed. "You mean my hair?"

She fanned her hand up and down. "The whole effort."

"I kept griping about my notoriety. My publisher's publicist did a great job, but it's made my life so public that I'm miserable. I can't go anywhere without people hovering, asking for a selfie, wanting to tell me what they've been through. My agent is desperate for book two, and I don't want to write it." Olivia sighed. "A private investigator is supposed to be discreet. Anyway, Callie suggested it after listening to me whine." Olivia grinned. "I can get in anywhere, now. No one recognizes me. I love it."

"And you think this new look is…discreet?"

Olivia laughed. "I thought I'd have a heart attack when Callie pushed me to do this, but once I caught the vision, I was done. Hair, makeup, different wardrobe, the works." Olivia stuck out her hand. "I even got a manicure."

Hazel stared at Olivia's hands, the tapering fingertips adorned with magenta polish that had worn around the edges.

"First one ever. And look." She made a pouty mouth to show off her lips.

Hazel laughed. "Monty never let you go to a salon?"

"I can't remember."

"Maybe you don't need to remember."

Olivia shook her head slightly. "Yeah, I don't want to go there. But the point is, I'm loving this."

Hazel took in the stunning platinum-blonde bob, dark eyeliner, bright lipstick. Leggings topped by a linen sheath, a chunky, silver necklace. Matching bracelets.

"Do you think Callie's responsible?"

"What do you mean?"

"She suggested it, right? But *you* made the choice."

Olivia brightened. "I did, didn't I?"

Hazel nodded. "Olivia, I think you are becoming your own person for the first time in your life."

Chapter Ten

"What's the matter?" Sherry asked, her big, blue eyes sparking concern. "Don't you like it here?"

The Harriman House restaurant server had seated us at a table next to the one Sergeant Hunter Faraday, and I had occupied two years ago, so I was a little misty-eyed. Back when the bloom of our romance had been exciting and new, I'd been fresh from the hospital, trying to recover my memory and find a road map to my new life. Finding out the truth had been impossibly hard, and I wonder now if I'd hurried past it, closing my eyes on purpose. "Hunter and I came here once," I said.

The server brought a bottle of wine and uncorked it.

"I would have never suggested this place if I'd known, Olivia."

"No worries at all. I need to move on. The guy—"

"The guy is crazy about you, and you need to pull the plug. Or rip the cord. However you want to put it, he should put a ring on your finger."

The server scuttled back to the table to pour the wine. I took a sip. "He proposed last fall."

Sherry's eyes went round as saucers. "What! Why didn't you tell us?"

"It didn't feel right. And I wasn't in the mood for input."

"I get it," she said and focused on the couple waiting for seating at the hostess station. "I think that's Hazel," she whispered.

My head whipped around. Sure enough, there stood my therapist. Laughing and flirting with some guy.

I'd known the woman three years, and I'd never heard her laugh like that.

I leaned toward Sherry across the table. "I can't picture her outside her office."

Sherry sliced her eyes toward Hazel and the man as they walked past. "Who is he?"

The man pulled out Hazel's chair and then bent down and kissed her.

I could not believe my eyes. Was my seventy-something therapist out on a *date*? I almost choked on my wine. "I don't know who that is, but you can bet I'm going to find out," I whispered.

Sherry shrugged. "She's human, too. Hey, but one thing is awesome…they didn't recognize you on the way to their table. Should you stay undercover?"

I chewed on my fingernail. "Maybe. Let's kind of watch."

Sherry lifted her eyebrows. "Do your thing."

We clinked wine glasses.

I had a tracking tile in my purse. Whether Hazel accepted it or not, I counted her one of the most important people in my life. For her own safety, I wanted to check out this dude.

"I'm headed to the restroom. Be right back," I told Sherry.

Head down, I slid past their table. In a fortuitous turn of events, her purse hung on the back of her chair. I dropped the small GPS tracking tile into it and told myself the small deception was for her protection. The two of them were so engrossed in conversation and menus that they didn't notice me.

I stole back to the table by a different route. Sherry's face was rosy with excitement. Or wine. Or both.

"Man! You're getting good at this."

I glanced at Hazel's table. "And now I'll come out of hiding. Watch."

"What are you going to say?"

"The things people say when they see other people they know in a restaurant. Y'know…normal."

"Right. Normal."

I slung my purse over my shoulder and sauntered over as if I'd only noticed them at this moment. "Hazel!" I exclaimed, my tone as shiny as a new penny. "Nice to see you out and about."

Hazel's head jerked. She blinked. Her reactions were telling. As Tom had taught me, micro-expressions were important. Her micros were freaking out.

"Olivia, how are you, dear?" She waved vaguely at her date. "Olivia, meet Pete."

Pete rose from his chair and reached out. I shook his hand. It took me a minute to get my hand back. The reactions I got to my new look amazed me. All the clichés about blondes…true. "Great to meet you, Olivia."

I pointed at Sherry. "My work colleague is over there. We hopped in to grab a bite before heading home."

Hazel was fidgety. And what the heck was up with this guy? Was it my imagination, or was he studying me like some rare insect he'd discovered? "I'll let you get back to your evening. Pete, nice to meet you. Where did you say you worked? You look familiar."

Pete smiled. "I didn't say."

Hazel stared at the floor.

I held Pete's gaze for a second. His response *totally* validated the tracker. I smiled and left.

Sherry and I finished dinner, paid the tab, and walked out. "So what do you think?" she asked.

I walked to my car and opened the door. "I think I have a long night ahead."

She grinned. "Be safe."

I raced back to my office, threw on my typical dark jeans and black, long-sleeve top combo that I used for surveillance. My tracking app told me Hazel's purse, and lover-boy Pete had lingered at the restaurant, so that meant two or three drinks. The blinking red light on the tracker's map began to move as I pulled the top over my head. Looking in the mirror, I realized I needed to hide this hair during surveillance, because Tom was right, it stuck out like a light bulb. I grabbed a hoodie. Looked at my phone.

The pinging, alert little circle moved in the direction of Hazel's house on the outskirts of Westminster. After checking in with Lilly, who was still bunking with Callie's daughter, I drove off into the darkness, wondering where this would lead and how Tom would feel about my after-hours, late-night skulking.

He would not approve. After all, it was pro-bono.

But he would understand.

I glanced at the larger, stronger tracker I'd brought with me. If I felt it was necessary, I'd attach it to Pete's car...if they'd been in Pete's car and he'd been invited into Hazel's house, I'd run his plate and go from there. Tom would kill me for the waste of a good tracker, but if I couldn't get it back, I'd buy him a new one. I needed to keep my own stash of those things, anyway.

As I approached her driveway, I registered two important pieces of information: the garage was closed, which meant her vehicle was inside. An unfamiliar vehicle was parked in the drive.

Nosing my car off the road into a secluded vacant lot, I parked and ran the numbers. A Hertz rental. That wasn't strange at all. A quick search of Pete's driver's license details revealed that he'd been charged with stalking a couple of years ago and lived in Owings Mills, Maryland, and racked up a couple of DUIs. The more sensitive files I was unable to access. Either outdated or sealed, but either way, my software didn't go deep enough.

The stalking charges had been dropped, but that made him even more creepy. I grabbed my tracking device—the expensive one with gorilla magnets and long-lasting battery life—knowing the law did not allow a private investigator to track someone without a reason. I brushed caution away as if sweeping a cobweb off the ceiling. Sometimes, breaking the law was necessary. Besides, though I'd not been hired to surveil the guy, he damn well needed surveilling.

I studied Hazel's home. The lights were on in the living area. Curtains closed. Shadows of one short, curly-haired person and one much taller male form walked back and forth. The shadows left the room. My heart beat in my throat. *Hazel, don't do it!*

I bit a fingernail and waited to see if her upstairs bedroom light would come on, feeling like a pervert. When a light came on at the back of the first floor, I heaved a sigh of relief. My guess was that she'd fixed them something in her kitchen, which gave me time.

A surge of adrenalin raced up my back. My fingers tingled. I exited my vehicle. The tracker in my hand felt sturdy and reliable. Sometimes my instincts were off, but not this time. I had a definite bad feeling.

I stole across the road. Circa-seventies-style homes with tidy, half-acre lots populated the street. A few lights remained on in the homes at this hour, and streetlamps hadn't been installed on this stretch of hilly suburbia. Darkness was a PI's best friend, Tom was fond of saying as we'd woven through the night in search of proof of an adulterous liaison or any number of investigation requests. I felt hugged by the dark as I crept ever closer to Hazel's driveway, but when I rammed my cheek into a mailbox, I cursed and flicked on my phone flashlight. Like sentinels, mailboxes marched down the street in each yard as far as I could see. I stepped away from the grass and onto the street, hoping no one would see a stooped, dark shadow in a hoodie creeping through the neighborhood and make an ill-timed 9-1-1 call.

I walked faster.

I approached the back of Pete's car like a cat stalking prey. Glancing at Hazel's windows, I dropped to the concrete and felt around under the car for any convenient metal to attach the magnetic tracker. My gloved hands ran into the ubiquitous plastic that had become all too common in late-model cars. Light blazed across the front yard. I heard the scraping of a door. Voices.

Dampness broke out on my forehead. I groped faster. Muttering under my breath, I took the glove off my right hand in a desperate search for metal. *There.* The reassuring feel of cold, hard, solid metal. I positioned the tracker and held my breath. Slid my glove back on.

"It's been a real nice evening, Pete," I heard Hazel say from her porch. "I enjoyed it."

"Me too," Pete said, his steps moving down the steps.

I stiffened. If I ran now, he'd see me.

His steps stopped. They changed direction and trotted back up the stairs.

I let out the breath I'd been holding.

"Did I forget my phone?" he asked.

Hazel tittered. They both went back inside.

I raced into her neighbor's yard and hid behind a boxwood shrub, peeking through the leaves. Hazel followed him back to his car, where they shared a hug. After Pete started the car, Hazel went inside. A few minutes later, I saw her bedroom light come on. Pete sat in the driveway, checking his phone. Bluetooth picked up a call. Incredulous at my good fortune, I realized I could hear pieces of the conversation.

"…any worthwhile information?" a female voice asked. Pete's voice, "the woman is rock-solid on the limits of her profession. Can't get a thing out of her." The female voice again, but I couldn't make out the words. What did they want from Hazel? Pete's voice returned. "Did you see the news about her house? The fire?" Burbles of response from the woman that I couldn't make out. This was *me* they were talking about. I closed my eyes. This intel is going to kill her. I crept closer.

"Yeah, she knew all about it. I confirmed that Olivia Callahan is her client by the way she acted when she introduced her at dinner tonight, but she can't share stuff they talk about in therapy or even that she's a client. I could tell, though. You were right about that."

I smiled. Way to play your cards close to the vest, Hazel.

Female voice.

"…made you?" Pete's voice. "Nope. This sweet, old lady believes I'm hot for her." He laughed. "It's sad."

Pete continued talking as he pulled out of Hazel's drive, into the street, and drove off. I sat back in the grass and stretched the kinks out of my legs. Who had Pete been talking to?

The neighbor's door flew open. Outdoor lights on each corner of the house came on. "Who's out there?" a voice demanded.

I shot up from the grass. "I'm just out for a walk. Taking a little break," I smiled.

"Well, don't scare people half to death!"

I strolled toward my car. Hazel's porchlight flipped on.

I ran.

Chapter Eleven

I stumbled into reception, pushing my hair out of my eyes. "Morning," I muttered.

"You look like something the cat dragged in," Tom joked as he sipped his coffee.

I sat in the chair across from Tom and pondered the day I'd accepted his request for an intern. Best decision ever.

"I *feel* like something the cat dragged in, too."

"Can't be easy sleeping on that hard-ass bed you got back there."

Sherry turned her face away so she wouldn't give away my secret. She had the kind of face that any self-respecting PI could read. She was dying for a chance to talk about my late-night bird-dogging. Who me? Sleep? Not last night.

"Yeah," I said, with a yawn. I stretched my arms above my head. "Didn't sleep, for some reason."

"How's the house comin'? Any progress on that case? Do they need an assist? From us?"

He smiled in that slow, fun way he had. Like an aging kid trying to talk a parent into giving them the keys to the car.

I laughed. "They do. They're stuck. But somehow, I don't think they'd want the victim on their payroll. They'll figure it out," I said, with more assurance than I felt.

"Don't you go sneakin' off without me," Tom said. "A fire investigation is a whole different animal." With a nod at Sherry, he strolled to his desk. We were an odd pairing, but it worked. I mouthed 'we'll talk later' at Sherry's questioning blue eyes.

I sat at my desk and opened my laptop. The calendar displayed on the screen told me we had an interview scheduled today. For the Dylan Palmer job.

"So what's going on with the Palmer investigation? It's been over a week and not a peep."

Tom smiled at me from across the room. "It's goin'."

I frowned.

After a pause, Tom continued, "You want to do that interview today?"

"Sure," I said, uncertain. "But we usually both go. You don't want to go to this one?"

"Don't you think it's about time to fly solo?"

I blinked. "You think I'm ready?"

"You're ready." Tom slapped his planner closed.

The man used the old-fashioned, refillable kind with paper in it and a place to keep a pen and business cards.

"Listen. We need to talk," he said. He jabbed his index finger at the two chairs in front of his desk. "Come on over here."

While I walked over into Tom's 'territory', he wheeled his chair around to his filing cabinets, pulled out a pile of folders a foot thick, and dropped them on his desk.

He pushed the pile toward me. "Want you to start goin' through these, okay? There's more where these came from."

My forehead furrowed. "But Tom, I don't know if—"

"Now don't you go doin' that," he fussed. "You knew this day was comin', right? You got a right to inherit my client base, and there's no one more deserving. And I'm here now, in case you have questions." He gave me a stern look under thick, gray, eyebrows. "It's settled." He thumbed through the folders, looking for something.

I struggled to believe this was happening. I thought maybe in ten years, but now?

I. Was. Not. Ready.

I tightened my jaw, my face like a vise. No way would I cry right here in front of him.

He found the file he was looking for, slid it into a desk drawer and, locked it, then handed me the rest. "Start on these. When you have time, contact these people and let them know I'm easing out and you're easing in. Remember… these folks are more than clients, they're good friends. You're gonna have to earn their trust."

"I will, Tom." I straightened my shoulders and picked up the pile. What had he hidden away, though?

Tom closed his eyes. His hand rested on his stomach. "Most of the time I'm not feelin' so good, now, but I'll only be a phone call away. Would you take on the interviews and surveillance? If I'm not havin' a good day, I mean."

"Of course, Tom."

Tom ran his fingers across the silver stubble on his chin. "You get that release from Sturgis?"

"He's waiting for my schedule to open up so I can get to Richmond for a thorough exam. But he's confident I'm able to handle this work. I mean, gosh, it's been almost three years since the incident. Also, the occupational therapist gave me a release."

He nodded. "Maryland is a little picky in that regard, so make sure you have 'em before you petition for the license."

I rose, holding the files in my arms. "Got it." I put the batch of files on my desk and walked back. "Go home, Tom. I'll take care of things."

"That interview this afternoon, it's tricky, so use your best female intuition."

I frowned. "Who is it?"

"Louise Waymire." He tilted his head back, looked at me under lowered eyelids. "I called Scott Waymire's wife, Louise. Might've hinted that we wanted to interview her for the possibility of an article."

My chin jerked into my neck. "Article for what?"

Tom was quiet.

I put a hand on my hip, thinking it through. "So. You called her to set this up, figuring I'd go along with it?"

Tom drummed his fingers on his desk.

"There's no article, is there?"

He smiled.

I stared up at the ceiling and sighed.

Tom threaded his fingers behind his head, waiting.

I glared at him and gagged a little, but said, "I'm in."

He shrugged. "Now, was that so hard?" He threw a tracker tile in my lap." In case you get the chance."

"One of these days, we're going to get caught, you know."

He shrugged. "I'm retirin'. Not much chance they'll catch me. What you do in your own firm is your business. Personally, I don't like runnin' around trying to find people. Waste of time when you can do it this way."

Gosh, I would miss this man. We just...got each other.

Lunch was a quick microwave affair, and the meeting with Louise Waymire wasn't until three, so I slow-walked my lane, relishing the warmth of the sun, the sound of birds. Since the fire, I hadn't had the luxury of sitting on my front porch in the evenings with a cup of tea, watching the birds. I missed it, but I did manage to fill their birdfeeders once a week.

I quickened my steps.

As I drew closer, I heard the sound of male voices, spied white work vans and sawhorses, and circular saws. Sounds of the buzzing saws and the smell of fresh-cut wood filled the air. Roofing supplies lay in front of my detached garage, and one of the crew climbed a ladder with a pile of shingles on his shoulder.

My beautiful, white front porch that spanned the front of my house sported a brand-new foundation and fresh boards waiting to be painted. The original porch lay in a heap to one side. I experienced a pang of regret that the porch my ex and I had worked so hard to restore was now only fit for the community dump. The death of an old friend.

"Okay, if I go in?" I asked one of the guys on the ground. He nodded.

I glanced at my watch. I still had a couple of hours. Skirting the piles, I walked across the new porch and opened the front door. Someone had re-painted the red screen door that I loved so much. They'd put my porch furniture in the den to get it out of the way. I slipped inside and headed to the laundry room behind the kitchen. I longed to open the windows, clean the floors. Buy new rugs. Not quite time yet, but soon. The area rugs had been tossed by the remediation people. My nose picked up the faint smell of mold, but I had been reassured that it would dissipate. The downstairs had already been restored. Bedrooms come next. I threw the fabric covers into the washer and turned it on. Opened all the windows in the house. Walked into the kitchen and opened the fridge to see if any food had survived.

My mouth dropped open.

The shelves had been rearranged to make room for it.

Daffodils and daisies in a vase.

My hand shook when I reached for the card.

"Love, a devoted Foofoo."

Okay. Now I was mad.

Chapter Twelve

Sergeant Faraday sat at his desk at Richmond PD Headquarters at 200 West Grace Street, hunched over reports, cursing the day he'd been promoted. The young patrol cop standing beside his desk eyed him. "Something wrong, sir?"

Faraday reached for the file the rookie had brought him. "Working out some things in my head, that's all."

"Understand, sir."

Faraday leafed through the report, then noticed the rookie was standing there, awkward and waiting and nervous.

"Dismissed, Donaldson," he said with a sigh.

"Yes, sir." The young cop saluted, spun around, and left.

Faraday rolled his eyes. "Rookies," he muttered.

His landline lit up with an unfamiliar number. He tossed the file on his desk and answered.

"Faraday."

"Hunter, it's Callie. Olivia's neighbor?"

Hunter's eyebrows rose. This was a first. His heart beat faster. "What's going on?" "Olivia's fine, Hunter. Sorry. I didn't even think you might—"

"That's okay," he interrupted, his voice brisk. No telling how much of this conversation would get back to Olivia.

Callie cleared her throat. "This fire thing? I don't know if there's a connection, but Olivia's been getting flowers. From her followers in that group. I wondered if you could look into it?"

"Flowers?" Hunter pulled out his notepad and started scribbling. "Why would that be a concern?"

"Daffodils and daisies. Twice. I'm concerned because they're from that freak fan club cult, Friends of Olivia. I figured they might mean something, and they do. I looked them up."

"And..." Hunter drawled in his warmest Richmond accent, "why did you say she wouldn't call me about this herself?"

Callie laughed. "I know you two are circling the wagons or something... I'm not going there. This is strictly from me. She's acting like it's no big deal, but with the fire and being out of her house and the PI thing—"

He grunted. "How's that going?"

"As far as she's concerned, it's the best thing that ever happened to her. I hope she knows what she's doing. It's a different world than thirty years ago. She won't listen to me, but...." Callie's voice trailed away.

"You're a good friend, Callie. I'll look into it, okay?"

"You won't tell her I called, right?" She paused. "You really care about her, don't you?"

"That's a fact," he replied, a flush climbing from his neck to his jaw. Did he just say that? To Olivia's best friend?

Crap.

Hunter stroked his upper lip. "Facebook group, the Friends of Olivia thing? I've looked in a time or two. Are there more?"

"Not as far as I know."

After they ended the call, Faraday leaned back in his chair, thinking. He glanced at his watch. Damn. Almost lunchtime, and he'd made plans to meet Shiloh.

Shiloh clutched her cell to her ear in the downtown deli as Hunter walked in. She held up one finger. He sat, folded his hands on top of the table, and considered how different Shi was from Olivia Callahan.

Shiloh's shoulder-length hair was light blond, whereas Olivia's hair was auburn. Shiloh was tall, almost as tall as his own six-foot-height, and Olivia was tiny...five feet, three inches or so. Shiloh worked out daily and liked to show it off with tight-knit tops and leggings. Form-fitting jeans when she was on the job.

Olivia would never wear stuff like that.

The first time he met her at her home in Glyndon, she wore the uniform of a busy mom—the bare minimum of jewelry, not much makeup, pullover, and Capris. Shiloh played up her assets to the max. Too much, in Hunter's opinion. He shrugged. Maybe it was the job. Sometimes she worked undercover as a hooker.

Shiloh jerked him out of his ruminations when she ended the call by slamming the phone down. His eyebrows rose.

"Problems?"

"Always," she quipped. "How's it goin'?"

He smiled. "I hate my job," he said.

"Knew you would," she said, slipping a straw between her bright pink lips to take a sip of her lemonade. "I couldn't do it. Wouldn't."

"They offer?"

"Yeah. Not for me. I like the street."

"Good way to get killed."

"Good way *not* to get lazy," she countered.

Hunter conceded the point. A waitress walked up, took their orders.

"How's Savannah?" Hunter asked.

"I like it. It's going well." She shrugged. "Come see me."

"I'll try," he said.

"How about in three weeks? I'm taking some time off. I'll show you around."

"I'll think about it." Hunter absently drew patterns on the table with his index finger.

Shiloh tilted her head. "You're quiet. That promotion must have you all tied up in knots. Can they slide you onto another unit? Something you'd like more than Major Crimes? What about Special Investigations?"

"Don't get me wrong, the paycheck is great, and I'm puttin' some away… but I don't think I'm cut out for it."

"I get it. One sniff of a drug bust, and I'm like a coonhound. Don't know how I'd respond to an office job."

Hunter lifted an eyebrow. "Coonhound?"

Shiloh waved one of her hands. "My dad used to hunt. He raised coonhounds. Had a whole flock of 'em. I can hear them treeing a possum or 'coon in my dreams." She shrugged. "What I remember is how excited he got racing along behind those damn dogs. I feel the same way about a drug bust."

And there it was. She *got* him. She got his job, she got the pressure, she got the street cred vibe. She got it all. So why didn't he want to pursue a serious relationship? He put his elbow on the table and his chin in his hand.

"It's okay, baby," Shiloh murmured. The server arrived with two plates, set them down, and left.

"What's okay?"

"You aren't sure about visiting me, which means once again, you can't commit." She shrugged. "Hey, you know me. I'm okay either way."

Hunter cocked one eyebrow. "Are you?"

Shi looked past him at the busy street outside. "Nope."

Hunter sighed. "Figured."

Chapter Thirteen

I teetered up the sidewalk of Scott and Louise Waymire's mid-sized home in high heels, hoping my cover would hold.

My cell vibrated with a text. Tom. Giving me a thumbs-up icon of encouragement on my first solo interview.

I smiled.

I studied the house. Redbrick, one story. Freshly mown yard. A blow-up kiddie pool at the side of the house and a red plastic wagon with a stuffed unicorn sitting in it. So they had kids. My research revealed that Scott had graduated from respected universities, with honors, and was up for partner with Schmidt & Schmidt downtown, a huge law firm. I took a deep breath. If Louise started asking questions, I'd make something up. Perhaps a graduate student assignment. I was flying by the seat of my pants here. Tom said he'd wanted to get a feel for the marriage in general, the family dynamic. I wondered, since my own twenty-year marriage had been such a disaster, if I could pick up on signals that alerted me to problems.

I'd better, or what had all that therapy been about?

I smoothed my skirt, tucked in my shirt. Tugged my hat into place. Minimum makeup. Prop glasses. I didn't want this woman to recognize me, ever. I knocked on a door with a brass doorknocker surrounded by a wreath of faux flowers.

Steps approached. The door opened. Louise was attractive and poised and had highlighted blond hair and blue eyes. Her smile was welcoming, and her teeth looked like the result of good orthodontia. Her arms looked solid and muscled as we shook hands. This woman took care of herself.

"You must be Marla. Come on in. Would you like something to drink?"

"Thanks for agreeing to talk to us, Mrs. Waymire." I stepped inside. The Waymire's home was picked up, smelled good, and the kids were school-age because I didn't hear the sounds of raucous toddlers. Louise showed me to their living room, then left to bring our drinks. Tom and I were stepping on all kinds of laws, and I was nervous. Was I only just realizing his rebellious streak of his? Maybe his diagnosis had thrown him into overdrive.

Louise bustled in, holding a tray with two black coffees, a creamer, and sugar. We prepared our coffees and talked about the weather. After five minutes, a pause presented itself, and I dove in.

"Shall we start?" I pulled out my notebook.

Louise picked at her skirt. Adjusted the watch on her wrist. Nerves. I watched her lips pucker for a fleeting half-second, and she touched the side of one eye. Disinterest. Disengagement.

She did not want to do this.

"Go ahead." Her eyes darted to the left. Another tell. She was about to say something that conflicted with the truth. "But I need to tell you that Scott is the only reason I'm doing this." Her smile was lopsided. Sign of mixed emotions.

"I'll be brief, Louise," I replied, digging out my cell. "Mind if I record? No one will listen to this but me." A lie, but whatever. Blame it on Tom.

"Rather you didn't."

"No problem." I tucked my phone back into my pocket. A little bell tinkled in the back of my mind. Why didn't she want to be recorded?

I went through a list of questions. Length of marriage, how many kids, Scott's upbringing, personal family life, people he wanted to invite to his fantasy dinner, people she wanted to invite to hers, Scott's favorite recreational activities and hangouts, his aspirations and dreams. Where they attended church. When I reached the firebomb I'd buried deep down the list, I stared at it a few seconds.

Louise rose, asked if I wanted water. I declined, and she walked into the kitchen.

She wants this to be over.

I listened to the sounds of the fridge opening and closing. Cabinets opening. Water pouring. The jangle of ice cubes. A large cat strolled into the room. A gorgeous cat, too…looked like a Ragdoll. I reached out my hand. The cat trotted over and put its head underneath. Louise got major points for the cat.

She returned. "I see you've met Hermes."

"Beautiful boy," I murmured.

Louise beamed. "He's a great cat. My buddy. Do you have one?"

I told her about Riot.

And just like that, we were best friends. Over cats.

A wave of conviction floated over me. I wasn't cut out for all this lying. I looked at my question. Lifted my gaze to hers. She sat on a light-colored couch across from me. A chalk-painted, white fireplace anchored one wall. The mantle held framed family pictures. They'd included the cat in their photos. A large, round coffee table divided the space between us. I pointed to a beautiful piece of pottery filled with beach shells. "Eastern shore?"

Again, Louise beamed.

This bonding thing was so easy.

"We bought a beach house in Ocean City. My kids are delighted." She chuckled.

I smiled. "That's wonderful. I've made some great memories at the beach, too." I addressed the list in my lap. "You've been so patient. You up for one more question?"

All warmed up and sunshiny toward me, she nodded. The smile was genuine.

"What has been your biggest regret in life, Louise?"

I looked at my pad, my pen poised over it. She couldn't know that my database had revealed a personal history marked with a patchwork of juvenile offenses. Her husband's PR firm or some other vested party had gone to great lengths to bury some additional sketchy offenses, but I'd find out what they were. Unless she answered this question with a lot more info than I'd hoped. Asking this question gave me no satisfaction, but her answer would reveal a lot.

Amused, she looked out the window and shook her head.

After a long silence, she gave me a look that made me want to crawl inside the fireplace. "You hit gold, didn't you?"

I did my best to look puzzled.

She closed her eyes and sank back into the cushions. "I told him this might happen if he ran for office. Can we keep this next part off the record?"

I put down my pen. "Done."

She raised her hands and drew air quotes.

" 'Neglected teenager desperate for attention.' Alcoholic parents, foster homes. An old story. I spent time in juvie. Records have been sealed, so..." She threw me a questioning look. "Scottie knew all that when we married. He loved me anyway." Louise's eyes grew damp.

I squirmed in my chair. I berated myself as the worst kind of human garbage.

Her voice soft, she continued. "In a way, he was my savior. He forgave me. And I've been different ever since. Marla, all that is past, and I've let it go. Can you? Can you give us a break and not put it out there for public disclosure?"

My fake persona slipped a little. "But don't you think... if the public does find out, that there is a good chance that they'll understand? That they won't hold it against you?"

Her jaw clenched, and fire lit her eyes. "People judge. If Scott wins this primary, I'm not always going to be at his side. I'll help in other ways, but I'm not about to let the damn media circus invade my life."

Boy. Could I ever relate.

This had been a mistake. I really liked Louise, now.

Tom shouldn't have put me in this situation.

I stood. "I think that'll do it, Louise. Thanks so much for sharing your life with me. I'll let you know when the article runs."

Which would be never. I gathered my things.

"What happens now?" she asked as she rose from the couch, her arms tight across her chest. No more buddy-buddy stuff going on, that was for sure.

"If this gets out, Louise, it won't be from me, okay? You have my word." Did I have scruples? I used to have scruples. How could I give her my word when I knew every stinking detail of this interview would go straight in a file that I'd hand over to Dylan Palmer?

I couldn't meet her eyes.

She nodded. "I'll...I'll let you see yourself out."

Like a whipped dog, I slunk away.

Chapter Fourteen

The Waymire interview needed sorting out. Tom would like the insights I discovered, but Dylan-the-scumbag would want more than that. If he knew about Louise's past, he'd crucify her. I couldn't let that happen.

I threw the covers back, jumped out of bed, and performed my morning stretches, toe touches, push-ups, and crunches.

I grinned as I soaped up and shampooed my hair. What a glorious feeling to be healthy and whole. I'd never take it for granted again. After the shower, I finger-combed my platinum curls and threw on jeans, slip-on sneakers, and whatever top I could find that wasn't in the dirty clothes. With a grimace at the small bedroom and the mess I kept leaving in there, I walked into the office.

No Sherry.

I glanced at my watch. It was early yet. She'd be here.

Wait.

Where was my phone?

I ran back to the bedroom and tossed my bed, ransacked the pockets of the clothes I'd worn yesterday. My hand slapped across my mouth. It couldn't be.

Had I left my phone at Louise Waymire's house?

I slumped onto the floor. No, no, no!

Password protected.

Yeah, but what if she'd found it the moment I'd left, and it hadn't hibernated yet?

What would she find?

I heard the barest vibration. A glimmer of hope trickled through. I rose from the floor and picked up the clothes on the floor in order to dump them in the washer. To my vast relief, the phone dropped out. I threw down the pile and clutched my phone to my chest in rapturous gratitude.

With a thousand pounds of disaster lifted off me, I started my laundry, then sailed to my desk and started rifling through notes and reminders. My phone buzzed. I looked at the lit-up screen and gasped. How many texts had I missed while I was showering? I snatched it.

Sherry.

Each text increasing in hysteria.

I called her.

"Where have you been?" she screeched. "Tom's at St. Agnes. He's in intensive care. You don't have anything much on your calendar today, right? Can you come?"

"I'm sorry! It was...I'll explain later. Yep. I'll be there in a flash."

I slipped the phone in my back pocket. Pulled the Smith & Wesson out of the safe and clipped it to my belt. "It must be bad if he's at St. Agnes," I muttered under my breath.

I flew out to my car, called Lilly on the way, and wove in and out of traffic trying to make good time, an impossible task during a weekday morning. Joining four lanes of irritable, stressed drivers going the same direction was *not* the best way to make it to downtown Baltimore in record time.

Sherry leapt up from the waiting room chair when I walked out of the elevator. "I'm glad you're here." Her huge, blue, sad eyes told the story. "His organs are shutting down."

I looked around. "Where's his family?"

Sherry shook her head. "I tried to find some. No wife, his folks have passed away. No cousins I could find." Her eyes wet, she said, "We may be it."

"Poor Tom. Will they let me see him?"

"They let me, so... I think they feel bad that no family's around."

The elevator opened. Hazel stepped out.

"Hi, girls. How's Tom?"

I blinked. "How did you find out?"

"Tom's been a friend for a long time. He has no one else." She flapped her hands as if to shoo away a fly. "Don't ask."

I blinked. Was there a story behind Tom's singleness?

A nurse approached. "Tom doesn't have long. An hour, maybe. Is anyone family?"

I sighed. "Not by blood…."

The nurse nodded. "Good enough. You guys can go on in. Don't tell anyone you're not family, okay?" She winked and left us.

With the hush of solemnity upon us, we crept into Tom's darkened room. I stood by his head, and Hazel stood on the opposite side of the bed and held one of his frail hands. Sherry stood at the end of the bed, her hands clasped behind her back. "Should we…say some words?" Sherry whispered. Tom picked up the oxygen mask. "Not dead yet," he rasped.

"Tom!" I picked up his hand on my side. "What happened?"

With effort, he turned his head toward me. "Told you. This time was always gonna come, gal. How was…"

I pulled up a chair. "The interview?"

His nod was weak.

"I found out some excellent information. We can use it."

He opened one eye. "*You* can use it."

"Oh, Tom," I murmured, stroking his hand.

"You got this. You're good, gal. You know what to do. Do it," he whispered, so softly I had to lean my ear to his lips to make out the words. He smiled, squeezed my hand. "Ready to go."

Hazel patted his arm, her cheeks streaked with tears. "Hey, old man," she said.

Tom didn't have the energy to open his eyes. "Seein' me off?"

Hazel smiled. "Something like that. We love you, Tom."

To my surprise, a tear slid down his face. The most emotionless man I'd ever known could cry.

Sherry turned away. Tom didn't display emotions…but Sherry displayed every single one. I could hear her whimpers, and in two seconds, we'd have full-scale blubbering.

Tom wiggled his hand in mine. "Tell her it's okay. Sherry girl. She's a good girl."

"She heard you, Tom," I replied, glancing at Sherry, who lost it all over again.

I told Tom about the interview, deleting the firebomb question. I assured him I'd review the files down to the last detail, that he'd left his clients in good hands. I promised him I'd take care of them. Hazel gave me a look. She was conflicted about my career choice. Along with most of the population in my orbit.

Except Tom. He had believed in me. Supported me. Encouraged me.

I loved him for it.

Hazel started talking about days long gone, when she and Tom had been in high school together, before Westminster had gotten so huge. When Carroll County was made up of farmland, barns, and acres of corn and cattle and horses. Tom smiled through all the telling.

The nurse checked in and whispered that his time was close, then left.

We continued holding his hands, watching this dear man leave his earthly body. He had poured so much of himself, his knowledge, his lifeblood into me. Passed on his secrets, techniques, tips. I wasn't sure what the future would hold, but I'd promised to carry on the work. I'd find a way to keep that promise. No matter what.

His breath rattled in his chest. His mouth drooped open. Tom's breathing became labored, harsh. A grayish pallor crept across his face, and his arms moved in restless bursts. I rubbed his hand. It was ice-cold. A doctor walked into the room.

"You must be Tom's family," he said.

We didn't bother to correct him.

"I'm glad you were able to be here," he said.

Tom emitted a blast of air, then time stood still.

The monitor plunged to its bottom-line death knell. Time of death was declared.

I stumbled into the waiting room, dropped into a chair, put my head in my hands. Without Tom, I felt helpless. Hopeless. It wasn't true. I knew it wasn't...but for now, I let my feelings have their way.

Hazel walked out and put her arm around me.

"What now," I whimpered. "He has no family. Has he selected a burial site? What does he want, cremation or burial? What about the funeral?"

Hazel patted my back. "Tom approached me a couple of years ago, Olivia. I'm the executor of his estate, and I have power of attorney. I've got this."

My eyes widened in shock. "Well, you must've been *really* close."

"Close friends are often better than family," she said and returned to Tom's side.

Chapter Fifteen

True to her word, Hazel took care of the funeral arrangements. She cancelled her appointments except for emergencies, and became a whirlwind of funereal activity. Tom, like my former divorce attorney, Earl; would be laid to rest in the same cemetery in the heart of Westminster. I was glad I'd be able to visit both at one time.

Small comfort.

I checked my calendar. Tom's celebration of life was this weekend. Tom hadn't been much for organized religion. We'd be in a park pavilion overlooking Carroll County's flowing hills. He'd have loved knowing that. Tom had liked wearing crazy socks, so attendees had been asked to bring a pair of fun socks that Tom would like, in his honor. Hazel had told me she was going to put them all in a basket, and people could pick out a favorite pair on their way out in memory of Tom.

I was amazed at Hazel's thoughtfulness. I hoped, somehow, that Tom would be watching.

I pecked half-heartedly at my keyboard. The meeting Dylan had demanded after hearing about Tom's demise had not yet happened. I'd given him status updates via email, but he requested a sit-down. I snorted. Exactly what I needed—a face-to-face with a bully on a power trip. When he'd discovered Tom's obit, he'd left a furious voicemail. How insensitive could someone be? Like it was Tom's fault that he died?

An email popped into the screen.

Speak of the devil.

I scanned Dylan's email, which declared in all caps that he'd need to check in by the end of next week, or we were fired.

I'd like nothing better. But I'd promised Tom I'd take care of things. I swallowed my anger and crafted a polite email with a choice of times. Punched 'send.' I looked up. "That was for you, Tom," I whispered. If Dylan had been my client, I would've told him to stick it where the sun don't shine.

He wrote back immediately. In a weeks' time, we'd meet in the same dive we'd met in before. I emailed back a thumbs-up icon.

He didn't deserve the effort of typing words.

Sherry had taken the day off. The office felt cold and lonely.

I stared at Tom's dented metal desk, his filing cabinets. Took a deep breath and crossed the divide. I gingerly sat in his chair, feeling like an intruder. His chair was an old-fashioned, wooden desk chair with a five-pronged wood base on wheels.

I began pulling out drawers. One of them resisted my efforts.

Locked.

My forehead wrinkled. The file! The file he'd pulled out of the pile and slid into this drawer when he'd handed files over to me. Where was the key? I planted my palms across the top of his desk, feeling for metal. I jerked out the other drawers and searched compartments. When that yielded nothing, in frustration, I approached the two metal filing cabinets against the wall behind his desk. Pulled out drawer after drawer and flipped through the file headings. But would he have put a tiny desk key in a file folder?

Probably not.

I studied the faded diplomas he'd lined up on the wall behind his chair in plastic, Dollar Store frames. In a burst of inspiration, I lifted each piece off its nail on the wall and looked at the back. The final piece… the one that held his current private investigator's registration…was a bingo. He'd taped an envelope to the back. I felt something hard inside the envelope. A shiver shimmied up my back.

I lay the framed registration on Tom's desk. I closed my eyes. My heart pounded in sync with my breathing.

After taking a series of deep breaths to prevent my own personal tachycardic event, I searched the drawers for something to open the envelope. A letter opener presented itself in a drawer. I clutched it in my ice-cold hands and after a few seconds of prayer, sliced open the envelope.

The key fell out on the desk.

A note slipped out behind the key.

My heart started its crazy pounding again.

The tiny key was weightless. I inserted it into the lock. The top drawer slid open.

I withdrew the secret file from the drawer and lay it on the desk beside the note.

I folded my hands together, and sat there a second. The sixth sense that had developed as a result of my TBI jumped around like popcorn in a hot air popper.

Tom's voice floated through my mind. *You've got this, girl.*

I unfolded the paper. Tom's bold, decisive handwriting covered two pages.

Hi there, gal, I knew you'd find the key. I'm passed on now, or you wouldn't be over here, pawing around in my drawers. Am I right? Ha.

This file holds some hard truths for you. Don't get all worried and skittish. You can handle it, but I wanted to prepare you, and I knew you'd go commando trying to find it after you saw me lock it away, which I let you see on purpose. Ha. If I were you, I'd hide the dang thing. Some folks aren't too keen on this info getting into the wrong hands. Please put it in a safe place, or burn it, or whatever, okay? You might need it as proof, though. Don't toss it until things work out.

My mind was exploding. Nausea climbed up my throat. What in God's name had Tom done? What had I inherited?

I grabbed a bottle of water from the fridge, stalked back to the office, and plopped down behind his desk, my nerves shredded. I drank half the water.

Next paragraph.

Your mom and I were close. Dang near got married. Maybe she told you about that, don't know. I cared a lot about her, but I was quite a bit older, and she still had her own wild oats to sow. Her father and I...well, let's just say some situations defy the law, family is family, and your dad's never going to forgive us.

My chin jerked into my neck. My dad? Tom had known my *dad?* Mom had told me he died. Or maybe she confused me with some of that doublespeak stuff she does when hiding an unpleasant truth. What had she told me? He'd left? He was dead? A hopeless drunk? He wasn't around, wasn't involved. Ever. I'd made a life thinking, hoping, praying that I didn't *need* a dad.

My God.

I sucked in a breath and kept reading.

Sophie might be mad at me for telling you your dad's still alive and kicking, so far as I know—but what can she do to me now? Ha. I've kept track of him because there've been threats of lawsuits and such over the years. Change the name of the firm soon as you can, and get rid of my cell phone. Your dad thinks it was all my idea, a lifetime ago, but it wasn't. I went along for the ride, probably shouldn't have, but it's done now. If your father thinks my firm petered out at the same time I did, that would be better than him knowing his daughter started up a new one on the back of my old one.

What idea? What collaboration? I glared at the file. Opening it might be the worst decision I'd ever made.

But Tom expected me to. And I promised.

I forced myself to read the grand finale.

Up to you whether you want to tell your mom what you know now. Family's a tricky thing. Maybe your dad's changed, but I doubt it. My suggestion? Don't find him. Take that for what it's worth. I wrote all this out in case I died before it got sorted out. I'm sorry I couldn't see it through to the end.

I let out an anguished cry. See *what* through?

One step at a time. One day at a time. Pay attention to who you take on as a client. If your gut tells you no, trust it.

Proud of you, gal.

Tom

I folded the note and put it back in the envelope after I took a photo of it. I would save the photo in a file marked with an innocuous heading in my private docs. Meanwhile, what do I do with the note? I couldn't toss it, no more than I could toss the memory of holding Tom's hand before he died.

My palms slid along the length of his desk. Closing my eyes, I tried to sense a whiff of his presence. Tom always wore Aramis. I could smell it a little. My eyes filled. Taking my time, I pulled open his drawers to see if there was something I could take, something to remind me of him. My hands pawed through the pens, fidget spinners, paper clips, and staple boxes. Through boxes of legal-sized envelopes, a tangle of rubber bands. One drawer held at least fifty sticky note pads of various sizes. I smiled. Cuticle scissors. Tweezers. A razor. A small hairbrush. His keychain. I picked up the hairbrush, dotted with whitish clumps of hair. Tom's attempts at trying to camouflage the balding areas by plopping hair wax on his hands and running them through the sparse, white tufts. Smiling, I picked out the hairbrush, and the keychain, wondering if any family would contact me to clear out his possessions. My gaze travelled to the coat rack he'd set up beside his desk. An old, raggedy sweater hung there. I hadn't really noticed it before. I lifted the sweater off the rack and pressed it to my face. The scent of Aramis and fine Scottish wool swept up my nose.

I had to save the sweater. I'd put it in a baggie to preserve the scent.

The door to reception opened. "Hey! I left my phone here yesterday." Sherry walked into the office. I must've looked as miserable as I felt because her jaw dropped. "What is it? What's wrong?"

I extended the sweater by way of explanation. "It's hard, that's all. Going through these files, thinking about Tom." I walked over and patted the top of the old metal desk. "This needs to go in our storage unit. Until someone shows up for it. Or doesn't."

She relaxed. This was something she could lean into. "Sure. I'll call a delivery service. I'm going to miss him, too. When's his Celebration of Life?"

"Tomorrow. I'll meet you there."

She nodded. "You need anything before I go? I gotta scoot."

"I'm good. Going to be a research day for me. No worries."

"Great. I'll see you tomorrow at the celebration." She left.

"Okay, Tom," I muttered, my hand on the file. "Here we go."

I flipped the file open. Fast. Like ripping off a Band-Aid.

Chapter Sixteen

There was a time and place for this conversation, but Sergeant Hunter Faraday was pretty sure it wasn't six p.m. on a Friday afternoon in the unit lieutenant's office.

Richmond PD Major Crimes' Lieutenant Nicholson continued shredding his request to be demoted back to the street. When the captain took a breath, Hunter chimed in.

"I apologize, sir, for the bad timing, but I'm not the man for the job. I'm unhappy with my performance."

"Don't you think *I'm* the one to be the judge of that?" Lieutenant Nicholson fired back. "How long have you been thinking about this, Sergeant?"

"A while, sir."

The captain stared out a window.

Hunter remained quiet. This may have not been the right approach. Or the right time. Or the right words. His jaw worked. His hands grew sweaty.

What if he lost his job?

Lieutenant Nicholson swiveled slightly in his chair. "How long since you've had a vacation, Sergeant?"

As if groping for the meaning of the word, he stammered, "V-vacation?"

Lieutenant Nicholson rolled his eyes. "How long?"

"Uhh…three years, sir."

"Effective immediately, you are taking six weeks. During this time, consider what you've requested. You want to give up a promotion *and* a pay increase because you don't like the admin duties attached to this job? A suck-up to the media once in a while? You've got a chance to make a difference, Sergeant. You can get out on the street at any time. No one's stopping you. You're the one in charge, for God's sake. Work it into your day. The paperwork duties will get easier with time, and you can get back out there with your team."

"Sir. The responsibilities are a world apart from what I'm accustomed to, and I don't know if I'm the right person for the—"

"Six weeks!" the lieutenant bellowed and rose to his feet.

Hunter's signal to leave.

Six weeks.

So much for asking for a demotion.

Hunter left the Richmond PD building with a box full of stuff he might need. Someone asked if he'd been fired as he trotted through the lobby on his way out. "Vacation," he mumbled.

He tossed the box in the back of his Jeep. "At least it's a *paid* vacation," he muttered to himself. He lowered the top on his Jeep and powered down the windows. Selected reggae music and turned it up loud. What was he going to do for six weeks?

He screamed out of the lot at full throttle, music blasting. The sun began its descent in an impressive display of oranges and golds.

His Bluetooth announced a call. Shiloh. He depressed 'end call' on his steering wheel. Five minutes later, another call came in. Olivia. He started to ignore the call, but his index finger hovered. With a sigh, he pressed the 'answer' icon.

"Hey."

"Hi," she paused. "You in a better mood now?"

"Than what?"

"We parted last time on...less than stellar terms."

He grunted.

"Listen, Hunter, do you have a few minutes?"

"I do. Actually, I have many minutes. Six weeks' worth of minutes."

"What? Why?"

"Strong recommendation for time off. To get my head on straight about my new job."

Olivia chuckled. "You had reservations about that a year ago."

Hunter's mind flipped back to the last in-person conversation they'd had when he thought—and he'd hoped that she felt the same—that they were heading toward a more serious commitment. He remembered how beautiful she'd looked that night, her hair a mess of curls around her face, eyes shimmering. He shook himself out of the images. *Get hold of yourself, man. The woman has spoken.*

"Yeah, well, and now I'm not sure about it. I sit at a desk most days. It's driving me up the wall."

Pause.

"I have an idea."

Hunter winced. "Can't wait."

"Tom Stark died, Hunter. My mentor?"

"I know who he is. I'm sorry for the loss. What does that have to do with your idea?"

"I…I…" she cleared her throat. "I have a client that's a problem. Plus, now it's me, solo. With the client list that I inherited from Tom. I feel kind of lost."

"Bottom-line it for me, Olivia." He enjoyed listening to each delectable morsel of humble pie she swallowed as she crept toward a request for his help. She hated having to reach out. His smile grew with each stuttering rationalization.

"And now that you're free for a few weeks? Maybe it's fate."

Hunter laughed. "Yeah, *fate,* if that works better for you. Gotta keep that 'independent' thing goin'."

Pause.

"I never said I needed to keep my independence intact."

"It came through loud and clear with your actions, Olivia. You are one difficult woman, you know that?"

Pause. "So you'll come?"

Hunter's eyes narrowed. He pulled the Jeep into his driveway. Walked into his condo, holding the phone to his ear. His condo looked like the typical, barren, cold hotel room. He'd had no time or desire to add homey touches, and the option of a visit to Glyndon appealed. Shiloh would have a meltdown if she found out. He'd have to sort that out.

Later.

"Is there a hotel close by?"

"You can stay in the office's guest room. Will that work? Or I'll pay for a hotel, but there aren't any very close."

"Where are you going to be?"

"Lilly and I are moving back into the house. This weekend. Can you come Monday?"

"How long?"

"As long as you want."

He ran his thumb across his lower lip.

Should he construe her answer as a good sign? *Quit thinking like that. She's done. No point.*

"See you next week," he said.

He walked into his bedroom to change into athletic pants and a T-shirt. He'd grab a bite and head to the gym. This vacation thing was looking better.

An hour later, Hunter emerged from the steam room. He got dressed, dried his hair, and—as fate would have it—walked outside at the same time Shiloh walked in. She beamed at him. "You never know who you're going to run into at the cop gym."

Hunter blinked. What was she doing in Richmond?

"I can see you're wondering why I'm here, but I've told you, remember? My perp has ties to Richmond, and so do I." She shrugged. "They're going to use me. No brainer. Anyway, I have interrogations scheduled for tomorrow. I tried to give you a heads-up, but you didn't answer your phone." She pulled her gym bag into a more comfortable position on her shoulder. "You going to be around?"

Hunter tugged his bottom lip.

She dropped the gym bag on a bench. "Okay. What's going on?"

He frowned. "Don't read anything into it before I tell you. Okay?"

Shiloh threw her hands up. "Oh. My. God. Here comes another round of Mercy's Miracle derangement syndrome." She jerked her bag onto her shoulder and up gave him a look. "You were done with that. Or, wait. *She* was done with that."

Hunter winced. It hadn't been fair to give Shiloh the impression that they might move in together. To be honest, he'd wanted to, but the timing hadn't worked out.

"She needs a cop. Since I'm off, she asked. That's it."

She raised her eyebrows. "You're off?"

"My Lieutenant's making me take six weeks' vacation. To 'think about it'." He drew air quotes around the last three words. "I asked to be back on the street. He didn't take it well."

Shiloh rolled her eyes. "Last I heard, she was full steam ahead on the private investigator track. So you're going to ignore policy, run out and help a PI even if it might mean your job?" She glared at him. "You know how tough the department is about off-duty cops and PIs." She placed a palm gently on his chest and leaned in. Hunter breathed in the scent of her shampoo and the light fragrance she always wore. "I'm done. *We're* done. Got it? Good," she whispered and walked away.

Chapter Seventeen

The day of Tom's Life Celebration started out with sunshine, but by one o'clock, light rain showers turned the sky a dingy gray.

When I arrived at the park, I found Sherry. We walked to the Pavilion, where Hazel greeted us. We both handed over our obnoxious sock purchases as requested.

"Tom would love these," she said with a smile. Her friend, Pete, stood behind the table, helping people sign in. A large sign rested in front of a basket overflowing with socks that said 'In memory of Tom Stark' Beneath this line was 'GRAB A PAIR'.

I chuckled. Tom would've loved the choice of words.

I was caught off-guard by Pete's attendance. I scanned the few cars in the parking lot. Yep. There it was, Pete's rental. I still wasn't sure why he was using a rental. I pointed.

Sherry gave me a look. "What?"

"Pete's car. We can pull the tracker."

"Ohhhh, yeah. Want me to do it?"

My eyebrows rose. "You know how?"

"If you put it on the rear, underneath." She folded her arms and fluttered her eyelashes. "You aren't the only one who's been learning about stuff."

"It's on the undercarriage. Maybe when people are focused on the podium."

She nodded. Sherry and I were starting to gel, and I took huge comfort in her support. I wouldn't be surprised if she didn't get her own PI license at some point.

I cast my eyes at the ground. “Nine o’clock.”

“Pete?” she whispered.

“Is he staring this way?”

“Oh, yeah,” she breathed. “At you.”

Sherry nodded at the podium. “They’re starting.”

A latecomer strode across the grass. I groaned. Dylan Palmer. Really? After he’d talked to me like it was Tom’s fault that he died before his case was finished? Why was he here?

I wasn’t sure how to handle it since he didn’t want people to know he’d hired an investigator. After the tributes concluded, I walked in his direction. I could at least be civil. “Nice to see you.”

His nod was curt. “Sad occasion.”

“Yeah.” I couldn’t think of what else to say. I was terrible at small talk.

“Look,” he stage-whispered. “We need something. My marketing team is screaming. We have to figure out how to position ourselves these last few weeks. Tell me you’ve made progress.”

“Tom spent hours surveilling, but found nothing out of the ordinary,” I told him. “Databases revealed traffic tickets. No felonies. No bankruptcies. So far, nothing we can use.”

Dylan stroked his chin and looked at me with those dead, flat, shark eyes of his.

Sherry walked across the grass and showed us the socks she’d selected in memory of Tom. “Look! I grabbed a pair.”

I fended off a smile. *Hilarious, Sherry.*

I introduced her to Dylan. As they chatted, Dylan lit up. Sherry was fantastic at small talk. With a side glance at me, she flipped him. “Olivia tells me you have an appointment next week.”

He rocked on his heels and stared at the grass. The adult equivalent of pouting. He wanted info, and he wanted it now.

I had the urge to put Dylan in a timeout. If ever I wanted to be reminded of the controlling abuser I’d married that now sat in a prison cell…five minutes with Dylan would do it. Did he think he had a snowball’s chance of getting elected? I didn’t.

He scanned the crowd, then glared at me. "You'd better have something substantial by then."

He walked into the crowd with a bright, shiny, smile.

My face screwed into a knot. This is the real reason he'd come. He was using Tom's Celebration to shake hands and kiss babies and talk about the election.

Sherry made a gagging sound. "How do you stand him?"

"I don't," I said.

She pulled something out of the front of her pants. "Look what I found," she whispered.

I laughed. "Forgot about the tracker."

She tucked it back into her pants. "I got you."

As we filed out of the park, my stomach did a little flip when I realized that Pete was *thanking people for attending* right alongside Hazel. The creep didn't even belong here. I was relatively certain he'd never met Tom. Thanks to the tracker, I knew where Pete spent his time, and it didn't match up with my idea of respectability. Hazel had a dangerous blind spot. It would be a sad day when I told her what I'd uncovered.

Pete turned in our direction and stared.

"Let's get out of here," Sherry whispered.

Eddie's Bistro was packed, but Callie had scored a table. I put my sunglasses in my purse, tugged at my still-unfamiliar, shorter hair, and wound through tables to the one in the back of the room where Callie sat.

"How was it?" Callie asked as I pulled out a chair.

"Sad. Sherry should be along in a minute." I ordered a bottle of wine. A pinot, this time.

"You back in your house yet?"

I nodded. "Tomorrow, thank God. The insurance investigator's report is in, forensics are finished. The fire investigator, Tasha, is keeping me in the loop on things, too. The house has been fully released back to me."

Callie sipped her wine. "You're changing the locks, right?"

Sherry walked in, flung herself into a chair. "Funerals wear me out."

I tapped the bottle of pinot I'd purchased. "Time to drink."

"Agree." Her eyes lit up at my choice. She extended her glass. "*Elyse* pinot? Are you kidding? Pour. Now."

We toasted Tom. After a respectable silence, Callie's eyes slid up and down my form. "You look great. Tell me I did a good job."

I sighed. "You did a good job. Here's the rundown, ladies—my new firm is Watchdog Investigations. I've applied for an LLC and hired the same accountant Tom used. I'm forging ahead next week with Tom's client base. Not overwhelming at all."

Because, dammit, I thought I'd have more time with him.

Callie smiled. "Congrats to you and Sherry, and best of luck. Where'd the name come from?"

"I got a dog."

Sherry's eyes widened. "You did? When?"

I played with the stem of my wine glass. "Yesterday afternoon. Y'know, between the fire and the possibility of Monty wreaking further havoc in my life…I figured a dog would be a good idea."

"What'd you get?" Sherry asked.

"A rescue. He's a mix of Lab and German Shepherd. They call them 'Shepradors'. The point is, I don't have time to train a puppy, and he'd been at the Humane Society a long time, so…I couldn't resist."

Callie leaned in. "He's the *best* dog. I'm watching him until she moves back into her house tomorrow."

"Aww, look at you! Will he be at the office?" Sherry asked. "I love dogs. Is he photogenic? We can feature him in the marketing."

"He's a brand new part of my life, so I need to get to know him first."

"How old is he?"

"Five." I sipped my wine. "He has *really* big teeth. Riot is going to have a heart attack."

We waved one another off with slightly inebriated salutations, and I ran by Callie's to pick up Marlowe to take with me to the office.

Marlowe sat in the passenger seat, watchful and mysterious, like his namesake. I pulled into my office parking lot, dreaming of the day 'Watchdog Investigations' would replace the 'Stark Investigations' sign. I sat in the car a minute, my hands gripping the wheel, watching the halogen lights blip on, listening to the cicadas sing. "Thanks, Tom," I whispered, "for all your hard work. You were…so important to me, and I miss you." My voice wobbled. "Rest in peace," I finished.

I picked up Marlowe's leash. We walked inside.

"It'll be nice to have some solitude, huh, boy?"

Marlowe sniffed the air, looked at me with his liquid, copper eyes, and slow-wagged his tail. I unclipped the leash. He sniffed his way through each nook and cranny. He followed me into my office. I sat at my desk and unlocked my middle drawer. Pulled out the TS file. Caressed it with my hand. Though I'd already scanned the contents, I'd been too emotional to wade into the deep. It would be good to process it alone, in the calm. The quiet. Without distractions.

I flipped open the file.

First, Tom's reports. The most important of which told me my grandfather, and he had hired (redacted) to mitigate the threat of bodily harm by Sonny Pellegra to my mother and her unborn child. Injuries and 'accidents' and hospital stays had been outlined in careful detail, including dates and copies of hospital records. Most of them, by my calculations, after he'd found out Mom was pregnant with me. The file held a half-inch-thick amount of police reports…but I knew the drill. Domestic violence wasn't talked about in the seventies and eighties, much less acted upon. Most women were too ashamed to come forward. For my mom to have consented to document this many events, Tom or my grandfather had to have been nagging her to do it. Tears rolled down my cheeks. What had Mom endured to keep me?

The date on Tom's report was March 25, 1980. The police reports were from the first through the fifteenth of March. A pattern of violence that escalated, and apparently nothing was being done. Tom and my grandpa must've concluded that they had no other choice but to take justice into their own hands.

I did the math in my head as I stroked Marlowe's back.

I was born November 10, 1980. Mom had been a month and a half along when the police reports started. Alongside the report was a copy of a Petition for Divorce, filed March 15, 1980. A restraining order was stamped the same day. Then another stamped two months later. Then another.

I threw my empty water bottle in the trash.

I knew from experience how difficult restraining orders were to enforce, even now. A determined guy could do damage in minutes, then disappear before the cops ever made it to the scene.

Forty years ago…when women's rights were a dim gleam in someone's political campaign…Mom must've been terrified of Sonny. From what I remembered of my grandfather, he was a tough old bird. Grandpa died when I was ten, but even as a little girl I sensed his over-protectiveness and the big 'family secret,' that colored everything. The secret that had caused my family to scream at each other and clam up tight whenever I was in the room. It hadn't made a difference to me back then, one way or the other. Secrets were for grown-ups.

I rubbed my eyes.

Forty-three years later, it had come full circle.

Darkness crept through the windows. I got up from my chair, stretched, then strolled the rooms checking locks and my security system. Marlowe stuck close. I scratched his head. Who would throw away such a fabulous dog?

A couple of the windows' blinds were open. I snapped them shut, a flutter of fear running through my chest. "Stop," I muttered to myself. Marlowe thought the command was for him and jerked to a seated position. I laughed.

I pictured my grandfather back then. His only daughter, pregnant, and so young. Throw in a guy that he couldn't possibly have trusted or approved of, and physical violence. He must've been crazy with anger and fear. I could see him hiring someone to take care of it. I tapped my chin. Seems to me, he had money from what Mom had told me about him. He must've paid someone a fortune. And since Tom had cared so much about my mother, he would've caved to whatever her dad needed in order to protect her.

I rubbed the back of my neck, thinking. It had never, ever occurred to me that Tom and my mother could've been involved. Tom's revelation in his note had been a complete surprise. She hadn't had the same feelings for him, obviously.

I stared at the documents strewn about my desk. The open file and the secrets it revealed. "Had mentoring me been hard for you, Tom? Had you seen my mother as a young woman when you looked at me?" I whispered, my palm lightly running across the pages. I shook my head. Mom must've been a force back in the day. I chuckled. Marlowe lifted his head and looked at me. "She's still a force, buddy," I told him.

I went back to the reports. Receipts with no explanation on the subject line. One for five thousand, another for five thousand two weeks later. Cash. No checks had changed hands. I pulled out files around those timeframes from the stash that Tom had given me. Nothing happened with Stark Investigations for two months after the date of the final receipt. Whatever the two men had arranged had knocked Tom out for a while. Had this been due to emotional reasons? Physical? What had happened to keep him off the planet for two months? What if he'd been the one to 'mitigate' the threat?

I pushed my hair off my face. No way. Tom's gentle demeanor and kind ways would never have allowed him to hurt someone. I was sure of it. Unless he was desperate. I picked out files dated six months after the event. Business had picked up. Lots of files, lots of 'paid' stamps on receipts. My forehead furrowed. Quite a few files did not have the requisite name label but a single letter: B.

Who was B?

Chapter Eighteen

Hazel slid an index finger down her list of appointments, then glanced at the clock and frowned. Had her client forgotten their appointment?

On cue, she heard footsteps trot up the rickety staircase from the street to her office door. Olivia knocked lightly and entered. "Sorry I'm late."

"Are you okay? You're *never* late."

Olivia grimaced. "I got a dog."

"How fun. A puppy?"

"He's five, but still. He has to go to the bathroom, and I have to pick up the poop, and he takes forever. Do all males act like that?" Olivia snorted her disgust. "Every male I've ever known takes forever in the bathroom. Anyway, I didn't sleep well last night, and on top of that, Riot's having a hard time and yowling his head off. So between the poop parade and my tomcat, it was a rough night."

"Interesting name," she said. "The crime detective in those books?"

Olivia grinned. "Cheesy, huh?"

Hazel motioned toward the back half of the large room that held her desk in one corner and the client space in the other.

"Let's step into my office, shall we?" The smell of toffee-flavored coffee permeated the room. Afternoon sunshine streamed across the floor through the bank of windows that fronted the space. Olivia settled on the couch.

"Where do you want to start?"

The barest shadow crossed her client's face.

"I'm struggling, Hazel."

"I can see that."

Olivia scooted to the edge of her seat on the couch and pointed her knees in Hazel's direction. "Look, I don't know how deep this therapist-client privilege goes. Is it both ways? For instance, if I tell you something and it's not…um…about me, are you bound by confidentiality guidelines to keep that quiet as well?"

"Anything shared in here is off limits. We've discussed this. The exception is when I feel you are becoming a danger to yourself or others…or I become aware of a crime."

"Okay." Olivia stared at her hands in her lap. Long seconds ticked by. "It's about Pete."

Hazel startled. "Excuse me?"

"You said you couldn't share this info with anyone, correct?"

"Right, but—"

"Yes or no?"

"Yes."

"This is going to be hard to hear, okay? But I care about you." Olivia straightened her shoulders, lifted her chin. "I put a GPS tracker on his car."

"What! Why? Besides, that's…*illegal*."

"Hence, my concern about confidentiality. Yeah, I committed a crime, but it was barely a crime. Besides, my motives were pure. Tom would be okay with it."

Hazel allowed a slight smile.

"The night I met him, Pete wouldn't tell me where he worked. Remember? You were nervous. He could've been threatening you for all I knew…and when he wouldn't let me know where he worked." I shrugged. "I had to do something. He was too…oh, I don't know…secretive."

The furrow between her brows deepened into the facial equivalent of a trench. "What did you do?"

"I drove to your house, hoping to get a lock on his vehicle. I figured he'd be there after you guys finished the meal. I was going to run his plates, but it was a rental. That alone makes me wonder. Did he mention an accident, or his car in the shop?"

Hazel slumped in her chair and shook her head. She riveted her eyes to the abundance of age spots on her arms and hands. Maybe Olivia's new career had her seeing crime behind every bush. Maybe not, though.

Olivia looked a bit lost.

Hazel cleared her throat. "I know this is uncomfortable, but go ahead. I need to know." She frowned. "You could be wrong, Olivia."

"Remember when he went back in to get his phone? It gave me time to connect my tracker. After Pete returned to the car, he took a call in the driveway. I heard most of it. Somebody is paying him for information. I bet they're also paying for the rental."

Hazel's eyes glazed. She rubbed her hands together, thinking. "Am I just an old fool?"

"No. No, you're not. The guy is good. What I don't know is why. What would he want from you? Can you think of anything? Do you have a huge life insurance policy, or a mad client, or anyone with an offense against you?"

"No, nothing." She laughed. "I think my biggest claim to fame is…." She looked at Olivia with big, round eyes. "You," she whispered. "Oh. My. Goodness. He's extremely interested in my practice. Most people are, but not like him. And…" Hazel scratched her cheek. "When he met you that night, he was entranced. I think he knows you're a client. He kept asking questions, and I kept putting him off. What if he wants to get close to me to get close to *you*?"

Olivia let out a sigh and closed her eyes. "That freaking 'Mercy's Miracle' syndrome. I wonder if it'll ever die. I'm sorry, Hazel. This might be my fault."

Hazel teared up. "I'm so stupid."

"Stop. Happens to thousands of women every day."

She sniffed. "The funny thing is…I knew it. I *knew* the attention was coming from some other place than a mutual attraction, or…or affection. I let it happen, anyway. After so many years, it felt good."

"I understand, Hazel. I do. I don't ever remember hearing you talk about a husband."

She shook her head, her wiry, salt-and-pepper curls bouncing. "There was a time that I thought…." Her expression grew wistful. Then she glanced at Olivia and looked away. Swatted the air. "Don't mind me. Drowning in regret about things that have already happened never brings a good result. I had plenty of relationships. I never liked the idea of marriage." She folded her arms across her chest. "Okay. You've told me. Shall we get back to you?"

Olivia shook her head. "Hazel, it's my turn to be a counselor. I know I'm breaking all kinds of protocols here, but I want to say something."

Her hand crept up to the crepey folds of her throat. "Olivia. I'm getting nervous about this. I took an oath not to cross over into personal territory, and I think it best you hand off these questions to someone else. Sherry, maybe? Or someone from the Westminster Police Department?"

I cleared my throat, straightened in my chair. "Okay, I understand. You're right. Just one more thing, okay? You need to know this. Pete hangs out at strip bars on The Block in downtown Baltimore, he gambles in Anne Arundel, and purchases a huge amount of whiskey at a liquor store in Westminster. He lives in a studio apartment in a run-down complex in Owings Mills. After following him a couple days, I get the feeling he's not such a good guy. Line up the truth with what he's told you. There. I'm done. I'll think about next steps, and take myself out of the equation."

Hazel paled. She fanned herself with her hands. "Good idea," she said.

Olivia rose to leave. "Someone will be in touch about this. Sorry to be the bearer of bad news."

"Thank you, Olivia," Hazel said as she walked to the windows that overlooked Westminster's Main Street.

Olivia watched her a few minutes, then left.

Hazel stared out the windows a long time. It started to rain.

Chapter Nineteen

The Fourth of July

I trotted downstairs and into the kitchen, tantalized by the wonderful smells of bacon and eggs. Mom put a mug of fresh coffee into my hands. "Happy Fourth, honey! I'm glad you're taking some time off. The repairs are going well, I see."

"I know, right? It's nice that we get a break from the hammering and sawing. Riot's been hiding under my bed for days."

"Aren't they about done?"

"Next week. I'm going to celebrate."

Mom laughed. "As you should."

Lilly ran down the stairs. "Hunter's here!"

My mother smiled. "You invited Hunter for the holiday, too?"

"Kind of," Olivia murmured.

"What does that mean?"

The front door banged shut. Hunter's booming laughter flew through the house. Mom glanced at me. "I'm glad he's here. And Lilly has a crush on him, in case you didn't know." She smiled.

"Most females do," I said.

"Mornin', ladies," Hunter drawled in his rich, luscious Richmond accent as he entered the kitchen. His gaze bounced around the room, then stalled on me. He sat on a barstool beside me at the breakfast bar.

"Hey. Happy Fourth. You get settled in down in the office guestroom?

Find the key okay?" I asked.

He nodded and stroked his cheek, puzzling through what was different about me.

He accepted a mug of coffee from Mom, thanked her. Stared at me over the rim of his mug as he drank. "We goin' undercover today? Seriously, we got somewhere to be? I can change. I brought some different hats and glasses and stuff."

I sighed. "We have nowhere to be today."

He reached for my hair and gave it a gentle tug. "That's not a wig?"

Mom laughed. "You didn't tell him?"

I scowled. "Would he ask my permission to get a different haircut or wear something other than khakis and blue button-downs?"

Mom kept laughing. I threw my hands up, glowered at Hunter. "See what you've done?"

"It'll take getting' used to, that's all." He looked down at his shirt. "You don't like my button-downs?"

I gritted my teeth. "That's not the point. The point is…it shouldn't matter."

Hunter quit talking, a smile teetering on his face.

Okay. Maybe I should've warned him before he saw me. Fine.

"Gray and I miss you coming over for dinner, *Sergeant* Faraday, since you're so busy now. Congratulations on the promotion, by the way."

Hunter cradled the mug in both hands. "Thanks, Sophie. Truth is, I'm taking a…sabbatical. I asked them to put me back on the street, and they didn't like it. So here I am," he said. "Via their strong suggestion to think about it for six weeks."

With a self-conscious finger-comb of my hair, I chimed in.

"I asked for his help, Mom. I'm…well, it's a lot, handling the firm without Tom. And now, he's left me with a mess."

Oops.

Mom started twisting her wedding ring. "What did he leave you with? Please tell me you're not considering something dangerous," she said quietly, her festive red-white-and-blue earrings swaying.

Lilly walked in, put her backpack and sunglasses down. "Any breakfast left?"

Hunter smiled. "Working on the Fourth?" he asked Lilly.

"It's okay. I get paid double." She sat on a barstool on the other side of me.

"When're fireworks?" Mom slipped a croissant, butter, and jelly in front of her.

"I think they've already started," she quipped, with a tilt of her head toward me.

"Hunter thought my new look was a disguise," I said.

Lilly almost choked. "That's hilarious. Wish I'd videoed that."

Hunter grinned. "I'll get used to it."

Lilly crammed the rest of the croissant into her mouth. "Gotta go. Be back around three, okay?" The front screen door banged shut behind her.

"Where's Gray?" Hunter asked.

"Had to work. I tried, but he had obligations. He said to tell everyone he was sorry he couldn't be here."

"Makes me glad I'm not married," I said. With a side glance at Hunter, I hastily added, "To a neurosurgeon."

Hunter's complexion mottled. Since I'd rejected his proposal last year, I'm sure that was a hard thing to hear. My bad.

"One of these days, though, I'll be ready." I avoided looking at Hunter or Mom.

How was it possible that I'd *made it even worse*.

Hunter picked up a croissant. "I'll be on the porch." He walked out of the kitchen.

Mom shook her head, fisted her hips. "When are you going to be more careful about what comes out of that insensitive mouth of yours? Do you hurt people on purpose?"

I lowered my head. "I didn't mean to."

"Work on it." She started putting dishes away. "He's a good man, and a good friend. You could at least be courteous."

I puffed out a sigh. "It's hard with the TBI, Mom. You know I have trouble controlling words."

"Olivia," Mom said, her voice gentled a notch, "are you going to go through life blaming everything on your brain injury? Isn't it time to move on and consider that you're recovered enough to start learning how to take three seconds to think before saying something you'll regret?" She turned, wiped her hands on a dishrag and leaned against the kitchen counter. "Get on out there and apologize. Don't blame it on the TBI, either. People are tired of hearing it. Sorry, honey, but someone has to be honest with you."

I walked outside. Dropped into my loveseat and kept my mouth shut. Hunter sat on the porch swing, rocking it with his foot. We listened to the birds, and the rush of wings as a cardinal pushed a chickadee off the feeder. The regal cardinals *always* won. I'd watched them for years, wondering which bird I was most like. A cardinal, probably. Maybe a woodpecker.

I looked at Hunter. "I'm sorry."

He smiled. "I know you didn't mean it. You can't help it, right?"

My forehead furrowed. "My injury happened three years ago. It can't be my default rationale anymore, Hunter. I'm sorry I'm not more sensitive. I'm going to work on it."

Hunter bit into his croissant. "Okay."

"We good?" I asked.

"We're good. What's the plan for tomorrow? You have the day off, right? I'll take care of the fireworks."

"Yes, I took the day off, and you don't have to buy fireworks. We're going to eat dinner, then head out to Oregon Ridge State Park, where there's a big fireworks display. We'll take camping chairs and leave around seven-thirty. Sound good?"

"Sounds great."

"Good. Enjoy the peace, because my irrational client Dylan Palmer is about to bite my head off because Tom and I didn't find much on his political opponent. I'm thinking dumpster dive is on our calendar, day after tomorrow."

Hunter laughed and laughed.

Then he realized I was serious.

Chapter Twenty

"You enjoy the holiday?" Sherry asked as I walked in the front door to the office.

"It was perfect," I said, going through the office mail on her desk. "I have a request." I took the envelopes for me and left the others.

Sherry stopped typing emails and looked at me.

"Didn't you tell me you wanted to be more involved in the cases?"

She grinned. "Anything to get me out of the office once in a while."

"Remember our friend, Pete?"

She leaned back in her chair, folded her arms. "Who could forget?"

"I had to tell Hazel what I found out."

Sherry nodded, thinking. "What'd she say?"

"I can't go any further with her because I'm a client."

She chuckled. "And I'm not. What do you want me to do?"

"I'm dying to get Hazel to build on this relationship, if she's willing. Pete has an agenda, and we need to find out what the heck he's doing. I bet someone's paying him to be a source. It's probably a reporter with a new slant on 'Mercy's Miracle.'

Sherry tapped her chin, thinking. "What if she's already told him to back off?"

I smiled. "Ask if she's willing to play along for a week or two, and we'll provide a road map. Correction...you will provide a road map. That you and I will figure out."

Sherry clapped her hands together. "I'm so excited."

I rolled my eyes. "You're always excited."

Sherry and I spent the rest of the morning working out details. She'd report back to Hunter if she had a question, and I would try my best to keep out of it.

Maybe.

I'd be hovering, though.

"What's so funny?" Sherry walked to the breakroom to grab her lunch from the fridge and heat it up in the microwave. She walked into my office, stirring the soup she'd heated.

"You calling her this afternoon?"

"Yep."

"She can't let Pete know we're onto him."

"I don't know her that well, but you do. I trust your instincts."

"She carries pepper spray. And she's been a therapist for forty years, so we don't need to worry about her people skills."

She blew on her hot soup. "I'll talk to Hunter if I run into a glitch."

"Tell her to make sure they're in public places. To meet him in her car instead of letting him pick her up."

Sherry smiled a patient smile. "Hazel's been around the block a time or two. She'll be fine."

I groaned. "I feel bad for putting you in this position, but a con like Pete can happen to anyone. When I think about my pathetic, twenty-year track record with my ex before he left me for the bimbo…and what happened with Niles…it makes me sick. Oh, and let's not forget the lying sack of garbage, Wyatt Harp. Over the past three years, my record is me: zero, dirtbags: three. Compared to me, Hazel's a tower of wisdom. Did I tell you she never married? What a brilliant idea."

Sherry laughed. "Don't worry, I'll keep you in the loop." She took a cautious sip of her soup. "Loosely in the loop. I'll be discreet."

I held up both hands in surrender. "She's all yours."

"I can't believe I'm doing this," Hunter grumbled as we crept down the dark street and across vacant lots and underbrush until we reached the Waymire's driveway. All along the curb, rich repositories of potential sat at the end of each home's driveway.

Trash day in the neighborhood.

I pulled my hoodie lower over my face. "I know it's beneath you, Sergeant."

"I'd only do it for you. Sherry called, by the way."

My cheeks heated up. "I had to hand off Hazel."

"She told me. I can be back-up for her. No worries."

I studied him. "I'm grateful for your help, Hunter. Thanks for coming."

"You bet. Sifting through garbage has always been my favorite thing."

A three a.m. moon hid behind the clouds. The street was pitch-black. In a stroke of luck, the City hadn't put streetlights down this stretch of road, and the darkness provided great cover.

Hunter flicked on his flashlight. The bright beam scared the crap out of me. "My gosh, you want to announce us to the whole block?"

He covered the beam with his hand. "Sorry," he whispered. "I can't even remember the last time I did this."

"Aim it better."

We both pulled on nitrile gloves. I lifted one of the receptacle's lids. We stuck our arms inside and raked away the mundane, and argued over what might be worthwhile. Scott's taste ran to Chinese, and his wife's to KFC. "Wow, they eat out a lot," I whispered.

"He's running for office. She's helping, not cooking."

We kept raking.

Hunter pulled out a receipt. "Ammo."

I sucked in a breath. It couldn't be. "What kind?"

He spent a few seconds studying it under his small—but mighty—flashlight. "FMJ."

"Let me see." I grabbed the receipt. "Louise signed for them."

"Careful, don't tear it. You got a baggie?"

"Hush," I groused, energized and tired at the same time. The two glasses of wine I'd had at dinner didn't help, either—my stomach bounced around like tennis balls on an escalator. The receipt was from Dick's Sporting Goods and dated a week ago. I dropped the receipt into a Ziploc.

"I'm interested in who the shooter is...Louise or Scott...or both?"

Hunter switched the flashlight to his mouth and scrounged through the trash with both hands. Thirty minutes later, we'd discovered Scott had a hefty beer habit (maybe it was Louise? I couldn't imagine), that Louise picked up the dry cleaning, their kids' sports uniforms cost an insane amount of money, that Louise liked to buy a lot of kids' clothes at Costco, they bought groceries at Wegman's, they didn't recycle, they had a big Trader Joe's habit, and once in a while, someone ate good, old-fashioned, Campbell's soup. In short, the ammo purchase looked a little hinky but didn't half of the country own firearms? "Hunter, can you find out if Scott owns a gun?"

"Sure. If I want to lose my job."

My eyes widened. "Why did I not know this?"

He laughed. "Y'know those scenes on TV that have a powerful official asking a deputy to look up whether someone owns a gun? Some moronic writer didn't do his research or had an agenda he wanted to advance, because it is illegal to produce documents that show gun registration. The FBI is not supposed to keep a record of that, but who knows what goes on behind the scenes? You can call in to check records for a felony or domestic conviction on certain dates, but gun registration? Making gun ownership public? Think about it. The bad guys would know who didn't have a firearm, and they'd be sitting ducks. A firearm registry is a bad idea, and there isn't a gun ownership registry in existence. Cops have to approach all calls as if weapons are involved. Long answer to a short question."

"Well, it's the only thing we've got. I'll run it down."

Hunter eyed me. "Are you going to let me in on how?"

"What do you think?" I grinned.

Chapter Twenty-One

Hunter stretched out on the guest room bed in the office and watched mindless TV shows. He and Olivia had organized the facts surrounding what they'd bagged from the Waymires' trash and had tried and failed to peel Sherry off the ceiling after she'd met with Hazel. He laughed out loud, thinking about it. Sherry had bolted back into the office so hyped that he'd had to tell her to take a breath and slow down. They'd purposely excluded Olivia due to the professional boundaries, but it was a small office, and she'd probably heard everything they said.

Olivia had told him that she thought Sherry might make a good investigator, and he didn't doubt it. Hunter had been ready to call it a day long before Oliva and Sherry locked the front door to Watchdog Investigations and went home.

He rolled over onto his side and plumped the pillows. Closed his eyes with a contented sigh.

Something hit a window. Hunter jerked upright. He heard soft voices. Maybe it was his imagination? It had been a long day, and he needed to sleep. He cursed and threw off the comforter. Pulled his weapon out of the nightstand drawer, found some shoes, and went outside.

He blinked at the brightness of the pole light. As he walked around the office structure, he thought about how good it had felt to sit at Tom Stark's old desk. Grudging kudos to Tom, especially after Olivia had taken him to the range over the holiday weekend. She was evolving. The familiarity with firearms, the changes she'd made to her appearance, and the confidence she exhibited impressed him. He could no longer kid himself – the woman was serious about the PI biz. Which made him wonder...did she need him anymore?

Something to think about.

He wrestled with the makeover. The platinum hair, the effortless way she'd slipped on another persona, bothered him. He missed the auburn curls, the warmth of her eyes, the air of innocence. But, as she liked to tell him, she 'wasn't that woman anymore.'

Would that affect his feelings for her?

An owl hooted. Something scurried through the grass. Raccoon, maybe. Hunter kept walking, his eyes searching and watchful. He hadn't forgotten that someone had committed arson on this property. Did they want to destroy Olivia's office, too?

He re-focused on his perimeter stroll. Hunter squatted down to inspect the dark green wiring that connected the security camera to an outlet behind the office and ran his hands up the tree trunk, and followed the wires as far as he could reach. Everything was intact. A large owl swooped so close that he could feel the flash of wings. Hunter gasped. "That'll get your heart pumpin'," he whispered into the dark. A rustling dragged through the brush. Hunter dropped into a crouch, put his hand on his firearm. With careful, quiet fingers, he unlatched it from the holster.

This time he was certain. He'd been hearing voices.

He saw the shadows of people behind the building, close to the guest bedroom window. The rustling stopped, then started up again. Someone was walking through Olivia's property.

Hunter paused, his gun held in both hands tight against his waist.

His cell vibrated in his pocket. With one hand, he took it out and powered it off.

A beam of light strafed the woods about fifty yards away.

Hunter drew back.

The beam zigzagged back and forth.

Was the videocam catching this? If these guys meant to do the building, he felt sure they'd reconned the place first and knew to avoid the cameras. He wiped sweat off his forehead.. They'd have no way of knowing that he was staying in the office guest bedroom. Would they?

He frowned. But the lights? He hadn't kept the place dark when the girls had left. He'd watched TV and gotten stuff from the breakroom. Had they thought it was Olivia?

The beam of light got farther away. Hunter followed. The full moon slipped from behind the clouds. Every tree leapt into focus.

He crept faster. Whoever it was had started running through the woods. He pulled out his cell to call 9-1-1.

Seconds later, something hard and solid rammed into his stomach, and before he could recover, his skull got whacked.

He dropped to the ground like a rock.

"Hunter."

He struggled to open his eyes.

"Hunter."

This was a voice he recognized. A woman. *Olivia.*

He tried to sit up, but it hurt. One of his ribs must be broken. Her light touch brushed his forehead. Her hand was cool and smooth. He worked an arm through the brush and tried again to push himself up.

"No. Don't do that. Here. Let me help you. Slow and easy. I called an ambulance. They're on the way."

Sunlight pierced his eyes. Pain shot through his head.

He looked up into her face. She'd been crying.

"Tell me what happened," she whispered.

"Heard something." Hunter held his forehead. "I followed them. I was checking the perimeter and heard a couple of guys. I should've been more careful."

He felt for his holster. Empty. Damn. "They got my gun."

Olivia smiled. "I'll look for it. They probably tossed it in the brush."

The ambulance screamed into the office parking lot. Voices yelled instructions. Doors opened and closed. Shoes clattered on pavement, then scuffled into the undergrowth.

"Here! Over here," Olivia called. She wiggled her phone. "They're tracking my location. Don't move. You might have a concussion."

"Judging by the pain in my gut, a broken rib, too," he said, wincing.

The footfalls drew closer. Olivia stroked his forehead. "It looks like you interrupted them setting a fire, or your living quarters would be toast."

"Bad joke." He smiled.

The ER team broke through the trees. Eased Hunter onto a body board, then hoisted him on a gurney. "They're not going to keep me down that easy, Olivia," he called as they rolled him away.

Hunter woke to a doctor telling him that he must have nine lives, because he read about the car bombs and that he'd had to replace two Jeep Wranglers.

"How'd you know about that?" Hunter asked, trying to shake off the sedation. He pulled out his IV. A nurse frowned at him, but took the IV pole away.

"You have street cred up here, Sergeant Faraday. On behalf of your efforts with local icon, Olivia Callahan. So yeah, our media works you in if you come across the screens in the newsroom."

"Great," he muttered. "And here I was, hoping to keep a low profile. I'd appreciate it if you didn't mention…any of this."

"So you're not here on business." The doctor made it a statement, not a question.

Olivia knocked gently and entered the room.

The doctor's gaze flickered over Olivia and back to Hunter. He offered his opinion that Hunter spend the night for observation due to a concussion and bruised ribs. Olivia put her hand on Hunter's shoulder. The doctor left. Hunter pulled his shirt over his head. "You ready?"

"The office guest quarters are out, they've made it a crime scene. All I needed was another flippin' crime scene in my life. You're feeling better, I see."

"I'll find somewhere to stay. Let's go." He slipped off the bed. Olivia held out her arm so he could steady himself.

"You sure you don't want to stay?"

Hunter rolled his eyes. "Never been one for hospitals."

"You can stay in my extra bedroom upstairs. I was told the investigation of the property wouldn't take long, and then you can go back if you want to."

Hunter cocked his head and looked at her. "You sure about the upstairs bedroom?"

"Of course. Lilly will be ecstatic."

"How about you?"

"I'll get to nag you to slow down. And make sure you eat."

Hunter smiled. "I like the sound of that."

"Will you?" Olivia asked.

"What?"

"Slow down."

Hunter grimaced at the pain as he bent over to pick up one of his shoes. Olivia took the shoe from him and slid his foot inside, then grabbed the other shoe to do the same.

Eyes closed against the dizziness, he told her she'd make a great geisha.

Olivia laughed. "Shut up. You're still having a hard time. I'd rather you spend the night in the hospital, Hunter."

"Yeah, well…no."

"Okay." She put on the other shoe and helped him stand. A nurse appeared with sign-out sheets and a wheelchair. He scribbled on the sheets, dropped into the wheelchair, and let the nurse wheel him out while Olivia brought her car around.

Hunter eased into the passenger side and closed his eyes. "Guess I'll take the rest of the day off."

"You think?" Olivia chuckled.

Hunter startled awake. It was dark.

He fixated on two things: one, he was in the guest bedroom of Olivia's home and had slept most of the day, and two, his head felt like someone had screwed it into the jaws of a bench vise and left it there overnight.

He rose from the bed a few inches at a time, then swung his legs over the side and waited for the throbbing to settle. Steps thumped up the stairs and raced down the hall to his door. He heard whining, then a bark.

Bark?

Lighter steps followed. Hunter walked to the door and opened it.

The human equivalent of a sunbeam of happiness greeted him with a dazzling smile. Hunter wondered how any human's teeth could be that white.

"Hi, Hunter, remember me? I'm Callie. Olivia wanted me to be here in case you need anything."

He pointed at the big dog beside her.

"What's that?"

"Well, it's a…wait, you're kidding, right? His name is Marlowe. He's Olivia's new dog."

"Didn't know she'd gotten a dog."

"I was keeping him for her until her house is ready to move back in. How'd you sleep?" She flashed that smile again.

His head ramped up the throbbing. "Could use some ibuprofen or something."

"Coming right up," She left.

Marlowe stared at Hunter with intelligent eyes the color of honey.

"Marlowe," he said, scratching the top of the dog's head. "That's a pretty big name to live up to, fella. You know any commands?" He paused. "Sit." Marlowe sat.

Hunter's eyebrows rose.

"Stay," he said, and walked to the end of the hall and back.

Marlowe did not move.

"Wow," he whispered.

Marlowe kept his eyes on Hunter.

"No rescue is this well-trained," he murmured to himself. He snapped his fingers and pointed to his side. "*Heel.*"

Marlowe got up and positioned himself to Hunter's left.

Riot appeared on the top stair and watched, his tail twitching like mad. Hunter chuckled. This cat was getting a major wake-up call.

He gingerly explored his scalp.

Callie appeared and handed him the pills and a glass of water. "How are you feeling?"

"Hell of a headache. The docs taped up my ribs and told me to go easy the next few days. I'll live."

He thanked her for the water. Tossed back the ibuprofen.

"Olivia had a client meeting. Should be back by seven-thirty or so. You're stuck with me 'til then."

"Not stuck with anything. Damn grateful."

Callie blushed. "Need anything else?"

"I'm good."

"I'm sure you're hungry…you've been out of it all day. Dinner's in the kitchen. I'll warm it up, okay?"

"Thank you. I'll be down in a minute."

Hunter closed his eyes against dizziness. He cursed his stupidity at being dropped like that. He must be getting soft. And he was supposed to be with Olivia right now, helping her with Dylan Palmer. The fact that she was alone with the guy killed him, but he couldn't even walk straight yet.

"Could you be any more incompetent, Faraday?" he whispered.

He walked down the second-story hallway and clutched the railing at the top of the staircase. He rubbed his eyes and tried to focus. He let out a long, slow breath. "Ready, boy?"

Marlowe rose and wagged his tail. Together, they slowly navigated the stairs.

Chapter Twenty-Two

July 7, 6:30 pm

I changed the meeting location.

Since processing the TS file, my gut told me one step ahead of Dylan Palmer might be better than one step behind. He hadn't been happy about a last-minute venue change, but at least I'd know the place wasn't bugged or populated by guys with guns.

My mother's words rang out loud and clear: *A little paranoia goes a long way, Olivia.*

Appropriate in the case of Dylan Palmer, asshole client and political candidate.

Like a cop, I sat with my back to the wall and faced the door. The only other occupants of the dive I'd chosen were a silver-haired couple, a bartender, and a server who sat at the bar glued to his phone. I'd ordered a martini. The attack on Hunter had shaken me up more than I wanted to admit. I figured a martini was preferable to a nervous breakdown. I'd order Dylan a drink, too, if he wanted one.

I lifted the glass to my lips.

The door burst open. Dylan's hair arrived before he did. In the bleak lighting of the place, his thick, silver thatch sparkled like a crown. The evil eye he shot my way didn't do his hair justice. I lifted my martini glass in welcome.

He reached my table in four angry stomps.

"What the hell? I wanted to keep this under wraps, Olivia." He scraped out a chair and dropped into it with a thunk.

My eyes roved the stygian interior. The place had been around since the dawn of time, and as far as I could tell, didn't draw crowds. Maybe ever.

"Dylan. Do you really think anyone here is interested in us?" I drew a circle in the air with my palm. "Take a look around. It's the most 'under wraps' place on the planet."

I sipped my drink. "Want an adult beverage?"

His lips pulled out of the pout. "Sure." He ordered a vodka tonic. He winced at the first sip. "No telling what kind of vodka this place uses, but I bet it's not Grey Goose."

"I'd take that bet," I said. The alcohol had taken the edge off, and now I didn't care who or what Dylan wanted, I was determined to remain ethical.

Okay, semi-ethical.

I pushed a folder across the table. "Here are the reports."

He nodded, raised his glass. "To Tom."

I did the same. We clinked.

He opened the folder and flipped through. "Looks thorough enough." He leaned forward on his elbows. "Why don't you summarize for me?"

Posed as a question, the muscle twitching in his jaw spoke otherwise. It was a command. Fine. My summary was simple. "I'll boil it down to two words, Dylan. No. Dirt."

Dylan's well-groomed eyebrows drew together. "How deep have you gone?"

"The first thing Tom did was dig into the software databases. We combed them together. Scott Waymire has a good record, Dylan. Nice, typical parents who stayed together, no police reports or drunk driving. Clean. No secrets that we found."

"Did you interview the neighbors?"

I frowned. "Of Scott's parents? That was not part of the deal."

"I told Tom 'whatever it takes.'"

I downed the rest of the martini. "It's *me*, now, Dylan. Not Tom. And if it crosses boundaries I shouldn't cross, I'm not going to do it."

He stared at me with those vacant, flat, eyes.

"I think it's best to focus on the Waymires, not the parents."

Dylan shrugged. "What else?"

"Award-winning quarterback in high school and college, both schools here in Maryland. Scott grew up in Towson, which is public knowledge, of course. I managed to grab some phone calls with three of his buddies from college days and law school. They had good things to say. Jock jokes and stories about frat parties...but nothing of any real concern. I did my best to get them to open up. Funny stories, but typical. Not criminal."

Dylan smiled. "You should've met with them in person. I promise you they'd have opened up." Chuckling, he finished off his drink. He wiped his mouth with his shirtsleeve instead of the napkin.

Which explained a lot.

I still couldn't wrap my head around him running for office. Who would vote for this guy?

I smiled. "I met with his wife."

"Good. How'd that go?"

Her detached response to my firebomb question ran through my mind. The hope that she'd not be a drain on her husband's chances of getting elected. Her fear that her past might be exposed. I could relate, and I'd be damned if Dylan would ruin the Waymires' marriage.

"Again, so *not* any dirt, there. According to my research, she's a homemaker and proud mom and wife. Period." I lifted my palms. "The only dings I've found on both of them are traffic tickets."

Dylan straightened. "DUIs? How many traffic tickets? A lot of them? Where?"

I shook my head. "Maybe six. Straight speeding. Over a period of ten years, Dylan. There's nothing there."

"Listen," he said, leaning so far over the table that his nose was a scant six inches from mine. "No one is perfect. No one. There's something. You just can't find it." He grunted. "Or won't."

How did he know? A smile twitched my lips. "That's not fair, Dylan. I'm doing my job."

"If you say so."

"We can call it quits right now. No problem. I'll get Sherry to send you an invoice."

Dylan looked away.

Though I kept my face blank, inside, I was jumping up and down like a two-year-old with cotton candy. Oh, please. Terminate this relationship.

He sighed. "No, you've already done the initial research."

My eyebrows rose into my hairline. "*Initial* research? How much 'research' are you expecting, Dylan?"

His eyes were cold. "Whatever it takes."

"Spell out your expectations, or I walk away."

Dylan's head snapped back. His lips parted.

I guess politicians aren't used to my brand of candor.

Mustering his wounded self-esteem, he barked, "We're done when I say we're done, Olivia. Get that through your head."

I stood up and slung my backpack over my shoulder. "You don't want me to work for you, Dylan. I don't even like you."

"How's it going, the fire clean-up and remodeling?" he fired back. "Didn't I hear another scare happened at your office? That a friend of yours ended up in the hospital?"

The attempted arson at my office hadn't hit the media yet. I stared at him. "How do you know about that, Dylan?"

"I hear things. I'm concerned about a possible a conflict of interest, and you have a lot of personal issues going on."

My internal radar flickered. "What conflict of interest?"

"Tom had a thing for your mom back in the day. Which would make him quite protective of her daughter. This is sensitive stuff we're dealing with. There can't be any long-lost love garbage factored into the job. Why didn't you tell me that Sophie Pellegra is your mom? You could be carrying some kind of bleeding heart torch for Tom." His thin lips formed a straight line.

We engaged in a staring contest that lasted so long it got awkward. I made a decision—go big or go home.

"Why would I keep that a secret? And why would I care if you knew my mother? It's not like I share details with her about what I do for a living. And Tom never mentioned one word about knowing my mom. He was a very private man." I chunked my backpack on the floor and crossed my arms. "Look, Dylan. I'm only doing this because Tom wanted me to see it through. I have no problem giving you recommendations for other PIs."

Why is he so interested in my mother? A single thought ran through my mind. *Get through the investigation and away from this jerk.*

Dylan lifted his hands in surrender and gave me a half-hearted grin.

"Apologies, Olivia. Sometimes I play the bad guy to see what shakes out." He lifted a shoulder. "Your mom moved away like…twenty years ago? To Florida or something, right?"

"How do you know my mother?"

"I guess I heard Tom talk about her," he said, not quite meeting my eyes. "I never really knew her. It's just…Glyndon is a small town. Baltimore Country, not so much. But if the media picks up a connection between Sophie and Tom Stark, it'll be an overblown mess."

He rose. "I respect you wanting to keep things clean, so let's proceed with the understanding that you keep digging, but not overstep your personal, uh, integrity." He shook the file folder in my direction. "This is a good start, but I need more."

My heart sank. I'd *so* wanted to get rid of this guy. A promise is a promise, though. I knew Tom well enough that he'd want me to finish the job. I wondered, though, what Dylan's reaction would be when I told him after this case that I was not only finished with the job, I was finished with *him.*

"I got little in the way of boundaries, so anything you have to do is fine with me."

We shook, and this time, his handshake was firm.

That was something, I guess.

Chapter Twenty-Three

"He knows who you are, now? How's that going to work?" Sherry asked.

I groaned. "I was awake last night, thinking—"

"You mean to tell me," she interrupted with a wide smile, "you can actually *sleep* knowing Hunter Faraday is lying in bed on the other side of your bedroom wall?"

"Very funny," I said. "Do you want to know what's on my mind or—"

Sherry waved her hand. "Only teasing. Please continue."

"Tom told me that if Dylan thinks I'm *not* continuing on with his firm, then he'll back off. I've already laid the foundation that I know nothing about the top secret file...uh, 'TS' file." Now all I have to do is convince him that I'm burned out and won't be carrying on Tom's good work...et cetera."

"We haven't started a presence on social media yet, so you want me to hold off?"

"What do you think?"

Sherry's large, gray-blue eyes roved the ceiling. "We're getting calls anyway from Tom's social media. It'll take a lot of effort to shut that down. Dylan will assume we're taking our own sweet time."

"He's in Canton. An hour away. Plus, he's winding up his campaign. He's a busy man. And no one is supposed to know he and I are doing business together."

"Let's think about that," Sherry said. I smiled. I could see myself setting her up with online PI courses. She had the natural bent for it, as Tom would say. I glanced up and high-fived Tom.

"Where there's no fuel, the flame goes out, right? He's convinced your main interest is a paycheck and keeping a promise to Tom, may he rest in peace. The only way he'd start wondering is if he does his *own* research into the Waymires and stumbles across something negative in Louise's history… then he might get upset."

I shook my head. "Not gonna happen. It's been way over ten years ago. To a politician, that's off-limits. He'd be subject to his own scrutiny, and I bet he couldn't stand up to it."

"Wonder what his dirty little secrets are?"

"Me too," I said as I walked into my office.

Tom's desk and file cabinets had been moved into reception for Hunter. Now, I had the whole office to myself. Sherry had ordered the 'Watchdog Investigations' sign to replace the one that said 'Stark Investigations,' but for now, we'd hold up on putting out a shingle until the mess with Dylan had concluded.

However, my heart skipped a few beats when I played out saying 'no' to the guy if he wanted to continue our relationship.

I heard the front door open and close, Hunter's greeting, and Sherry's simpering reply. I wish my girlfriends would get over it and accept that, yeah, Sergeant Faraday should be a model in a cop calendar and get on with life. I flicked through more emails. Hunter walked into my office and sat in one of the armchairs, and told me the mattress in the upstairs guest bedroom had been perfect.

"Great," I said, distracted by a visual of Hunter on the guestroom bed. Possibly naked. I watched him under hooded eyes, hoping with all my heart that he couldn't read minds.

"So what's on the agenda for Watchdog Investigations today?" His head whipped around. "Where's Marlowe? Isn't he supposed to be onsite during the workday?"

I smiled. "You like him, don't you?"

Marlowe strolled out of the guest quarters, wagging his tail, and flopped down beside Hunter's chair. "Morning, buddy," he said, ruffling his ears.

I brought Hunter up to date on my plan to push out the Watchdog

Investigations launch.

"You don't have your license yet, do you?"

"In three weeks, I will."

"If you pass the test."

"I'll pass the test."

"Gray give you the release you needed?"

"He will. By the way, I ran by Dick's, they let me look at footage. I could tell by the way Louise handled her firearm that she's the shooter in the family. I mean, that doesn't rule out Scott, but it's information."

He nodded. "Okay. She owns a firearm. Not illegal. So what else do we need to do for Dylan Palmer?"

"He wants to find dirt on Scott Waymire. You know that."

"Yeah. But do you?"

Good, intuitive question. Subliminally I didn't want Dylan to win his political race because he was such a douchebag. Was I biased? And if so, was it affecting my work ethic?

Yeah.

But definitely not because of my mother. I still didn't understand how that figured in, but it was a big, fat, dangling thread that connected to the TS file. I was sure of it.

"I want to give him his money's worth," I said.

"This is what I'm thinking... if I can find out when their sports stuff is, I can do a little investigating out in the sunshine. Observe Mommy and Daddy's interactions. Maybe chat up teachers and friends. How's that sound?"

"Fine. But how are you? Shouldn't you be resting?"

"Ibuprofen is my best friend." He put his hands on his hips and glanced around the room. "Am I still in reception at Tom's desk?"

"All yours. Let Sherry know what you need." That empty place in my heart that Tom used to occupy sagged against my soul. He'd been the leader, the instigator, the compass of my burgeoning career. And now...overwhelmed didn't even begin to cover it. I rubbed my eyes.

"Here." I handed him Dylan's file. "The reports I've given to Dylan, and some of Tom's notes and mine. I think we should spend another three days or so pretending that we're working hard to vilify Scott."

Hunter took the file. "Okay. Anything else?"

I shook my head. "Not really, but there's something you should know."

Hunter chuckled. "What now?"

"I haven't told you about the flowers."

He gave me a look I couldn't decipher.

"Two times now," Bouquets with flowers that have *meaning*, for God's sake. They've been the same each time. Daisies and buttercups. Jonquils. Whatever they're called. They mean resilience, hope. Strong little survivors. The daisies mean innocence. Purity. New beginnings." I stared out the window in my office. "Sorry I haven't told you."

"You left out one of the most important meanings." He smiled, crossed his arms. "True love."

I frowned. "How would you know that?"

"Callie is a good friend, Olivia."

I took a second to absorb that statement. "Wh-wh…" My brain fumbled the words. Retro effects of a TBI happened in bewildering or stressful moments. "So, Callie?"

"She called and asked me to assist because she thought it was strange. Have you gotten any more deliveries? I already have my own personal investigation started into the Foofoo nut jobs, by the way. Just so you know."

Seconds passed as I internally connected dots. Callie had clued Hunter in to the bouquets because she'd been worried, and Hunter had looked into the group because she'd asked him to. Should I be offended? I wasn't sure.

"I'm going to join 'Friends of Olivia' with an alias," I said, with a smug lift of my chin.

Hunter smiled. "Already done. You don't have to."

Okay. Now I was offended. I hopped out of my chair. "And when were you going to tell me? What if I'd joined, and you thought I was one of them?"

Hunter lifted his hands. "You didn't," he said. "Non-issue."

Olivia. Take it. It's a gift. You can't do everything.

Hunter spread his arms in supplication. "I'm here to help, remember? I didn't tell you because Callie wanted it kept quiet. Otherwise, I would have."

After five more minutes of posturing and pouting, I answered his question. "No to any more flower deliveries. And do I get to know what you found out?"

"Sure. Now?"

I nodded. Hunter set the Dylan Palmer file aside and dropped into a chair.

I sat in the chair beside his, separated by fifteen inches of accent table. Oh, how I wished I'd *never* been crowned 'Mercy's Miracle' or endured the media attention around my assault, injury, and rehab, but then like an idiot, I had to go and write a *book* about it. As a result, this rabid following had morphed into something sinister.

Did I want to know what Hunter had discovered? So soon after Tom's death, and in the middle of a difficult investigation?

No.

You can't bury your head in the sand and hope things will work out.

Hunter watched me process, the only sign of his tension a biting down on his lower lip. He'd had plenty of experience with the aftermath of my TBI, and he probably suffered from flashbacks of my seizures. "I'm okay, Hunter," I reassured him.

He let his arms dangle over the sides of the chair. "The primary topic in the group right now—it's a private group, by the way—is finding your dad. I thought he was dead…?" The question hung in the air.

Licking my lips absently, I thought about that. Had I not told him? Add that to the long list of things I forget on a regular basis. "Hunter, my father is *alive*."

His chin jerked. "Okay. What's the story on that?"

"Mom never talked about him much. When I was old enough to ask, she gave me the impression he'd died and changed the subject. I never knew what happened. She kept all that inside, I guess, but…." I stared at the carpet. Fidgeted with the pen in my hands. "Tom knew," I whispered.

Awareness dropped from the heavens like a wispy cloud. "It's all connected," I muttered, almost to myself. "The fires, the TS file…Mom, Tom…everything."

Hunter frowned. "What the hell is the 'TS' file?"

"Tom left me his files...in essence, I inherited his clients, right?"

Hunter leaned forward, elbows on knees, eyes locked on mine. "Yeah."

"There was this one file. He locked it in a drawer and gave me the rest. I was curious about it. Later, I found out that he made sure I saw him lock it away so I'd know where to look for it after he passed."

Hunter's jaw clenched, his cop mind grinding through possibilities.

"The file indicated an event forty-three years ago that involved my mother's father and Tom. Now, this is the kicker...Tom told me that he and my mother almost got married. Mom never told me that. There's got to be a reason. And Tom didn't mention it when we worked together either. Don't you think that's odd?"

Hunter leaned back in his chair and rubbed his forehead. "This gets more and more complicated," he muttered.

"Anyway, Tom locked that file away to highlight it. He had a plan all worked out. I'm discovering the information in the file is something he wanted me to know. Something pivotal." I paused and rubbed my hands together. How much did Hunter need to know? Should I keep going? Didn't he have enough on his plate already?

I looked at his face, the warm, chocolate eyes dark with concern and the stubble he hadn't had time to shore up because he'd been so busy helping me. Hunter was the most generous man I knew. And yeah, he'd want to know everything.

I cleared my throat. "There are people that do *not* want me to uncover what happened in that file."

Hunter's forehead wrinkled. "A forty-plus-year-old case? Why?" He turned this new information over in his mind. "Do you think the fires are related? What the heck is in that file?"

I shrugged. "A lot of it's redacted. For a reason, I'm sure. That's what I'm trying to figure out. It was never an active investigation...I think it was covered up or people were paid off. Something. And my *father*...is apparently a guy with a temper and a grudge. Tom said I shouldn't look him up."

"Huh." Hunter mulled this over. "So now you have two angry men on your tail."

I grinned. "Three, including you."

"Very funny." Hunter's lips pressed together. "This is serious stuff, Olivia."

"I know," I whispered.

We shared a moment of silence. I was crushingly grateful for him. His presence had reduced my stress by half. His support meant the world. "Good thing you called me in, Olivia."

"You have no idea," I said.

We stared at each other.

"You have a whiteboard?" he asked, rising from the chair.

"Sherry!" I called. "Break out the whiteboard."

Chapter Twenty-Four

Hazel took a last peek in the mirror in her bathroom, touched up her lipstick, and walked to her living room to wait on Pete.

She drew the curtain back. Pete had not arrived. With a sigh, she slumped onto her couch. "I'm too old for this cloak-and-dagger stuff," she muttered, wondering if she had time for a quick shot of Schnapps.

Bad idea, since Pete was taking her somewhere 'special' he'd told her, and she was sure the event would include alcohol. Too much booze would cause a slip of the tongue, and she couldn't chance it. For now, she hoped that he wouldn't pick up on any difference in her attitude toward him.

A car pulled into the driveway. A door opened, then closed. Steps proceeded from the driveway to the short sidewalk and up the stairs to her front door. He knocked.

Hazel took a deep breath. "You can do this," she whispered. She puffed out her chest. Opened the door.

"Hi, gorgeous. You ready for a great night?"

"Ready." she trilled, her voice an octave too high. She gripped her purse and followed him to the car. He opened the door for her. On the passenger seat lay a large, tissue-wrapped bouquet of daisies and daffodils. "How lovely!" she exclaimed. "Let me run these back in the house and put them in a vase. I'll only be a second."

She hastened inside, threw the flowers in the trash, and called Sherry. "Quick. Tell me what kind of flowers Olivia's been getting."

Sherry told her and added that her timing was impeccable because Olivia had received another one an hour ago on the front porch of her office.

Signed, 'Love, Your special Foofoo.'

"I'm getting into Pete's car, and guess what I find on the seat?"

Sherry gasped. "No."

"Pete must assume that I know about the Foofoo bouquets. He would've assumed that she shared that in our sessions, right? Maybe it's a test."

"What's your card say?" Sherry asked.

Her fingers like wood, she pulled the flowers from the trash and found the card. "It says 'Love, Pete'."

"Maybe you should reschedule, Hazel."

"Not a chance," she declared. "He's overplayed his hand, my dear. Now I know he has something to do with this group."

"Or someone in the group is partnering with him."

"I have to go…he's waiting."

"But—didn't you tell me you were going to meet him from now on? Not ride with him? Olivia wanted me to make sure to tell you that."

Hazel's eyes widened. "He insisted that he drive. I thought—" She frowned. "You're right. I'll make up something."

Hazel ended the call. Sucked on her lower lip. Her stomach was in free fall. She went into her bedroom to her bedside table and pulled out a fresh cylinder of pepper spray, and tucked it into her purse before she returned to Pete's car.

"The flowers are gorgeous, thank you," she beamed, opening the passenger side door of Pete's car. "You know what? I forgot that I made plans to run by and check on a friend after dinner. Do you mind if I take my car?"

Pete scowled, but offered up the name of the restaurant. "Wanted it to be a surprise," he grumbled.

"It will be. I've never been. I can't wait."

"You pulled out all the stops tonight, didn't you?" Hazel remarked, her demeanor softened by a glass of sauvignon blanc.

Pete leaned forward over the white tablecloth. Candles flickered on the table and the dim lighting showed off the chiseled planes of his face to full advantage. Hazel had been gobsmacked by this attractive man's interest.

She should've known he was up to something. She smiled a secret smile. Pete smiled back.

She'd hand him back his stupid scheme on a silver platter.

"You look beautiful tonight, Hazel. The thing is, I've...enjoyed the last six weeks so much that I...I...."

"Me, too, Pete," she responded, working hard to keep from gagging. Perhaps she'd been an ignorant, old fool for a while, but all that was about to change. With a smile borne on the wings of thoughts about her starring role in his fall from grace, she responded. "You what, Pete?"

He stared at her. She saw a flicker of distaste in his eyes. Or was it avoidance? Observing him as a therapist instead of a romantic interest, she interpreted his 'tells' easily. She couldn't wait to hear the next thing that fell out of his lying mouth.

He reached for her hand. "I want us to take it to the next level, Hazel."

She choked a little on the wine. "You do?"

"Don't you?"

She leaned in. "Tell me why you think we should take this to the next level."

His head jerked a tad. His eyelids fell to half-mast. "Well, I...I think you're unique and I want us to be...closer."

Hazel almost laughed in his face. Closer?

"And...and..." He cleared his throat. "I think I'm falling in love with you."

Hazel downed the rest of her wine. He'd say something *this painfully dishonest* to get information out of her? What were the stakes here?

Hazel mock-sighed. "Pete. I had no idea."

He frowned. "You didn't?"

"This is sweet of you...to arrange a nice dinner at a wonderful restaurant to share your feeling, but I have no plans to commit. To you or anyone."

"So...you're saying no? To *me*?" His eyes flashed his disbelief.

Yes, dipwad. Surprise!

"Let's enjoy," she suggested, digging into the entrée that a young man had placed before her with great flourish. "Enjoy the meal. Enjoy conversation. Let's not complicate things with words like 'next level.'" The young man danced around to Pete's side and placed his meal with the same flourish, then slipped away.

They ate in silence. Pete drank another glass of wine. He'd had two and now worked through a third. Hazel had been careful to limit herself. Phase One of 'solicit information' was underway.

"Have you heard what's happening in the Glyndon area?"

"Maybe," Pete said, morosely picking through his meal.

"Someone's setting fires."

Pete's hand stilled on the fork. "I heard about that. Do you know anyone that's affected?"

She nodded. "A friend of mine's house was targeted. It's been ruled arson."

Pete's reaction would tell her a lot. Hazel finished eating, set her napkin aside. Picked up her glass of water and drank. "How was your dinner?"

"Not hungry," he said and put down his fork. "I can't quit thinking about Olivia Callahan since you introduced us that night at dinner. I hope she wasn't involved. It's awful how bad things keep happening to her." He shook his head.

"How could you possibly know that? Yes, it was Olivia's house. You must be clairvoyant." Hazel grinned. Now they were getting somewhere. "Her fans, The Friends of Olivia group? They've already sent flowers. They must be a nice bunch of people, those Foofoos."

Pete rubbed the back of his neck. "Friends of Olivia? What's that?"

"Her fan club. They call themselves the Foofoos. You know, like that singer, whats-her-name, Taylor Swift, that's it. Her fans are the 'Swifties'. Well, Olivia's are the Foofoos." Hazel chuckled. "I think I'll look into joining. I'm not much for social media, but I can figure it out."

Pete frowned. "Why?"

"I want to help. Maybe they do nice things for her on a regular basis."

Pete stared at the floor.

"It's so interesting. The flowers you gave me tonight are the very same ones that she's been getting. Isn't that funny? I guess that combination is popular."

Pete tugged at his collar.

"Now," Hazel said, "I'd love to hear more about *you*, Pete."

As she'd hoped, the wine had loosened his tongue and then some. She tried to look interested.

Chapter Twenty-Five

Hunter felt along the dashboard of his Jeep for his binoculars.

He'd brought powerful binocs, tracking tiles, political brochures in case he wanted to play door-to-door volunteer, and a couple of changes of clothes and assorted disguise items. The street was his first love, always had been.

What a rush.

He missed this.

A block away, the door to the house he'd been surveilling opened.

Hunter zoomed in with the binoculars. Louise and some guy walked out onto the front steps, and they spent quite a while playing tongue hockey before they parted.

"Bad, bad, girl, Louise," he muttered. He took photos, but it was too far away for them to be clear. He frowned. How could anyone be that stupid? Especially if the spouse was running for political office? Straightening her short, tight skirt, she looked right, then left, before she dashed to her car, hair blowing in the breeze. She got into a dark green Subaru and started it. In short order, she killed the engine and ran back into the house.

"Cool," Hunter murmured.

Raking his hands through his hair in an attempt to convince it to behave, he then pulled on oversize sunglasses and topped it off with an Indiana Jones-style hat. A simple door-to-door nuisance that no one would remember. He picked up the pile of brochures and meandered down the sidewalk of the seedy suburban neighborhood. Shaggy yards, junk cars, and a few broken windows painted the story of a once-thriving neighborhood fallen on hard times. As he walked down the sidewalk, a Doberman charged him in full devil mode through a chain link fence. He gave the yard a wide berth.

Since it was a political season, no one would give a door-to-door volunteer a second thought. Louise's laugh tinkled through the air when she reappeared on the stoop. They embraced again, and she returned to the car. Hunter stepped in front of the car and gave her a big smile. "Ma'am? I'm sure you've heard of Scott Waymire, who's running against the incumbent. Are you voting?" He offered a brochure. "We have to kick out Dylan Palmer. My bet's on Scott Waymire. He is the future."

A puzzled look crossed her face as she took the brochure. "But these… aren't supposed to…" She stared at him. "This isn't his district. How did you get these?"

"From his headquarters, ma'am. Is there a problem?" Hunter grinned again.

"No…I just…"

"Vote for Scott! You won't be sorry."

"I will, I…."

Hunter tilted his head. "Anything wrong, ma'am?"

"I'm fine," she muttered, staring at the brochure.

"If you need to talk…." Hunter continued, letting the thought dangle.

"I'm…dealing with a lot right now."

"I understand. Last night, my wife told me she'd dropped ten grand on the ponies. How do you like that?" Hunter shook his head. "Nobody's perfect, I guess."

Louise grinned. "My husband has such a tight fist on money that he squeaks when he walks."

Hunter chuckled. "I hear you."

"Did she win, at least?"

"No," Hunter told her.

"Marriage is complicated, Louise mumbled, shoving the brochure in her purse.

"That's a fact."

Louise looked at him. "Who are you, again?"

Hunter beamed his smile at her once more. "A faithful foot soldier in the Waymire army, ma'am. Don't forget to vote. You have a good day."

Hunter walked down the sidewalk, pretending to knock on doors until Louise had left the area. He took a picture of the license plate of the car in the driveway of the house Louise had visited, then the address and name on the mailbox. He walked back to his Jeep. "What a crappy world," he muttered.

Louise was still in the business, and her husband didn't know. He'd have to prove it, but he figured she was hooking or working sex traffic. A simple affair? Maybe. But from what Olivia had told him about the woman, she felt like a pro.

Next, close-up photos. Tonight, maybe. Dylan Palmer would get his money's worth, but a marriage could be destroyed.

Yeah, the world was a crappy place sometimes.

He glanced at his watch. He could make the Waymires'son's ballgame.

The bleachers were filling up. The rain had shifted north, and the sun popped out. Humidity was high, and mosquitos nipped at Hunter's arms. He swatted them away. The field was next to a local park. Kids raced around. People walked dogs. Knots of parents sipped cokes and chatted before the game started. A dad and his young son threw a football back and forth. Norman Rockwell might as well set up his easel and start painting.

Hunter spotted Louise's green Subaru and pulled down his baseball cap. He'd traded the sunglasses for clear nerd-glasses and changed into a T-shirt with a Lakers logo on the front. Louise wouldn't recognize him. Scott had arrived as well. The two of them walked together to the bleachers, holding hands.

Hunter stood twenty yards from the bleachers, watching. In blissful ignorance, Scott slid his arm around his wife as they walked. At the foot of the bleachers, he hopped up first and offered his hand to help her up the steps. "Huh," Hunter grunted, sucking Diet Coke through a straw. "Yeah, if I didn't know I'd married a hooker, I'd be a happy camper, too."

He frowned. Maybe Scott *had* known and forgave her. He imagined the tearful scene, the repentance, the promises never to let it happen again.

Then he rehashed the scene he'd witnessed at the guy's house. Not exactly repentant behavior.

Refs called for the Little League game to begin. Players took their places. Scott's ten-year-old son was a short, hefty kid in the outfield.

While Scott and Louise focused on their son, Hunter crept up the other side of the bleachers and worked his way across until she was two rows behind them. He sat and focused on the players. It was easy to chat up parents in this type of setting. He simply rooted for their kids' team, and like the parting of the red sea, parents in his orbit bought his story about checking out the area and spilled their guts in detail. Especially when he suggested he might want to check out the same neighborhood as the Waymires. In the middle of the hooting and hollering at the refs, someone introduced him to Scott. Louise turned around and smiled, but didn't recognize him without sunglasses, a dress shirt, a hat, and a pile of brochures under his arm. Hunter had no negative impressions of Scott. Zip. In his opinion, Scott was a good—albeit clueless—guy. Louise, on the other hand, smelled like a hustler.

He sucked on the Coke straw and got nothing but ice and spit.

One woman pointedly had not engaged. When she got up for a break, Hunter was quick to follow.

He arranged bumping into her behind the bleachers. "Hey. Aren't you... didn't I meet you back there?"

She laughed. "You met most of the parents *but* me, I think. My name's Sally. I overheard you say you're moving here?"

"Maybe." He grinned. "How do you like it? Is your neighborhood around here? I've been driving the area, thinking my family would love it."

"Sure. Oh, it's okay. I've lived here most of my life, so...it's home."

Hunter planted his feet, crossed his arms. "Tell me why I *shouldn't* consider moving here. That's what matters, right? Anyone can say the usual things. What I don't get is the gritty truth." He smiled.

Sally fidgeted. Her eyes darted back and forth.

"Come on, Sally. My family's safety is my priority. You understand, right?"

"I don't like to throw people under the bus."

Hunter was quiet. He'd perfected the art of waiting out awkward silences in interrogation rooms.

After a lengthy pause, she sighed. "Look. I heard you say you were thinking of moving to Hightower. The neighborhood the Waymires live in." Sally drew air quotes around the name 'Waymire' with a slight grimace.

Uh oh, Hunter thought. Here it comes.

"It's...so over the top. They have neighborhood parties, kids' playdates, bouncy houses."

Hunter held his arms out to his side. "Isn't that good for the kids?"

"Well, yeah, but..." she looked away. "There are rumors."

He cocked his head at her. "It's information. You aren't throwing anyone under the bus."

Sally glanced left, then right. Crossed her arms. "There are odd things going on over there," she murmured. "Questionable activities with kids and moms. Everyone talks about it. The people coming and going out of their house?" She shook her head. "*I* wouldn't move to that neighborhood, for what it's worth." She turned and walked in the direction of the restrooms.

"Wow," Hunter breathed and pulled out his cell as he walked back to his Jeep. "I'd say that was worth an afternoon of kids' baseball. He punched in Olivia's number.

Chapter Twenty-Six

I stood on the front porch and waved as Lilly raced off to an early meeting at the Y. So many threads ran through my mind. First, I was curious how the evening went with Hazel and Pete. Next, after I'd gotten a brief call from Hunter last night, all hope of a clean slate for the Waymires had drifted away. Dammit, Dylan had been right. Everyone had something they wanted to hide. I knew I should remain objective as a professional, but I (so far) liked these people, and besides, anybody would be a better choice than Dylan Palmer for Maryland State Representative. I dreaded listening to Hunter unpack the details today.

The morning sky was powder blue and held a thin whiff of rain on the way. A bank of clouds drifted across the sky. I'd refilled my bird feeders, and now the cardinals and orioles fought. An eastern towhee showed up and, to my delight, a couple of bluebirds. I could watch them all day, but Dylan had me on a short leash. With a sigh, I pulled open the red screen door, pushed Riot out of the way with my foot, and went inside.

Hunter walked down the staircase, Marlowe at his side. Riot slunk underneath the foyer table and stayed there. He was still pouting about Marlowe.

I laughed. "Looks like you've made a friend."

Hunter's hand drifted to Marlowe's head. "Yeah, this is a great dog. Shoulda had him at the office the night of the arson attempt."

I nodded. "Would've been a good idea."

"No doubt."

"Help yourself to whatever's in the kitchen, okay? Lilly and I already ate."

Hunter grabbed a bowl of cereal and sat at the breakfast bar. I walked to the kitchen counter and leaned against it. Thunder grumbled in the background.

"So. How was yesterday?"

"Got a lot done," he said, munching cereal. "I visited the kids' school and found some staff wandering around. They're off in the summer, but still...they do stuff here and there, and I got lucky. Public school, by the way, not private. Anyway, I told them I was a friend of the Waymires and thinking about settling in the area. They opened up about every detail. Someone should tell them there are privacy issues, for God's sake." He shrugged. "I caught the baseball coach on the school grounds. Friendly guy. Waymire's son plays baseball, daughter does gymnastics.

I waited.

"I'll be busy today, getting some better shots. My bet is on her for the, uh, win?"

I chuckled. "Gosh. I liked her. I hate that we've found something."

"We'll see. Never know."

"Okay, so you'll be in Reisterstown?"

"In and around." Hunter took out his phone. "She's on the move. I'm headed to the office first. Whose idea was the tracker?"

"Tom's."

"Good call." He took off.

The morning passed quietly enough, and I was grateful for the calm. I popped into reception just as Hunter opened the door to leave.

Sherry's cell chirped. She flapped her hands at the phone. "This is Hazel. *Wait,* Hunter. This should be epic," she said. She put the phone on speaker.

"Should I stay?" I whispered.

She shrugged.

I stayed. To hover.

"Good morning," she said. How'd it go with Pete?"

"He wanted to take our relationship to the 'next level.'"

"Wow. What was your reaction?"

A few beats of silence ensued. My forehead wrinkled. She couldn't have... let him railroad her, could she? Hunter narrowed his eyes.

Hazel laughed. "Had you for a minute, didn't I?"

My heart started beating again. I groaned.

Sherry shook her head at me and mouthed, 'be quiet.' "Yeah, you had me there, Hazel."

Hazel snickered. "In all seriousness, Sherry, it couldn't have gone any better. I played him like a violin. I haven't had this much fun all year."

I glanced at Hunter and smiled.

"Tell me about it, Hazel." Sherry grinned at Hunter.

"I acted like the flowers were a coincidence, and he bought it, but I could tell he was concerned that I knew Olivia got some at the same time."

"Wow. Great job, Hazel."

"Told him I wasn't a 'commitment' type of woman, and he was offended that I hadn't fallen at his feet in gratitude or something. The look on his face was classic."

"I bet. You manage to hold it together?" Sherry asked.

"I have untapped talents."

Sherry laughed. I shook my head.

"Anyway, he's such a narcissist that he can't resist talking about himself. Plus, he was drinking. He dragged out his past, his misspent youth, his deranged father, an incarceration. He is also obsessed with another book from Olivia. For some reason. I'll be taking my pepper spray any time I'm with the guy. Which I doubt will be much from now on, but he loves the attention."

"Incarceration?" Hunter asked.

"Didn't show up for a DUI, I think. They threw him in a correctional facility so he wouldn't kill anybody. I learned he is a recovering alcoholic. A very *recent* recovering alcoholic who fell off the wagon last night."

Hunter frowned. "When? What dates?"

"Within the last couple of years. That's the impression I got."

I closed my eyes.

"Where?" Sherry asked.

My throat began to close.

"Maryland Correctional—"

"Hagerstown. Same as Monty." Sherry's head whipped around toward me.

Hunter's jaw clenched.

"We'll have to think about this. But great job, Hazel. We can build on this stuff."

I nodded my approval. Sherry smiled.

"So now we have a *definite* connection. It's more than we had before," Hunter added.

"I did it!" Hazel hooted like a three-year-old.

"Yes, you did, Hazel. Hunter and I are very proud of you," Sherry said.

I pictured her dancing a little jig in her office. She reminded me of Mom, with the gentle clanking of bracelets and earrings as she moved. I could almost smell her Chanel through the connection. "Got a client in five minutes. Talk later." Hazel ended the call.

No one spoke.

Hunter started for the door. "Good job, Sherry. See you later."

He walked outside and got into his Jeep. I walked over to the window and watched him. From the look of it, he had some serious cogitation going on. Neither of us would ever forget the pain Monty had caused both of us. The trauma might start all over again if Pete and Monty had made some sort of pact in prison.

In a bizarre twist of fate, the assault that had almost killed me had turned out to be the thing that saved my life. Funny how life works. The way my brain healed will forever be a source of wonder to me. I was so *different* now—the complete opposite of the woman I'd been with Monty. If not for that, I'd probably still be with him.

I shuddered.

Monty still considered me his wife, though we'd been divorced almost three years. As far as he was concerned, I was his property, and he resented the fact that I wasn't his passive, codependent wife anymore. My mind flew back three years, when Hunter Faraday had been an investigator in my assault case. We'd been trying to get my memories back, so he could build a foundation to get a search warrant for the attacker's house. Monty was livid about the time we spent together. I closed my eyes, remembering.

A harsh knock at the screen door interrupted us. I apologized to the investigator and walked to the door. Monty frowned at me through the screen. Why was he here? In violation of a restraining order?

I stepped outside. Monty moved aside, but not much, like a disgruntled child in line that didn't want to give up his spot. His jaw clenched.

I crossed my arms and held his gaze. Two could play this game.

Eventually, I sighed and blurted, "What?"

He jutted his chin toward the house. "A little cozy with that investigator, Faraday."

"What do you mean, Monty?"

"Just sayin'."

"Just sayin' what? For God's sake, Monty, I can't figure out this doublespeak thing that you do."

His eyes darkened. "You're my wife," he seethed.

"We're separated, in case you forgot. And a restraining order is a real thing. Did I forget to mention that? Or are you ignoring it? I need you to leave, Monty." I spun around.

He gripped my upper arm. His sour breath smelled of alcohol and rage.

Detective Faraday exploded from the foyer, wrestled Monty's arm off me, and twisted it behind Monty's back.

Monty blanched. "What the hell, man?"

He gentled his hold. "We all calmed down?"

The memory floated away. I rubbed my arm. I could still feel the pressure of his hands.

Marlowe walked in and sat beside me. I kissed the top of his head. Sherry had gotten involved in returning emails and paying bills at her desk. I went back to my office.

An email arrived from Sherry that a date had been set on my calendar. I clicked on it. New client appointment at eleven. "Who is it?" I yelled from my office.

"She wouldn't say."

The last thing on earth I needed right now was a new client.

I got up and walked into reception. "Since when are we making appointments for people that don't give you their information?"

She shrugged. "I can cancel it."

"Never mind," I huffed out. "Did Hunter leave you anything?"

She swirled her chair around to her laptop. "He emailed reports last night." She punched a key. "It's sent."

"Thanks." I walked into my office and sat in my caramel leather, crazy expensive, ergonomically correct desk chair that had been worth every penny.

I scanned Hunter's report. The Waymires had been married twenty-two years, had moved six times, and had two kids aged ten and twelve. The kids did well in school, had friends, and behaved. Louise had accomplished a lot in spite of many setbacks, and I was happy for her.

I read on.

Mother volunteers at school, dad participates in kids' sports activities, according to the coach.

I chuckled. Hunter must've chatted up everyone there to get this kind of personal stuff. No bankruptcies, no domestic violence reports, neighbor complaints, not even a barking dog complaint from the security department at their homeowners association. On to Louise...

Hunter had uncovered her past drug use and juvie record, and...my eyes grew round.

Prostitution.

Uh oh.

Now *that* was something you didn't run across much. Dylan would be downright jubilant at this discovery. This was a tough one. Should I skirt around the truth? Soft-pedal it, hoping Dylan doesn't dig around and find these records? Hunter had access to the same databases I did and more.

Dylan couldn't have access to our software options. Could he?

I tugged on my ear, thinking.

I studied the report again. The prostitution charge had been eighteen years ago. Before they'd gotten married.

I ran a hand through my hair. Now what? I had an obligation to my client, jerk or not.

I chewed on a fingernail and thought about how much I missed Tom. I also thought about how hard my heart was beating.

Sherry was deep into organizing the file cabinet when I walked in. "I'm having some kind of meltdown. Stress, maybe?"

"TBI-related, maybe?" she suggested, her voice soft.

"Ugh," I groaned. "I need to check in with my neuro. Sometimes, I get these emotional, crazy, runaway events. But they taper off."

Sherry trotted from her desk to sit beside me. "I'll wait it out with you."

After a few minutes, my heart stopped acting like a racehorse. "It's over. Thank you, Sherry," I smiled in relief. "Have you kept in touch with Hannah? It's been a year, right? Since she moved?"

"I see her on Facebook and Instagram, but everything's roses and sunshine there...nobody posts the bad stuff. We message back and forth sometimes. She asks about you. I fill her in on your news since you have become allergic to social media."

"Let's call her." I grabbed my cell and punched in her number.

The call went nowhere, and voicemail didn't pick up. I frowned.

"So. She and her new hubby moved to Florida? North Carolina? I can't remember."

"Niceville, Florida. And she always tells me things are good."

"She change her number?"

Sherry lifted her hands and returned to her desk. "I'll message her and see if she has a new number."

"Okay. I have to get back to it. We've discovered some incriminating stuff about Louise." I shook my head. "I had her all figured out. I liked her."

Sherry brightened. "Use me! I'll do more legwork if you want." he pursed her lips. "Do you want to discredit the information or validate it?"

I laughed. "You've got your hands full with Hazel's case. Besides, somebody's got to babysit the office."

Sherry batted her eyes at me. "And Hunter."

"Stop," I said. "He'll be with me, anyway, when I share this stuff with Dylan."

Sherry laughed. "Ohhhhh. Of *course,* he will."

Being the boss had its benefits.

Chapter Twenty-Seven

"Where's my eleven o'clock appointment?" I asked, walking into reception after a hectic morning. "Who did you say it was again?"

Sherry looked up from her laptop. "Uhh…they cancelled."

"What? Why?"

"She didn't say," she said, and resumed typing. "When are you going to let me do some social media marketing? I know you want Watchdog off the radar, so Dylan won't know, but we don't exactly have a full pipeline, y'know."

I laughed. "Who knew you were the goddess of sales? The election is in less than a week so we have to wrap it up. Hang on a little longer. Create, but don't post." I walked back to my office.

Ten minutes later, Sherry peeked around the door. "Come on in," I said.

Sherry's hands twisted together. "It's…it's…well, Dylan's here."

What was he doing here? "Did you forget to tell me he made an appointment? I have to be out of here pretty soon."

"No," she whispered, her eyes wide. "He just dropped in. What do you want to do?"

"Tell him I can give him ten minutes. Otherwise, he needs to put something on the schedule."

"Okay."

I patted my hair into place, checked my lipstick. "Stay," I told Marlowe, pointing to a spot on the floor. He dropped.

I walked into reception. Dylan didn't smile. We shook hands. "I don't remember an appointment. Did I miss something?"

"A situation has developed. I wanted to discuss it in person," he said, his voice flat.

"I only have a few minutes, Dylan."

I took him into the office. Marlowe stared at him, then curled up on the floor by my chair. Dylan bit the inside of his cheek.

What was going on?

I sat beside Dylan.

His steel-gray hair stuck out at odd angles, and his clothing was wrinkled, like he'd dashed over to see me right out of bed. Something must have turned over his apple cart.

"What do you need?"

"Before I start, is my report completed?"

"We'll have a full report," I mentally calculated and hoped I was being realistic. "By tomorrow afternoon."

Dylan brightened. "Great. I'll have time to shoot it over to my PR team." He frowned. "There is something to shoot out, isn't there?"

I sighed. "You'll be happy," I said. "We're still verifying, so I don't want to say anything yet."

He smiled. "I needed some good news."

"How's the race going?"

A thundercloud slid across his face. "That's what I wanted to talk to you about. Not good. My polling's in the tank. It's hard to believe."

No, it's not.

"My wife left me."

Now, there's a shocker.

After a few beats of silence, I managed, "I'm sorry, Dylan. That must've been hard."

He pushed out of the chair and stalked around the office detailing all the reasons this was his wife's fault and not his. In minutes, Dylan was jabbing his finger into the air and shouting.

Marlowe growled and bared his teeth.

I made him lie down. I didn't need a dog-bite lawsuit before we even announced the opening of Watchdog Investigations.

I focused on Dylan with one eye on Marlowe.

"She knew how much this meant to me!" Dylan insisted, his eyes watery and red.

He sank into a chair. "You got booze in here?"

"Tom kept some. Vodka tonic, right?"

I strode to the breakroom hoping Marlowe would contain himself while I tried to remember where Tom had stashed his vodka.

He downed the drink in three gulps and left.

I heaved a sigh of relief after his car left the parking lot. What Hunter had discovered would fill in a lot of gaps. I pulled my cell out to give him a call but decided it could wait.

It had been a long day, and it was only one p.m.

Chapter Twenty-Eight

I was on my second cup of coffee the following morning when Hunter's Jeep rumbled into the lot. I glanced out the window.

In his typical pumped-up testosterone-and-fire manner, he burst out of the vehicle and stalked inside.

"What are you doing here so early?" I asked.

He dropped his backpack and files on the temporary desk Sherry, and I had set up. "Let's get this done."

"You worked last night, I see."

Hunter scratched his stubble. "I want to get this over with, Olivia. You don't want Dylan Palmer around, and I can't stand the guy." He grabbed his coffee. "Where's Sherry?"

"It's seven-thirty in the morning, for God's sake Hunter. Not everyone jumps out of bed wide awake and raring to go at five a.m. How about we go into my office?"

I closed and locked my office door behind us. Hunter and I settled in our usual spots. He followed my gaze around the room. "You ever think about Wyatt Harp?"

"Can't help but think about it, he built this building, and I bought into everything he told me. Haven't forgiven myself yet."

"Finding out he had a nephew put him over the edge. You got caught in the crossfire."

"At least I had Tom to help me through it back then. I feel lost without him. He could spot the bad guys a mile away."

"Wyatt in Hagerstown Correctional?"

I nodded. “How ironic is it that he and my ex are in the same facility?”

“Wyatt and Monty deserve each other.”

“They deserve max security,” I huffed. “The jails are overcrowded, and that’s the only reason they’re not. The last time Lilly went to visit her father, he told her he and Wyatt rarely spoke. Wonder why?” I straightened in my chair, crossed my arms. “Okay, let’s see it.”

“Here’s the latest.” He handed me his phone. On it were photos of Louise talking with several different men. One had a woman in the background, and she didn’t look happy.

“Spent half the night following her. I feel bad for her husband.” He winced. “Either she has a drug habit, or she’s hooking. Looks like Palmer gets to keep his seat in the House.”

I frowned. “Where does Scott think she is when she stays out late?”

“What I want to know, too. How deep do you want to go with this?”

“We don’t have much time, Hunter. Election’s in less than a week. In other news, Dylan came in yesterday all weirded out and told me his wife’s filing for divorce. He wants to get our findings out there to keep his constituents’ minds on a bigger scandal than his own.”

Hunter smiled and stroked his lower lip with his index finger.

I groaned. “What?”

“Hey, did I ever tell you how much I like undercover work?”

I tucked my hair behind my ear, opened my mouth to say something, but didn’t.

“I kept eyes on her ‘til three a.m., and then I figured I might as well finish out the night, so I made a little trip downtown.”

“Let me guess. To Canton?”

Hunter lifted his eyebrows up and down. “Dylan’s stomping grounds. You’ll never guess.”

“Hunter…”

He lifted his palms. “Okay, okay. Dylan’s gay.”

My mouth dropped open. “Never in a million years.”

Hunter chuckled. “Right? I mean, it’s not that big a deal…unless you’ve passed yourself off as a conservative, tough guy, your whole career. I mean…

look at these." He took his phone out of my hand, scrolled and handed it back to me.

"My God. Where…did you…was this public?"

"He got a little carried away with grief, what with his wife leavin' and all." His voice dripped sarcasm. "This was on the sidewalk front of a bar. I guess he had to drown his sorrows, y'know…since his cover left."

"No wonder he was spooked when he dropped in yesterday."

"Never know, do we?"

"I don't know how to use this. Or if we should." I paused. Stroked my chin. "Maybe he's bi? Maybe they had an arrangement?"

Hunter grunted. "Either way, I think Dylan Palmer has a lot of stuff to hide. Scott Waymire's wife's side hustle is one thing, but Dylan has his own problems. I guess he can come out before the election, but I doubt that'll win him any votes. Be a big headline, though."

"No kidding," I said, thinking. "You think Scott is clean?"

He nodded. "Can't find a thing. A neighbor told me about some hinky stuff…questionable people and kids in and out of their house. It may be something to track down, but I can't see a guy runnin' for office havin' anything to do with sex trafficking. Especially kids."

"Our job is to find something on the Waymires. Full stop. Dylan's about to explode. He's desperate for something to give the media. I hate to do this to Louise, but we have hard proof. Get me the information, and I'll write the reports. Send me the photos, too, and I'll order 8x10s. You need to be invisible. When this breaks, Baltimore PD may get involved."

"Maybe," Hunter said. "This is what I think—I think Scott is a die-hard romantic that believes everything his cute, sexy wife says. And she might be trafficking right under his nose." He blew out a breath. "So after this, you're done with Palmer, right? Didn't Tom suggest you let go? Not look for your dad, I mean?"

Hazel's voice hurtled through the fog of my indecision. *"Trauma lives on in our bodies. It continues to cause agitation, rage, and heartache. These symptoms are pieces of the past that haven't been laid to rest."*

I made a quick, emotionally significant u-turn.

"Hunter, I can't simply 'let go' of my past because I don't remember all the pieces of it. Perhaps that's a good thing, but it doesn't feel like that to me. It's a big hole I need to fill. Tom's file and the note insisting I stay away from Dylan and not seek out my dad…." I shook my head. "I'm pretty sure he would understand that I can't walk away without knowing what happened. After I dig up the truth, then I'll walk away."

An idea flashed through my mind. "I think those photos of Dylan might come in handy."

After lunch, Sherry walked in with the news that she'd finished formatting the reports on the Dylan Palmer investigation. She'd emailed the file and printed out hard copies. She handed me a 9x12 manila envelope.

I went through the documents one by one. Hunter had been thorough and precise. I got a bit teary-eyed at all he'd done for my firm. Free of charge. His assistance had allowed me to gain a little balance in my upcoming role as CEO of Watchdog Investigations, and the close of Dylan's investigation meant Sherry and I could pull the trigger on social media and marketing venues she had ready and waiting.

My cell jangled with my agent Agatha's ringtone. I stared at the phone in my hand, wondering how it would feel to throw it—and Agatha—against the wall.

She must smell blood in the water.

My blood.

I answered.

"Well, hello there. Been a while."

Agatha's voice was chirpy. Agatha wasn't the chirpy type. I frowned. "Yep. How's it going?"

"Oh, you know. Same old, same old."

I wasn't sure what agents did every day, but I went with the flow. "Yeah. Same."

"That's not what I heard," she chided me.

My waxed and shaped brows drew together. "What did you hear?"

"Olivia. You know this is public record." She tittered a few seconds. "It's fabulous! Your house burning? Add that to the fact that you've built a career from the ground up. I already have a working title. "Up from the Ashes." She tittered again. "That's *so* overdone, though. I'll keep brainstorming."

I covered my eyes with my palm. "Agatha, how many times do I have to tell you I don't want to write a second book?"

"But dear, your public is dying to know. How are you taking it? The persecution, the danger, the threats hanging over your head?"

I frowned. "What threats?"

I waited through the dead air. I wondered if she accidentally hit 'mute'.

"Well, not threats…" she continued, faltering. "But I can imagine what you've been through. And, of course, I keep up with the 'Friends of Olivia' group, and those people, well, they should be—"

"You joined the Foofoos?" I interrupted. "Why would you do that? They're a bunch of dingbats, Agatha."

"Oh, piffle, Olivia. I need a global view. That includes the dingbats." More tittering.

"The answer is no."

"Olivia, will you think about it? Please? Pretty please? There's a nice advance waiting in the wings, too. I've created a bidding war."

I was furious. "How can you create a bidding war when I'm not going to write the book? Agatha, you're impossible!"

"That's what makes me so good, dear."

I took a beat to calm down. Marlowe lifted his head and held his tail at an alert half-mast.

"Agatha, you know I appreciate what you've done for me, but I don't want any more notoriety than I already have."

After we ended the call, Sherry placed a soothing hand on my arm. "I heard. The old bat," she said.

I muttered an expletive. "Would you do me a favor? If Agatha calls the office, tell her I'm out. Or busy. Or whatever. I'm blocking her, so the next thing she'll try is our landline."

She nodded. "She wants the second book."

"Yeah."

She looked at me under lowered eyelids. “I kinda do, too.”

I threw my pen at her.

Chapter Twenty-Nine

"Mornin'" Hunter said, as he walked into reception where Sherry and I sat scrolling through our phones.

"Morning," we responded in unison.

I was exhausted and dreaming of a vacation in Aruba. For a month. A month with no Dylans, no presumed dead but rebirthed fathers, and no jailbait exes. I set the phone aside.

Hunter noticed the absence of my typical chipper mood. "You havin' one of those things that you have?"

I almost laughed.

Almost.

"I miss Tom," I whimpered. My chin trembled.

Hunter got in my face. "Don't do this."

I looked away. "Maybe I'm not cut out for a detective career."

"Nobody is when it gets tough. And the tough will pass. Okay? I've been so scared I didn't know if I could make it, and I did. You will, too. You have the skills and the instincts of a cop. All you have to do is hang on. Persevere."

"And I can shoot," I added, my voice wobbly but stronger.

Hunter laughed. "Yes, you can."

Sherry smiled, her elbows propped on her desk, her chin in her hands. "Y'all are so cute."

I frowned. "The situation is not 'cute,' Sherry."

She studied her laptop. "I know, I know. You're both attending the Dylan Palmer appointment at three, right? What's the location?"

"Same place on Reisterstown Road."

Her fingers flew across the keyboard. "Any special instructions?"

"If you don't hear from us by close of business, assume we're dead."

"That is *so* not funny, Olivia," Sherry quipped. "By the way, I cannot find Hannah."

I sighed. "Okay, well, let's get together on that later."

"Hannah?" Hunter squinted at us.

"You don't have to think about it, Hunter."

He nodded and went back to his desk.

I loved that the man did not pry. When I asked him to drop stuff, he did. As long as it wasn't about me. If it *was* about me, he was a human crowbar. Monty had been the opposite of Hunter Faraday, uninterested in my decisions, hopes, dreams…unless it benefited him in some way. *And I'd let it happen.*

Learned behaviors die hard, but I was confident I had fought my way back to a new normal. Though I didn't remember a lot of specifics about the twenty-year marriage to Monty, my emotions did. My reactions to certain situation were bizarre, and with Hazel's help, I'd learned that they were triggers from an event in my past that I may not even remember. The process of letting go is difficult when a TBI is involved, and Hazel keeps explaining that I should grieve the loss of my former self, but allow the range of emotions to cycle through.

All fine and dandy, but I'd sure like to know which emotions go with what event, and how to manage the process.

I walked toward my office, listening to Hunter and Sherry trade barbs.

I smiled.

The relationship with Hunter was so about *me* that I didn't know how to handle it. Hazel said this reaction was normal for a woman brought up without a loving, involved father in the home…and add to that twenty years with an abusive controller. The assault three years ago had put the final nail in the coffin—the death of my trust in men.

I lingered in my office doorway, watching Hunter. Fresh from his morning shower, wearing rumpled khakis and one of his ubiquitous blue oxford button-down shirts. From experience, I knew the rumpled part was a decision. His khakis had knife-sharp creases when on the job. He regarded being here with me as a vacation—no ironing allowed. I smiled. With the still-wet, wavy, brown hair falling into his eyes and his shirt sleeves rolled up to the elbows, he looked like a college kid even though he was forty-four...forty-five?"

"Hunter. You have a birthday coming up?"

"You remembered," he replied, not looking up from his laptop. "I was plannin' on taking you to dinner."

I laughed. "On your birthday, you want to take *me* to dinner."

He smiled. Sherry gave me a look.

At that precise moment, I prayed my trust issues would take a hike where this one solid, awesome man was concerned. Hunter Faraday was worth trusting.

The rumble of thunder provided a backdrop as Hunter and I drove to Kelvin's Bakery in Pikesville to meet Dylan. We hadn't talked much. Both of us hoped this would be the last we'd see of Dylan, but I wasn't so sure. The term 'bad penny' came to mind. Aren't bad pennies supposed to return at the most inopportune times or something? I looked at Hunter. "How you feeling about this?"

He glanced at me. "Fine."

"Just 'fine'?"

His lips turned down. He navigated a lane change. "You know as well as I do the guy's trouble. You carryin'?"

"All the time."

"Good."

I smiled. "You expecting a shootout at the OK Corral? In the middle of Reisterstown?"

"Never know."

My stomach growled. When had I eaten last? I couldn't remember. I glanced at the dashboard clock. We had twenty minutes to spare. "Can we hop into a Chick-Fil-A or something?"

Without a word, he screamed across two lanes. I heard some serious cussing from angry drivers, and when I opened my eyes, we'd landed in a Wendy's drive-through.

Hanging onto the Jeep's grab bar for dear life, I managed, "Six-piece chicken nuggets and a Diet Coke, please."

Ten minutes later, I was myself again. Blood sugar, check; pulse rate, check; steady vision, check. Dr. Grayson Sturgis—Mom's new husband and my neuro—would be proud that I'd taken my own vitals before driving to an appointment where I might have to use my gun.

Dead calm in the face of impending doom. That was me.

Hunter zipped his Jeep Wrangler Rubicon four-door into the tiny parking lot. Right behind us, Dylan pulled in. We walked into the deli together. Hunter picked a chair facing the door. The other two were up for grabs. I sat in the one beside Hunter, and Dylan snatched the small, black, wrought-iron chair and placed it backward, then straddled it. It was so out of character for him that I had to smile.

Dylan spoke around the toothpick he had in his mouth. "You never seen anyone sit like this, Olivia?"

"Sure," I said. "Hallmark movies. Westerns."

He took the toothpick out of his mouth. "Whatcha got for me?"

Hunter handed him a thick 9x12 envelope. Dylan grunted his acknowledgment and thumbed it open.

"Dylan, we found little, if anything, on Scott Waymire. His family life seems healthy and normal. They have friends. Support." Hunter sighed. "His wife, Louise, is another matter."

Hunter and I waited as Dylan flipped through the pages and photos. After three minutes, he patted the documents into a tidy pile and slid them back inside the envelope. Holding the envelope bent in half with his huge hand, he jabbed it at each of us like a laser pointer. "This has made my day. You needed a little pushing, but you got it done." Dylan pressed the envelope to his chest. "I'm going straight to the local CBS and NBC affiliates after this, and you guys have made it possible for me to talk 'new developments'. Those idiot talking heads love 'new developments.' Their tongues will be hangin' out. My PR team is going to break out the Champagne." He cackled with delight. "The divorce won't even make it to the six o'clock news. It'll be a two-inch block paragraph at the bottom of page forty in the Baltimore Sun."

"Glad you're satisfied, Dylan." I slid him an invoice.

"I'll get my assistant to pay the invoice. Look. I'm sorry if I was out of line in some of our communication. It's the pressure. Next time we do business, it'll be better. Promise." Dylan stuck his arm out, expecting a handshake.

I folded my arms across my chest. "I think you should find a different investigator, Dylan. Let's call it even. I did this for Tom. Now it's over."

He frowned. "That doesn't make any sense. You've been *trained* by Tom. You know his methods, and we have history. Seems like a slam-dunk to me." He shrugged. "I'm always needing an investigator for something. Tom owed me, you know. I thought you understood."

"Understood what?" I asked, with an innocent look on my face. Of course, I knew what this scumbag wanted, but I had a backup plan in the event of coercion...which I'd hoped to avoid. Did he think Tom had clued me into their relationship? And if so, why would he think I'd be interested in signing on? Did he think he could manipulate me like he'd manipulated Tom?

My eyes narrowed.

Dylan grunted. "The arrangement we had," he mumbled. I watched as his eyes slid left and right, trying to assess how much I knew, how much I didn't know. He had assumed I'd be happy that he wanted to continue our working relationship. Even I knew that assuming was a dangerous thing to do.

He turned his chair around the right way, sat, and crossed his arms. "I see no reason why we shouldn't continue this relationship."

Hunter tensed.

I reached in my bag, pulled out an envelope, and put it in front of him on the table.

The thick furrows of his forehead squeezed together. "What's this?"

"A conclusion to our business," I said.

He pulled out the photos. His chin quivered. A rosy red hue climbed from his neck all the way up into his hairline. He slammed the photos facedown.

"Where'd you get these?"

"Can we agree that you won't be needing our services? That it is in the best interests of both parties that we end on the satisfying note of 'job well done'? The release form is in the envelope. I'll wait." I had the insane urge to turn my chair around backward and sit in it like Dylan had.

Hunter's arm inched toward his weapon.

Dylan looked like he swallowed a piece of roadkill. After long seconds, he said, "Look, I was out of my mind that night. My wife had told me she was walking out and with the election and all...." He gripped his hands together on the table and scowled. His left leg jiggled up and down like it had a life of its own.

With a sigh, he searched through the envelope for the release form. "Guess I had you guys all wrong," he muttered. With a flourish, he signed his name and slid the form in front of me.

Hunter's arm relaxed.

I rose from the table. "Good luck, Dylan."

Dylan grabbed the photos and jerked from the chair. It clattered to the floor. With an angry grunt, he kicked it across the room. The manager trotted out from behind the counter. "What the hell, dude?" he asked, holding a pair of tongs.

Dylan glared at him, then me. "I have your guarantee these photos will remain between us?" he whispered.

"Of course," I said.

Dylan put the toothpick back in his mouth, flung the door open, then slammed it good and hard behind him.

I flinched.

His vehicle roared to life in the parking lot. He must've burned rubber a full block.

I melted in relief.

Hunter reached across the table for my hand. "Good job, boss."

Chapter Thirty

The next morning, I had trouble getting my brain to function. The meeting with Dylan had done a number on me. With a sigh, I unlocked the office door. Marlowe barked from the car. I laughed and went back to the car to let him out. "Sorry bud, I have a thousand things on my mind today." We walked inside. He ran to my office. I put my stuff down on my desk, and started to make coffee.

My phone buzzed. I didn't know the number. "Hello?"

"Olivia Callahan? You're an emergency contact on our victim's phone. Wanted to let you know that Hazel Magellson is at Carroll Hospital Center in Westminster. She's stable."

I gasped. The caller gave me the short version— Hazel's house had been set on fire, and she'd sustained injuries. My hands shaking, I ended the call, leaned forward over my desk, and prayed that she'd recover.

Sherry walked in. "What? What is it?"

I opened my eyes. "Hazel's at the hospital in Westminster. Someone set fire to her house, and they think she was assaulted. She has a broken nose. And...and the smoke! What must that have done to her lungs?" Tears pooled in my eyes. "She's in her late seventies, for God's sake. What kind of monster would do this?"

Sherry stood there, arms akimbo, gaping. "What can I do?"

"Cancel the morning's appointments," Olivia told her. "Keep Marlowe close, okay? Lock the door. I don't know who the heck is doing this, but I don't want to put anyone else with close ties to me at risk. Call Hunter and tell him to meet me at the hospital. I'll keep you informed."

I ran out the door.

Once I got out onto the highway, I called Hunter about a hunch I wanted to track down before I came to the hospital. He said he'd stay with Hazel until I got there. With a jerk of the steering wheel, I turned my vehicle in the direction of Hazel's house, and stomped on the accelerator.

Raw determination clenched my jaw. I'd do *anything* to keep my friends and family safe, and I was going to find out what was going on with these fires. I realized it was a pattern now. They were connected. Someone had an agenda.

Hazel's street sign came into view. I drove slowly down the street and parked opposite her house.

A single hose arced a stream of water on the home, but it looked like they'd started to wrap things up. The clean-up firefighters walked the perimeter. I choked back a sob. Hazel's lovely home looked like a bedraggled, soot-stained husk. Half the roof was gone, and no telling what it looked like inside. I got out of my car and approached.

"Olivia!" Tasha waved. "Figured you'd show up."

I waved back as I walked into the front yard. "I had no idea how valuable it is to have a fire investigator for a friend. Any ideas?"

"Off the record, it's a disorganized mess, but I haven't been inside yet. Maybe it was accidental. Did Hazel smoke? Do you know if she liked candles? Did she have electrical issues in her house?"

"She didn't smoke, and I don't remember candles. I've only been in her house once. I barely remember the floor plan."

"You guys done in there?" she yelled at the firefighter walking around with an extinguisher.

"Five minutes," he told her. Two firefighters wrapped hoses, and the one holding the extinguisher stood apart, his gaze burning a hole into me. I gasped when I recognized him.

Why hadn't I known Pete was a firefighter? Oh yeah, because he wouldn't tell me where he worked. "Hold on, Tasha, I need to talk to this guy."

My hands curled into fists. I started walking toward him.

His eyes darted back and forth. He put down the extinguisher and pulled off his mask.

"Pete," I growled.

"Hello, Olivia. This is a sad day. How is Hazel?"

"I find it odd that you're here instead of her hospital room."

He licked his lips. "This is where I can do the most good. I wasn't sure...I mean...whatever. I was close, and they called me in. I-I didn't have a choice."

"She's stable, but they're keeping her for a while."

Shock registered for the briefest second then flitted away. "Thank God. I didn't know if she'd survive this. It was a hot, fast fire."

Olivia folded her arms across her chest. "Where were you before you suited up and rode in to save the day, Pete?"

He frowned. "Why?"

I waited.

Pete's jaw tightened. "Hazel is special to me."

"Sure she is. And she blew you off. Like, what, two days ago?"

Tasha approached. "I can go in now." She eyed Pete. "Were you here at inception?"

Pete gave her a look.

"What did you see when you got here? Were you working inside?" she prodded.

"It spread quick. It was hard to put out, the wind blowing like it was. She was lucky to survive." He kept staring at Tasha. "Is that it?"

Tasha glanced over her shoulder at Pete as he left. "Pete's been at every fire the last few months. He's an odd guy. The volunteers rotate, but he's been at every one."

"Volunteer? As in volunteer firefighter?"

Tasha nodded. "Yeah."

"He knew the victim."

Tasha frowned. "Okay."

I drew air quotes with my fingers." She calls him her 'special friend'."

Tasha stared at the blackened brick exterior of the home. "I'll keep that in mind moving forward, thanks. I'm going in now. Talk to you later."

My cell buzzed.

"Where are you?" Hunter asked.

"Pete was at the scene. He's a volunteer firefighter," I told him. "How did I not know that?"

A blip of silence. "Is that significant?"

"Maybe. He's been at every fire the last few times."

"First responders are short-staffed. Could be a coincidence."

"Doesn't feel that way to me, Hunter. Could you keep him on your radar?"

Hunter laughed. "You have a lot of faith in me."

My cheeks warmed. "Yes, I do. Headed over to the hospital now, okay?"

After a poignant pause that made me feel like an awkward teenager with braces and an inferiority complex, we ended the call.

The hospital's elevator doors whooshed open.

I headed to the nurses' station.

"Olivia," Hunter called.

Sailing by the nurses' station, I walked past three patient rooms, two wheelchairs, and a group of medical interns to get to him.

"I hate hospitals," I muttered as I approached.

Hunter smiled. "So you've said."

I nodded. "She lucid?"

"See for yourself." Hunter opened the door for me. He leaned against the doorjamb, half-in, half-out, his eyes watchful.

I stiffened at the sight. Tubes snaked from her tiny arms and chest. A monitor blipped, and two IV poles framed the bed, each holding bags of liquid. Hazel's complexion matched the silver of her hair. Her cheek felt dry and soft as I stroked it gently. Her eyes fluttered open. Her parted lips held a permanent reddish cast. At the sight of me, her mouth started working. She clutched my arm.

"Hunter and I are both here. How are you feeling?"

Hazel's eyes teared up. She raised an arm and made an angry sound. I leaned in close and lifted the oxygen mask. I couldn't make out the words. I tried my best to lip-read.

One arm waving erratically through the air, she squeaked "Indoh. Indoh. *W-Win.*"

Window?

"Window?"

Hazel bobbed her head and jabbed her index finger at her ear.

"Hear. Heard. Window. Heard window."

Hazel bounced her head up and down. "Precious."

Tears trickled from under the mask and down her wrinkled cheeks. "Precious," she repeated.

I frowned. "The bird? Your canary?"

She nodded. "Duh... *Die.*"

My eyes widened. "Died? In the smoke?"

She shook her head. "Kill."

"Someone killed Precious?"

She nodded, trying hard to get a breath. I slipped the mask back over her face and patted her hands. Why would someone kill a bird? Little birds like that just keel over one day without explanation, right? I wasn't a bird person, so I didn't know.

"Windows. I thnk she heard windows opening," I told Hunter.

"Good. Tell forensics that. They're probably already there."

"On it." I walked to the door. My hand on the doorknob, I turned. "Thanks, Hunter. You okay here?"

He gave me a two-finger salute. "I'm invisible."

"Not to me," I quipped.

He smiled.

Chapter Thirty-One

"Have you seen the front page this morning?" Sherry asked as I walked into the office.

I shook my head. "Sorry I'm late. Lilly is trying to cram all the mother-daughter conversations into these last couple of weeks. She's excited about moving to Richmond in August, but she's nervous, too."

Sherry nodded. "Sure. I get it. But...look."

I took the tabloid-sized local newspaper from her. Carroll County's local daily was a rarity—local news with no agenda other than truth-telling. I frowned at the headline that jumped out at me. 'Scott Waymire on Defensive as Palmer Strikes Back'. Scanning the story, which continued from the front page to the interior, my jaw dropped. Dylan had changed the narrative completely. The evidence about Louise had been thin, and we'd told him so. A photo of a shocked Louise caught in the parking lot of a local grocery store accompanied the article. I sucked in a breath. I'd liked her, but if she had been pulling stunts that reeked of infidelity or worse, who was I to hold back the truth?

Still.

I was torn. The major papers, news stations, social media would love this. The scandal would race all over the globe in minutes. Boom. Reputation destroyed. It didn't seem fair.

Hunter walked in. "Good morning, ladies." His eyes fell to the headline. "That's too bad. I guess I hoped she'd get a break." He shrugged. "Hard to hide that kind of lifestyle for long."

I pushed my hair off my forehead. "Yeah, but this looks like she's a diehard slut…implying that Scott is complicit. What do you bet rumors of 'open marriage' start flying around. From what she told me, she'd repented of things she'd done in her past. Changed her life. How can I feel so bad for her when the photos clearly show a secret life?" I walked into the breakroom for something to drink. "Have you seen the Sun, Sherry? Is she in there, too?"

"Way back in local news. Small article. No photo."

"At least that's some comfort," I muttered.

"The job," Hunter said as he sat opposite me, "…is to dig out the facts and give a report to the clients. Keep feelings out of it. It's not so easy." He chuckled. "You'll get a dose of humility soon enough. People don't exactly love a PI."

I grabbed my phone, scrolled through social media. It was awful. Louise is a slut, whore, and various other nouns that shouldn't be allowed in the English language. How could I have been so wrong about a person?

"Dylan Palmer used our investigation with the intention of blowing it up into some world-shattering issue. No mercy at all."

"Not everyone slobbers all over someone who isn't her husband. From my photos, maybe several someones. Why are you defending this woman?"

I jabbed my arms across my chest. "Scott is a good guy."

"That may be true, but he's also blinded by his wife's charms."

"What Dylan did is overkill," I shot back.

He gave me a crooked grin. "Maybe Scott won't accept the truth. It's easy to overlook someone's faults if you're crazy about them."

I looked at him under hooded eyes. Was he talking about me? *Us?* Or maybe…

"Like me and Monty?"

"Were you crazy about him?"

Sherry had been stapling pages together, but she stopped.

I stared at the ceiling, trying to piece together an answer. On the surface, the answer was a huge *no*, but I think the relationship had been more complicated than a single, two-letter word. "In a clinical sense, I can't say I ever loved him because I probably didn't know what real love looked like. He was a duty. An obligation. I was grateful he took care of us and provided for us, of course. But, what's the definition of 'love' anyway? Isn't that the age-old question? Is it sizzling hot feelings? Is it trust? Faith? Security? A decision?"

Hunter cocked his head. "I think it's all of those things."

Sherry stifled a smile when she looked at me. I rolled my eyes. Her thoughts were so loud I could almost hear them: 'what is wrong with you? This man is incredible, and you're an idiot to keep him hanging', and furthermore, can I have him?'

"I don't know what I felt for Monty," I admitted. "I can't remember. Maybe I'm not supposed to."

"You have no idea how relieved I am to hear you say that," Sherry said in a small voice.

"All you moms tried to get through to me, didn't you? Before the assault, I mean, when our kids were growing up. Before Monty left me for the younger, greener grass of the bimbo."

Sherry grunted. "After a while, we gave up. It's like...you put on this cute little homemaker mask and pretended things were fabulous...only we knew they weren't. We were never sure if it was an act."

"I don't think it was an act. Hazel says Monty was a replacement father since mine was absent. She might be right." I shrugged. "But why would I gravitate toward a man like that just because I didn't have a dad in my life? Is it a law or something?" I frowned.

"How's Hazel doing today?" Hunter asked.

I gave the paper back to Sherry. She picked up her stapler and resumed her tasks.

"She's nagging me like a leaky faucet. So I know she's getting better."

An hour into trying to make sense of the notes on my desk and assembling them into some kind of order, my cell lit up with a call. My mother. I stared at the work on my desk...the phone...the work on my desk...the phone. With a sigh, I took the call.

"Hey, Mom."

"Hi, honey. Got a few minutes?"

"Yeah."

"How are you? Is the investigation completed?"

"They have a suspect."

"That's great news. I hope that's the end of it." She cleared her throat. "I was reading the paper this morning. Did you see the smear job Dylan Palmer did on Scott Waymire? Dylan Palmer really knows how to erase his competition, doesn't he?"

The furrow deepened between my eyebrows. "Why are you following that?"

She sighed. "Can you spare a few minutes?"

The hair on the back of my neck stood straight up. How did she know Dylan Palmer? I pushed away from my desk. Turned my chair so I could look out a window instead of the pile of cases.

"I'll take the time, Mom."

"I guess I haven't been quite, uhh...transparent. It's time that I was. Dylan Palmer is a part of my past I can't avoid anymore. That's why I called. It's time you knew."

I silently agreed. It was time. *Past* time.

She'd led me to believe my dad was dead or somewhere in an alley shooting up, that he didn't care about me and never would. Why? Tom's letter had up-ended my world. "Mom, I want to be transparent with you, too. I know my father is alive. Was everything you told me about him a lie?"

She gasped. "Olivia, what's happened? Are you sure he's alive?"

"I found a sensitive file after Tom's death. I wasn't sure how to approach it, but since you brought up Dylan, your timing is perfect." I left my desk, walked to one of the guest chairs. "I always wondered why you didn't give me any information about my father."

"Honey, I'm so sorry. I hoped I'd never have to tell you."

"Mom. You don't need to keep coddling me. I'm *fine.* The file I'm talking about was redacted, so I have questions. And after I read Tom's letter, I was more confused than ever. What the hell happened?"

Mom sniffled. Wait. Why was she crying?"

I gave her a minute.

"He left a letter?"

"Yeah. He said to tell you that you can't do anything about keeping his mouth shut now, and, 'ha-ha.'" His words. "So you guys were complicit in something. What was it?"

She was quiet.

"*Why* didn't you ever tell me about my father?"

"What good would it have done?" she blurted. "Your dad was a dangerous man. He reminded me of Monty. Didn't you ever wonder why Monty and I never got along? When your father left, it was the best thing that ever happened to us."

"Tom's file indicated he was forced out, Mom. I'd like to know more about that." My voice faltered. Talking about a father I'd never known turned me into a five-year-old that wanted her daddy to swing his princess up onto his shoulders. "Did he ever ask to meet me?"

After a pause, Mom said, "He didn't want me to go forward with the pregnancy, honey. I went ballistic on him. The thought of terminating the pregnancy was never something I could do. We fought over it many times, and the last time he put his hands around my neck with the intention of killing me. I was done. But it wasn't easy to get him to leave me alone."

I closed my eyes and waited for her to continue.

"There were other incidents. When I say he was dangerous, I know what I'm talking about. I nearly died that night. After I got out of the hospital and realized you had come through the ordeal healthy, I swore he'd never have contact with you. No matter what I had to do."

My heart raced. A simple razor slit to my wrist would've been easier than having this conversation.

"I never wanted you to come in contact with him, and I didn't want you to know how cruel he was. For the record, I did *not* know he was alive. Tom kept up with him, but I asked him not to tell me anything, and he didn't. He was thoughtful that way."

Tom kept up with my father? Why?

"Tom's letter said that he and Grandpa hired someone. 'Mitigate' was the word he used. What did that mean?" I asked.

"Your father was in the hospital for weeks." She sighed. "I never heard another peep. My attorney sent the divorce documents, he signed. That was it."

I tapped my chin, thinking. "Was he supposed to die, Mom? Did 'mitigate' mean 'murder'?"

"God help me. I almost wish they *had* sent him straight to hell, where he belongs."

Something clicked in my brain. Long seconds passed. I let my emotions slide away and clamped my investigator hat firmly on my head. "Mom, what was his name? The guy Tom and Grandpa hired?"

"Think about it, Olivia. By the time you met him, Tom was a shell. He used to be vibrant and strong. The most confident guy I knew." She let out a long, drawn-out breath, as if the act of breathing physically hurt. "The minute I saw that headline this morning, I knew what had happened. Anything Dylan wanted or needed over the years, Tom had to agree. It wore him down. Tom would've never supported Dylan in a bid for re-election. Never."

I thought about Tom and Dylan's little pissing contest during the meet-up at Kelvin's. "Mom, Tom was hoping to wrap up whatever he and Dylan had going on, but he died before he could make things right. Tom told me in that letter to pay attention to who I took on as a client. I bet he meant Dylan. He said to trust my gut." I smiled. "Tom trusted my gut, y'know. He got me."

"Your grandpa and Tom didn't count on the backlash from Dylan, and I'm sure Tom never meant for Sonny to end up in a hospital for three weeks. They must've beat him to a pulp. They were both looking at accessory or assault charges. Dylan used it as leverage. Tom told me they were sending a message, but he couldn't have known how bad it would be. All he did was hand off Dylan to my dad. None of us knew how far Dylan would take it, and it was Tom and my father's word against his. Who knows? Maybe there's a long trail of people he's blackmailed."

My mind jerked to a stop. The 'B' files floated in front of my eyes. *Blackmailed.* All those folders marked 'B' stood for blackmailer.

I listened to Mom breathe. To keep all this inside for so many years must've been awful, and my heart went out to her. I wasn't sure what I'd do with this info, but that didn't matter right now. What mattered was the truth and restoration. Closure. A laying aside of guilt or shame. I appreciated her for baring her soul and loved her all the more for it.

"Anyway, Tom got backed into a corner that lasted the rest of his life. Dylan couldn't take a run at my father because he had a heart attack and died a year later. I blamed myself for that," Mom whispered.

"Thanks for sharing all this with me," I said.

We were quiet a few beats.

I tried to think of something positive that would take our conversation out of the sewer that contained Dylan Palmer. "You'll be interested in this, Mom. After Dylan's investigation concluded, I made him sign a contract he would no longer need my services. I didn't realize how deep his sleazeball-ness went with Tom, but now I understand why he wasn't happy about it." I thought about that meeting. "In my own way, I blackmailed him, too, so I guess Tom would get a good laugh out of that."

"Wait. He was your client?"

"I didn't know anything about what happened forty years ago, but I had to finish the assignment. He was *Tom's* client. I worked with Tom, so his clients became mine. Tom died right in the middle of the case.

"So you found something on his opponent." She sighed. "I can't believe you're wrapped up in this. I guess it was too much to hope that I could spare you from knowing. I wanted to keep you from all that violence and regret. I wanted you to have a fresh start, a normal life." She snorted. "Then Monty came along, and here you were, on your own journey with a man just like I'd had—perfect on the outside and rotten on the inside."

I looked at the clock on my wall. It was ten in the morning, but I needed a drink. A big one. "Mom, how does a person go through life never knowing who their father was? Anyway, it should be a relief to you that I'm done with Dylan." I made a little disgusted sound. "What I cannot believe is that people are voting for the guy. It blows my mind." After a beat, I continued. "Do you know where my father lives now?"

"Honey, I don't think—"

"Mom. I have to meet him, you know that, right?"

Seconds ticked by.

"You'll regret it."

"I can take care of myself."

"He'll twist you into a thousand little pieces and leave you bleeding on the floor. Please."

"After all these years of thinking that he's dead or missing, I want to eyeball him. Let him know I am a living, breathing person. Where is he?"

"Tom kept tabs on him. I never wanted to know."

"What's his name?"

"Sonny Pellegra. Unless he changed it."

I rolled his name around on my tongue. Sonny. Sonny Pellegra. "Anything else I can use? Social? Marriage certificate? Hospital records?"

"I got rid of anything to do with him. His name isn't on your birth certificate, either."

"You got rid of anything to do with him…except me."

"Olivia…"

"Bad joke, Mom. Sorry." After a few more tense minutes of feeling like I was picking at a scab, we ended the call.

Why had I talked to her like she was in the wrong for not wanting him to hang around? It took me twenty years and a romp with a stranger that almost put me in a grave to realize I'd married the ultimate scumbag, so why would I be angry that she waffled about his existence all my life? Maybe she believed it would be better for me to think my dad had faded to black and floated around in the netherworld than to give it to me straight: that he'd been an abusive, violent tyrant that had wanted to get rid of me.

I tilted my head back and closed my eyes. The old adage was right—sometimes, it *is* better to let sleeping dogs lie.

Chapter Thirty-Two

One day until the election

Hazel struggled to her elbows, then pushed up to a sitting position. What was she doing in a twin bed? Her nose twitched. Antiseptic, strange smells. Hospital room. Memories flooded her mind. She frowned.

"Nurse!" she yelled. "Nurse?"

A nurse rushed in, an irritated look on her face. She pointed at the call button on the bed. "We have a remote for that. You don't have to upset the whole floor."

Hazel slid her legs over the side of the mattress and shuffled to the mirror. Every arthritic joint in her body screamed. "Oh, my," she whispered as she looked into the mirror. With trembling fingers, she touched her bandaged nose, the purplish eyes.

"How long have I been here?"

"Three days," the stocky nurse answered. "You were in a lot of pain when they brought you in. We kept you heavily sedated. We took you off the IV this morning. I see you're much better today," the woman's voice was testy.

Hazel glared at her. "Get up on the wrong side of the bed?"

The nurse rolled her eyes and stalked out of the room.

A quick peek into the closet let her know someone had bought clothes for her. It took a while to shower and get dressed. She found her purse in a drawer.

She put on sunglasses to hide her scary-looking black eyes and snuck out to a waiting room to call Sherry. Three days was enough in here.

Sherry answered on the first ring. "Hey. How are you, Hazel?"

"Irritated. Frustrated. Angry. If I think of more descriptors, I'll let you know."

Sherry chuckled.

"I'm alive, that's about it." She coughed, cleared her throat. "I guess they sedated me for three days. I lost three whole days, and I have things to do. First, I want to see my house."

Sherry rubbed the back of her neck. "Are you sure? Are you feeling good enough to—"

The irritable nurse skittered around a corner into the waiting room. "What are you doing? You can't get a wild hair and leave your room without telling anyone." She gripped Hazel's arm. "Back to the room, young lady."

"Who is that?" Sherry asked.

"Let go of me!" Hazel told the nurse, jerking her arm away. "It's the nurse from hell," she whispered. "Get me out of here."

"Be there in twenty."

Hazel shoved her head out of the passenger-side window like a puppy, letting the wind catch her face a few minutes.

She sighed happily and took off her sunglasses after she powered up Sherry's car window.

"Whoa," Sherry said.

"They broke my nose with the back of a shovel," Hazel explained. "At least my house is still standing. Can we go inside?"

Sherry nodded. "I don't see a reason why not. There's no yellow tape."

"Is that strange?"

"I don't know. They could've cleared the scene already."

Once inside, Hazel walked through the home in a fog. The living room and dining room lay in ashes and rubble. The bedrooms weren't quite as bad, but certainly not livable. White, gummy, melted sheetrock footprints tracked through the house. The smell of mold and mildew permeated.

Hazel emerged from the short hall. "Now I know what Olivia went through."

"I called your insurance for you, and I think they've already been out. I told them to send your mail to the office for now. We want to help."

She put her fists on her hips. "Tell me the truth. Do you think Pete did this?"

"We aren't sure yet. They found prints on a window. You kept saying 'window' when you were in the hospital, and we had them check. Did you open any windows that afternoon?"

"I had the A/C on, and there is no way I would have opened a window."

"One was open. In the guest bedroom. So we think someone expected you to be at work."

Hazel gulped in some air and patted her chest. "I did hear something, Sherry. I thought it was my imagination? What kind of person kills a tiny bird? Precious was dead on the floor of his cage. He'd been fine an hour before. His little chest was caved in. What kind of disturbed person would do such a thing?"

"You're sure the bird didn't die from the smoke?"

"Absolutely not." Hazel folded her arms. "Precious was gone from his cage before the fire started. I was walking around the house looking for him. When I went back to his cage, he was lying on the bottom. That's when I noticed smoke. Do you think it was a robbery?"

Sherry stared at smoke and water stains on the ceiling. "I think someone wanted you to go and check on the bird." She wrinkled her nose. "It stinks in here. Do you have chairs in the back?"

The yard looked cheery and green in contrast to the blackened husk of the house. Sherry dusted off two chairs.

"You were found on the floor in the living room. If you'd been walking around your house doing stuff, a simple blanket or extinguisher would've taken care of it, Tasha told us. But the perpetrator decided to knock you out. I don't think that was part of the original plan. I think the plan was another fire, and you were in the way." Sherry shook her head. "What we don't know is why they set the fire. They found a candle holder."

"I wasn't using candles that day."

"Pete was one of the volunteer firefighters at the scene, Hazel, and I don't know why he isn't being held pending trial. It doesn't make sense. Did you know he was a volunteer firefighter?"

"He never mentioned it," Hazel said. "Maybe he planned it that way."

Chapter Thirty-Three

Evening before election

I watched Sherry help Hazel out of the car. My heart melted at the sight of my sweet therapist's bruised and battered face. She held onto Sherry as they walked up the sidewalk to my front porch.

Hazel beamed. "Like my new look?"

Sherry and I laughed. I put my arms around Hazel. "I'm glad you accepted my offer. It's great that they finished the office repairs just in time. Hunter's fine staying upstairs in Serena's old room. You can stay as long as you want."

Hazel waved a hand dismissively. "It'll only be a week or so until I sort out somewhere else to live."

"Sure. There's no way I was going to let you waste away in a hotel when I have a perfectly fine guest room at the office." I smiled.

"Thanks for inviting me to dinner. Is Hunter here?"

"He's coming later," I told her as we went inside and sat down to dinner.

"No more Foofoo bouquets, then?" Hazel's eyebrows arched. She picked up her fork.

I put a finger to my lips. "Shh. I haven't told Lilly."

Hazel glanced at Lilly. "Too late, I think she heard," she whispered.

Lilly flipped her strawberry blond hair over one shoulder as she ate. "What bouquets?"

"It's nothing."

"Mom!"

I focused on my daughter. "They've stopped. I had two weird bouquets and—"

"I had one, too." Hazel offered, chewing a bite of grilled chicken breast.

The twilight melted into a deep indigo outside the dining room window. I longed to sit on my front porch with nothing on my mind but watching the birds and enjoying my tea. How long had it been since I'd spent significant time out there? Seemed a lifetime ago. Before the fires. Before I'd become Tom's intern. Before the book had been such a raving success that my agent had all but threatened me with a lawsuit if I didn't write another one.

A long time.

"Mom. As you were saying?"

I sighed. "Honey, are you familiar with the Friends of Olivia?"

She nodded. "I get kidded all the time about the Foofoos. My friends think they're a bunch of wackos."

"I do, too," Hazel said. "Olivia, did I tell you I found out that Pete's in that group?"

"Hunter told me," I said, forking my salad and stuffing a huge amount of spring mix and cherry tomato into my mouth.

Lilly's eyes widened. "Who's Pete?"

I frowned at her. "Never mind."

"Really, Mom? I asked you to be more transparent." She popped up from her chair, threw her napkin on the table. "I'll find out for myself. I doubt you guys know how to join a private FB group, anyway." She ran upstairs.

"Peter Hayes," Hazel called after her.

I grinned. "She's not mad, just annoyed. I *would* like to know more about his Foofoo status, however."

Hazel picked up her plate and silverware and walked to the sink. "Isn't the election tomorrow? Seems I remember in our sessions you were concerned about it."

I nodded. "One of my clients is involved. I don't know how it's going to play out." I crumpled my napkin into a ball, tossed it onto my plate, and scooted my chair back. "My biggest takeaway from working a political investigation is never trust a politician and never *be* one, either." I snorted in disgust. "How does a person decide to run for office if they don't have a squeaky-clean background? Do they think no one will find out?"

"It's a network. People get paid off, promise to do things. But when those people get corrupted, the promises mean nothing."

"I'll never work a case like that again. Talk about disillusioned."

Hazel laughed. "I have to believe there are some good politicians out there."

I stretched out my legs, crossed my ankles. Looked at the plate I was too lazy to take to the sink. "You feeling okay?"

"I'm a tough old broad."

"No, you're not," I countered. "You're a *sweet* old broad.

An easy silence drifted into the room. Stars began to prick the night sky.

"Let's have tea. On my porch."

Hazel beamed. "Wonderful."

We settled on my floral, white wicker furniture with the tea tray between us. The night temps had cooled to an amiable seventy-two degrees, and a breeze swept across our faces. A three-quarter moon had risen above the trees, and lightning bugs lit up the yard like a party.

Hazel sipped her tea from one of my best bone china cups.

"Better times ahead, I'm hoping. You've made such progress, Olivia."

"I'm hoping to overcome being a clueless airhead."

"You're succeeding."

"High praise from you."

"Well-deserved. You've done the hard work." She set the teacup in its saucer. The clink of good china made a musical sound against the backdrop of frogs chirruping in the night. A fox slunk across the lane and into the brush. A faint light shone halfway down the curving lane that led to my office building, and after that, the highway into the historic town of Glyndon. Headlights probed the darkness and started up the lane. The light made eerie patterns through the trees that populated my five acres. Hunter had put such huge tires on his Jeep that it sounded like an artillery tank as he drove up the lane and parked. When he jogged across the yard and up the steps to the porch, my heart skipped a beat or two. Or three.

"Evenin' ladies." He flopped into a chair and eyed the teapot. "Yes, I believe I will."

I chuckled. "Go get a cup and saucer."

Hazel tilted her head as the red screen door banged shut. Riot scurried out of the way. "Marlowe at Callie's?"

I nodded. "Yeah, she likes the dog. I loaned him out."

Hunter reappeared with a mug instead of a teacup. I frowned. "You can't drink proper hot tea in that thing."

"Watch me," he said with a grin.

"Sacrilege," I whispered, but poured and added two sugars and cream.

Hazel's bright eyes missed nothing. I could almost hear her thoughts. *Why aren't these two married yet?*

Hunter leaned back in his chair, his eyes on the stars. "Man. It's so gorgeous out here."

"Isn't it nice in Richmond, too?" Hazel asked.

He laughed. "Not like this. I'm a cliché. Single, middle-aged cop with a condo."

Hazel gave me the side-eye.

I thumped her on the back. "Stop."

"In answer to the obvious," Hunter quipped, his eyes full of mischief, "Hazel, you must know I already asked. She turned me down."

She put down her cup, leaned back, and pursed her lips. An owl hooted in the distance. Another owl answered.

"How are you feeling about that?"

My mouth dropped open. Wasn't this like…a transgression of patient privacy or something? How could she ask him that question?

Hunter looked at me and lifted his palms in resignation. "She sends mixed signals. After a while, a man gets tired."

"And keeps other women in reserve as a backup," I shot back.

The furrow between Hunter's eyebrows deepened. He put his mug down. The cry of bobwhites punctuated his silence. After the pause, he continued.

"You will be happy to know that because I've had a hard time letting go of the thought of us together, Shiloh walked away. For good, this time." He cocked his head and stared at me a few seconds. "One of us needs to make up their mind. And it isn't me." He stood, stuck his hands in his pockets. "Thanks for the tea. I'll be going to bed." The screen door slammed shut behind him. Another, softer slam occurred upstairs when he went into his bedroom.

I twitched at each slam.

Hazel poured herself more tea.

Lilly appeared behind the screen, stooped to pet Riot, then walked outside. "What's up with Hunter?"

Hazel and I said nothing.

Lilly rolled her eyes. "Fine. None of my business. But this Pete guy? Did you know he started that group? He got the whole Foofoo thing rolling. It's his group. And he's really into you, Mom. He's not under his name, by the way. Members use an alias, it looks like, or some stupid made-up handle. But he put his real face on his profile, and I recognized him from Mr. Stark's funeral. He goes by 'MiracleChaser.' Okay, now you know, goodnight." She went inside.

"Good night, honey," I called, stunned.

Now I knew what?

Hazel's complexion paled. Her hands trembled in her lap. "Does he know where you live?" One hand made its way to her throat. "I'm sorry I was such a fool. This whole thing could've been avoided if I'd made better decisions. Maybe we need the dog back."

"We've got Hunter and a restraining order, and as I've said before—"

"You have a gun and know how to use it," she interrupted.

"Exactly," I said, with more confidence than I felt.

Hunter's door flew open upstairs, and he stampeded down the stairs and onto the porch. "Olivia, we've got a problem."

I stared at him. What now?

"Louise Waymire? She's on the job. She assists Special Investigations with victims of sex crimes. We've blown her cover, and I'm not sure if we ruined their sting or if they can resolve this." his voice trailed off.

"Wait. Who told you that?"

"I worked trafficking in Richmond for a while, and when I was working your case here with Baltimore PD, I met some of those cops. They gave me a courtesy call. Not a happy call, either," he said.

"But..."

He cursed. "No 'buts' this time, Olivia! I screwed up. You screwed up. No wonder she was so confused when I approached her the other day with the flyer." He glanced at Hazel. "Sorry, we're going to finish this conversation elsewhere." He propelled me down the stairs and into the middle of my front yard.

"I got it all wrong. She's helping dismantle child prostitution rings. All that talk about kids and women in and out of the Waymires' home boils down to a safe house that processes them on their way to shelters. She camouflages it as birthday parties and kid activities. That's why all the paraphernalia in the yard. I'm sure she went straight to her team to ask them how to handle it. He slapped his forehead. "I don't think they realize I'm in the area. They called to ask me to tell *you* to back off. She's in a volatile situation now, with Dylan throwing Louise's photos around like free Hershey bars. The department is trying to figure out what to do."

I stared at the night sky, my mind blown. "I was doing what Tom asked. He'd already set it up, and he couldn't have known she was working with the police. She working with the Westminster PD?"

"Baltimore County Child Abuse Unit."

My gut had been right. Louise was clean. "This is going to be fun."

"Maybe this is no big deal to you," Hunter said, my smirk adding to his stress level. "But *I* could lose my job if I'm made." Hunter's frown deepened. "What do you mean, 'fun'?"

"Clearing Louise's reputation." I slitted my eyes. "You could've said no when I asked you to come."

He nodded. "Should've."

"You can say you picked up on a 'situation' or whatever while you were off-duty. Nobody knows you're anything but a friend helping a friend. Louise isn't going to know who you are, Hunter!"

Hunter's jaw clenched. An artery throbbed in his neck.

I waited him out.

Finally, he let it go with a long blast of air. "Nothin' I can do now, I guess."

I thought about how to get him to settle down. I batted my eyelashes at him, or tried. My eyelashes were about as existent as snail's teeth. "I'm staking out precincts tomorrow. Would you be up for helping? One of us at Dylan's home base, and the other at Scott's? I'm expecting a lot of volatility."

Hunter stroked his chin stubble, thinking.

I'd successfully re-routed him. Good for me.

"I think I'll make some anonymous 'tip' calls and get a few extra eyes on the polling places."

"Right," I said, with a glance at Hazel on the porch. I stretched, rotated my shoulders. "I'm ready to go to bed."

Hunter gave me a look. "About damn time."

I laughed.

He moved in so hard and fast that I didn't have time to react. Held me tight enough to crack my ribcage and kissed me with a primal ferocity. I melted into the kiss, weak in the knees when it ended. He cradled my cheek in his hand, gave me a long, slow smile. As I stood there wondering what that had been about and if we could please do it again, he turned and strolled through my front yard, up the porch stairs, and past Hazel without a backward glance.

My cheeks burning, I returned to the porch.

"That's what I'm talkin' about," Hazel said, and lifted her teacup daintily to her lips.

Chapter Thirty-Four

Election day, July 20

I tried to hear Hunter's voice on my phone in the hubbub around me. Voters snaked around the building, chatting and excited. 'VOTE WAYMIRE' volunteers bobbed signs up and down. A food truck rumbled into the parking lot and started setting up. I could barely hear with my cell pressed hard against my ear and turned up all the way.

"Listen, I got the biggest butt-chewing you can imagine. Lieutenant Nicholson is not moving on this vacation thing. I got the message loud and clear. I'm a friend. Hanging out. Period. And my vacation time was extended an additional two weeks because I dared ask to get involved in any official capacity."

"You can go if you want. You're not on a freaking leash, Hunter. What do you see at Palmer's polling place?"

"Dylan Palmer, glad-handing his ass off."

"He walking around like the King of Everything?"

"Yep."

The comfortable chatter of poll workers and voters filled my ears. Every once in a while, signs would wave, and I'd hear choruses 'We Want Waymire' or 'Waymire for the Win.' I scanned the crowd. Scott Waymire was working the crowd so hard I figured he'd have a case of lockjaw in the morning. Louise sat at a table behind the sign wavers, looking a little tattered around the edges. She must be furious. I'd promised her that her history wouldn't come out, and Dylan had torn her reputation apart on the basis of the photos that Hunter had taken. Why had I chosen the Waymires' polling place for a stakeout, anyway? I turned away from her in shame. If she recognized me, it wouldn't be pretty.

I vacillated between a desperate hope that I'd avoid a defamation lawsuit, and disgust at what Dylan Palmer was capable of. The assignment with Dylan had been under the auspices of Tom Stark Investigations, not my new firm, and I hadn't been on his payroll, so they couldn't pin 'employee' on me. At least, that's what I planned to say if dragged into court.

"Hunter, I hope you're hanging in the back, so Palmer doesn't know who you are."

He made a rude sound. "Who cares if someone recognizes me? I'm here to—"

His voice vanished.

I stared at the phone. Had his phone died? No, I heard background sounds. And the pop-pop-pop of…wait. My forehead scrunched.

"Hunter? Hey! You there? What's going on?"

I heard screams and shouting. Someone called for 9-1-1. The thuds of Hunter's racing steps, and his labored breathing wormed its way to my ears. "What's happening?" I cried, my hand an iron claw around the phone.

"Shooter," he managed through gulps of air. Then the phone went dead.

I squinted through the crowd to make sure I didn't have my own shooter to deal with. Louise was still at the table, and I spotted Scott on the other side of the library grounds. Things looked hunky-dory here.

Thus fortified that my little bottleneck of the election cycle was on solid footing, I fled to Palmer's base station. Dread flooded my stomach. What was going on? It took a full fifteen minutes before I screamed into the parking lot and skidded to a stop. Bounding from my car, I fielded some nasty, ill-mannered attention from a couple of drunk guys, then dashed around looking for Hunter. The TV news stations had already set up. I scowled. I considered them worse vermin than ambulance-chasing attorneys. Thankfully, they looked right over me as a potential story angle, thanks to my new platinum hair and cheeky outfit. Silver linings.

Where was Hunter? What had the shooting been about?

I spotted a couple of ambulances. To my great relief, I found Hunter well apart from the ambos. *Easy does it. Whatever happened can't be good.* I slowed my pace to a crawl, processing the scene. Hunter knelt on the manicured library grounds lawn, his hand on a woman's shoulder. Her tortured wails pierced my heart. Where was the victim? Had the ambos already transported the victim to the ER? I crept closer. Blinked. The woman on the ground with Hunter was Dylan's *wife.* Something must've happened to Dylan. One ambulance had its back doors open. I peeked inside.

A first responder pounded the vic's chest, sweating and swearing at the same time. He paused the resuscitation efforts, turned toward another man, and said something, allowing me to get a look. I gasped. Dylan Palmer lay on his back shirtless, pale, and still as a haddock on ice. A paramedic glanced my way and slammed the doors shut. The ambo started singing as it pulled away.

Hunter looked up and lifted a weary shoulder. I gave him a cop-nod. He said something to the woman, then handed her off to a uniform. The uni led Dylan's wife to the other ambulance and placed her on the rear of the vehicle. Two somber cops approached her, their hands on their weapons. Hunter headed toward me.

"Let's find a quieter place to talk," he said.

We left the ruckus behind and found a bench. I couldn't hold in my questions. I mean, who could?

"His past catching up with him? An angry constituent? A Waymire supporter? A mistress?"

He held up a palm. "I'm trying, here. Give me a minute. It's been a blur." He shook his head. "I would've never...."

Breathless, I urged, "Never what?"

He stared at me with bleak eyes. "His wife. Remember? He had that private meeting with you, unannounced, to let you know his divorce was pending. That she'd left him."

I frowned. "What does that have to do with anything?"

He put his hands in his pockets. "Is there any way she coulda gotten hold of the photos?"

"I gave a set to Dylan." My eyes widened. "Wow. You think she found them?"

Hunter's mouth curved into a half-smile. "You think maybe we shouldn't have given him copies of his tongue down the throat of another guy?" He flicked his hand as if swatting a fly away. "You never know. The fool should've hidden them better, I guess. Maybe she found out some other way. But his secret's out. It's all over the news."

"She shot him?" I whispered.

"She chased him all over the field with a revolver, screaming her head off. All his indiscretions caught large on video. When he talked to you that day, I imagine that was only one layer of a great, big, smelly onion."

I thought of Tom, his feet up and cozy in front of a fireplace at his home in Glory, and hoped he'd been able to participate in this cosmic twist of justice. I wished he'd lived to see his blackmailer taken down. However, nobody deserved to die this way, even a creep like Palmer. "Will he make it?"

Hunter shrugged. "Not sure. He took three bullets. Either way, his political career is over."

Chapter Thirty-Five

The morning after dawned with zero perilous calls from captains or revenge-bound husbands, or disgruntled clients. I'd picked up Hazel from the office and brought her to my house for breakfast in hopes of helping her make calls. Whatever she needed. I grinned as I listened to her bark orders into her cell phone. I marveled that even a shovel-shattered face and inferno-obliterated home couldn't get the best of her. She was my hero.

She shot me a disgusted look from her spot on the swing. "Contractors! Insurance companies! What did I do to deserve this? She threw her hands in the air. Her phone clattered to the floor.

"You're connected to 'Mercy's Miracle,'" I said, my voice droll. "It's inevitable."

The sun inched above the trees, and morning dew sparkled like diamonds on the grass. The trees bracketing my lane had fluffed out in their best deep-summer-green now, and the branches reached across, creating a droopy, leafy arch. Cardinals, finches, and orioles in full-on breakfast mode swooped in and out, taking turns at the feeders.

I breathed a sigh of contentment.

The last couple of days had worn me down to a nub. I'd given Sherry time off, and Hunter spent a lot of time walking my property and thinking. My office was locked up tight, and I checked the security system every couple of hours. I wasn't sure when we'd re-open, but it didn't matter. We'd all needed a break.

"What'd they say?" I asked, chewing a mouthful of eggs.

"They're backed up. I don't have a finish date yet. Insurance will pay for a rental, so I need to start figuring out where to live. There are lots of rentals close to my office."

"You feeling good enough to be on your own?"

She waved one of her hands around. "I need my own place, and I'm going to PetSmart this morning. I have to line up furniture to rent, too."

"Sure you're ready for a new bird?"

"What are you, your mother? It was a *bird*, not a dog like your Marlowe, here." She reached down to pet him. "What a good boy."

Marlowe's tail thumped. He'd taken an instant liking to Hazel. My golden ginger tomcat had settled into his normal doughnut pose inside the screen, watching us. He'd grown used to Marlowe, and I pictured them cuddled together on his dog bed at some point. I couldn't wait to take a photo when that happened.

"I'm going in today. Paperwork."

Hazel studied me. "This has been a lot for you. What's going to happen now that Dylan Palmer has passed? He was your client, wasn't he?"

I guess it doesn't matter that you know, now that he's gone, but yeah. Really he was Tom's client, but...semantics. I got it in the middle after Tom died." I drank some of my coffee. "Scott Waymire coasted to an easy win. I think the other side's contesting that, though. I don't know much about the political system." I chewed the last bite, swallowed. "That'll be my last political client, though, I guarantee it."

I heard Hunter thumping down the stairs. The red screen door squealed open, revealing a suitcase straining at its zippers and Hunter in jogging pants and a T-shirt.

"I'd ask where you're going, but I'm an investigator, and I know things."

He smiled, parked the luggage, and sat.

"Have you had your coffee yet?" Hazel asked.

Hunter shook his head. "You offering?"

She poked a tiny index finger in the air, which ended in an immaculately painted red fingernail. She'd done her nails. Another reassuring sign that she was on the road to her old self. "Yes. I'm offering. Back in a jiffy."

Hunter smiled. Hazel opened the screen door. Riot moved out of the way as slow as possible, an irritated look on his face.

"That woman is amazing. I'm glad I've gotten to know her a little."

"She thinks the world of you, y'know."

"Nice to hear," he said, then lapsed into silence.

We both started talking at once.

"I need to hit the road," he said. "I'm glad I was able to help, but I did risk a lot in coming. It wasn't the best idea." He looked at me longer than necessary. "But it showed me how much I care about you."

I looked at my fingernails. Unlike Hazel's, they had scraggly chips of leftover polish from my first manicure. They were hideous.

How long were we going to continue this tap dance? I knew the time had come to take a stand, but I was wobbly.

The story of my life. Wobbly.

I sighed.

I did care. I cared a lot. But as Hazel and I had discussed ad nauseam, my distrust of the male species ran deep. And now the awesome news that I'd had a father all along, and he'd discarded me like a piece of garbage. How could I trust any of them?

"I take it the feeling isn't returned," Hunter said, watching conflict scroll across my face.

Hazel returned with a steaming to-go cup.

"Thanks," he said, rising from the chair. I rose with him, and we started walking to his Jeep. After ten days of in-the-trenches-together time, this dreadful awkwardness between us felt foreign. Painful. He put his luggage in the back, then leaned against the Jeep and eyeballed me.

A heartbeat of silence passed.

I couldn't let him leave without explaining.

"Hunter, I care about you, too. A lot. But it's not fair to expect you to stand by while I work out my trust issues when you expect a blushing bride, all radiant with expectation and the wonder of marital bliss."

He winced.

I spread my arms. "See? These crazy words come out of my mouth and…and… I'm still developing into a 'person' after the blasted brain injury that keeps tripping me up. I'm blunt, outspoken, and even rude. I run toward situations I should stay away from. How can I expect you to live with that?" I fought back tears. "Besides, I can't leave to go live in Richmond. I love my house. *You* sure aren't going to move." I crossed my arms and looked away.

Hunter grinned. "Huh. So you *have* thought about it." He took my hands in his. Studied my face. "I've lived through most of that with you, Olivia. I've seen you evolve. Watched you change." He stroked my hair. "Did I ever tell you how hot I think you look this way? I had to get used to it, but the bottom line is, you're coming into your own. I'm wondering if it's fair of me to expect you to consider a proposal of marriage from a Richmond cop when you may find a lot better man than me right here."

A tear straggled down my cheek. "There *is no* better man than you, Detective Hunter Faraday."

"Sergeant," he corrected softly.

"Whatever."

He laughed. "So. A stalemate, then?"

I leaned in to kiss him. Gentle. A promise. "Until next time, Sergeant," I whispered.

"I look forward to it." He tilted his head. "I think."

With the roar of his Jeep's V8 and the growl of enormous tires, he left in a cloud of dust.

I'd enjoyed the few days of reprieve, but it felt good to be back in the office.

I stroked my minimalist, mid-century desk, admired my organizational trays and fresh-minted business cards.

With Hunter gone, I had to face facts. The mad torcher was still out there. I was convinced Hazel's house had been an outlier. The consensus was Pete, but that was almost too easy. What are the odds a volunteer firefighter would be setting fires, anyway? Pete had been interviewed, his place tossed, each fire scene examined for his fingerprints. They came up with were partials of Pete's and Dylan's fingerprints on Tom's ancient metal filing cabinets, which he explained away as the two of them being in Tom's office once upon a time. We had no way of verifying since Tom was deceased—and the story was plausible. My vote leaned toward Dylan. He'd been desperate to uncover any information Tom had stowed about the assault on my father. How desperate, I wondered?

I put an elbow on my desk and dropped my chin into my hand.

Was Hazel safe? Was I? Was anyone who knew me safe? What were the fires about? My house and office had to be about the Mercy's Miracle persona—the victim identity that I longed to put behind me. I wished I could burn all those damn books out there, but no, it had to go and become a best-seller. On the bright side, nobody expected me to pop up as a PI, and the makeover helped. Media didn't recognize me at all. I'd enjoy it while it lasted. At least I could walk around without a dozen mics in my face.

"Sherry!" I called.

She raced into my office and grabbed a chair. I came out from behind my desk and sat opposite. "I'm trying to figure out fires now. We have any strange calls in the past week or so that you jotted down to talk with me about? I know I've been out of my mind. I'm better after a couple of days off. You doing okay?"

"No worries there, Olivia. Hunter gone?"

I nodded. "We can move his desk back into storage."

"Too bad. I know you'll miss him."

"I don't want to talk about it."

After a beat, she continued. "Okay. What do we have?"

"I've been through the reports. They're operating on the premise that mine was arson, two were accidental, Hazel's was linked to me, and the office building was linked to Tom, or me. *I'm* the common denominator. It's depressing." I raked my hands through my hair. "The Baltimore Fire Investigation Bureau touches base now and then. Tasha has been great at keeping me current on status. An arson judgment is on the books where my house is concerned, but no leads except Pete, and there's no conclusive proof. Whoever did this didn't take anything of value. This is personal."

My gut gurgled with nerves. "I've distanced myself from these arson events long enough. Dylan and the chaos surrounding him took all my focus. It's over. Time to move on."

Sherry tilted her head. "Is it?"

"Shut up. I need a soft place to land. Even if it's obtuse."

She smiled. "Obtuse? I don't even know what that means. I'm talking about Pete and Dylan. Together. Did they know each other? Did you tell me you confirmed that?"

I shook my head. "Just a suspicion. Tasha seemed to think they did, however. Which I thought was odd, because she barely knows who Pete is." I shrugged. "She gives me updates. Not supposed to, but I get the feeling that she has my back. So. Back to my original question: weird calls?"

Sherry flipped through the small notebook she kept. A shadow crossed her face when she came to one of the pages.

I frowned. "What?"

She licked her upper lip. Her knobby, long fingers played with the page.

I tightened my grip on the armrests of my chair.

She tossed the notebook in my lap. "Here."

I picked it up. In her tidy handwriting, she'd noted, 'Olivia's dad?' beside a number with an area code I'd never heard of. My hands shook. "Why is there a question mark?"

"It's a South Dakota area code. Pierre, South Dakota. It's the capital. The Foofoos are trying to find your dad, and I don't know if it's a trick or the real thing."

"When?"

"Last week."

A full month after, I'd discovered the man was alive.

My mind flipped back. I discovered the file the end of June. It was the end of July now. How many people knew I wanted to find dear, old dad? And why were the Foofoos so fired up about it, before I even knew of his existence? I closed the notebook, handed it back to her.

Sherry tilted her head. "I see those wheels spinning."

I smiled. "Spinning, but not going anywhere."

"Who would want info about your dad?"

I laughed. "My agent, for one. She's asked about him for two years. She can't stand that I have no idea who he is, and has the idea that she...*we*...can wrap the next book around 'finding daddy'. As if it'd be some sort of tearful reunion."

"Why wouldn't it? You want to find him, don't you?"

My eyes narrowed. Had I told her about my conversation with Mom?

Should I?

No.

Okay, yes.

Sherry straightened in her chair. She sensed an information drop of epic proportions.

I swallowed, hard. "Mom and I had a heart-to-heart the other day. Short version is that my birth father decided snapping her neck was a better solution than birth control. Anyway, he was a dangerous guy. And he didn't want Mom to have me." I paused, thinking how to put it. "Her dad decided to get rid of him, so Tom gave him the name of some thug. My father had no choice but to leave after the beatdown."

Sherry blinked. "That's horrible, Olivia," she whispered.

"I got so used to 'not having a dad' that I stopped talking about it. She must've given me the impression that he'd died. She always insisted we were better off without him, and gave no indication he was alive. In her defense, she actually didn't know...she asked Tom not to keep her advised about his whereabouts." I smiled. "She and Tom were close. Tom never told me, or Mom either. Don't you think that's weird?"

Sherry drummed her fingers on the accent table beside her chair. "Not weird if you are trying to protect your kid from trauma. I remember when you found the TS file. How *shocked* you were. I didn't know that you'd talked to your mom and filled in some of the blanks. That totally explains why Tom and your grandfather plotted to get rid of him." Sherry crossed her arms, stared at the floor. "Is it on record?"

I laughed. "Here? You are aware of how small Westminster is, right? Glyndon is even smaller. Tom shared long, detailed narratives during our surveillance about how crooked the cops were back then. He said it was a 'club' and he was considered an outsider. I'm pretty sure a police report wouldn't have done any good. The only report is the TS file and that's why Dylan was so worried."

"Dylan?"

Had I left out the part about Dylan? "The man my grandpa hired was Dylan."

Sherry's mouth fell open. "My gosh, I had no idea," she whispered, thinking it through. "But after meeting him, I can *so* see it. Wow."

"Maybe Dylan was part of the 'club' Tom talked about. All I know is that Sonny—my father—was furious about the pregnancy." I smiled. "How's that for fatherhood? So no, I don't think our reunion will be a happy one, and I don't think I should write another book with him as the cornerstone. Gross. He made Mom's life so miserable that her dad decided to take the law into his own hands. Tom didn't even know Dylan at all, nor did he know a brutal beating was coming down. All he did was give her father a name. Mom told me that my father was in the hospital for weeks."

"Boy," Sherry said. "You and your mom both got involved with men that turned out to be a nightmare. Is this a family curse or something?" She grinned.

"These guys are cons. If a woman isn't prepared...she believes all the romantic traps and lies these guys like to play with. Anyway, I believe in facts, and information is power. I'm going to *meet him*. First step. Find him. Mom doesn't know where he is, and she kept his name off my birth certificate. Would you do a deep dive on Sonny Pellegra?"

Sherry's forehead wrinkled. "Sure, but...why would you want to meet him? He sounds like an animal."

My cell vibrated on my desk. "I have to. I'm sure of it." I picked up my call.

Chapter Thirty-Six

On my way to meet the girls for our Wine & Whine, a tall, middle-aged man with graying hair and a shaggy beard walked down the sidewalk. I wouldn't have given him a thought, except I recognized him as Graham, Callie's ex.

My first investigation assignment had been a simple surveillance. I'd taken lots of photos of Graham in compromising situations, and here he was, walking straight toward me. Hunter's words rose to the surface: *People don't exactly love a PI, Olivia.* Graham's expression when he saw me confirmed it, for sure. I hoped he didn't have physical comeuppance in mind, but you never knew. Due to Tom's adroit instruction, I now carried mace, a piercing whistle on my keychain, and a cute, manageable switchblade. I didn't have my gun tonight, but the knife would do in a pinch.

"Hi, Graham. Hope you're doing well these days."

"No thanks to you," he said.

Okay. There it was. The bait.

I now understood why he and my ex had been good buddies. According to Callie, they'd maintained that relationship to this day. I wondered what kind of person maintained a friendship with someone like Monty. Pushing aside my better intentions, I poked the bear.

"How're things with Monty, Graham?"

"Why would I know?" He stuck his hands in his pockets.

I shrugged. "You should find better friends, that's all."

He studied me. "How's Lilly?"

"She's crazy excited about starting college in Richmond. Like your Amy."

He nodded. "That's right, they're rooming together."

"They are." I tried to keep walking, but he persisted.

"I plan on visiting often."

My pulse sped up.

"I'm sure Amy will look forward to father-daughter time," I said, hesitant.

"I'll make it a threesome. Happy to have Lilly along. Maybe Serena, too."

"Not sure that's a good idea, Graham."

"No bother at all," he said.

My mind raced through the facts: one) he could pump my daughters for information and get back to Monty with it, two) he hated me since I'd been the one to prove to Callie he was having an affair, and that would most likely translate to sharing his venom with my daughters. Good sense told me to draw a line with this man.

A big, freaking line.

"I'm sure Amy would prefer father-daughter time without her friends along." I gave him a steely-eyed look. "I hope we understand each other."

Graham stepped back a pace or two. "I didn't mean anything. Don't you recognize when someone's trying to do something nice?" He turned and walked away. Score a win for me, but I felt like I'd been slimed. No matter how he tried to paint it, the offer to include my daughters sounded like a threat, and I didn't trust anyone who made it a point to keep up with my ex.

Sherry and Callie were waiting for me in the restaurant just ahead. I stared, thoughtful, at Graham's back as he retreated down the sidewalk. Graham had been lingering outside the restaurant before he'd walked in my direction. Had he been stalking Callie?

I almost tore the hostess's head off when she couldn't locate the Wine & Whine group's table. *Thanks for the bad mood, Graham.* She finally found them in a separate room in the back.

This was a new spot for our group. I took in the shiny chrome and white, marble tabletops, the monochromatic swirls of gray and tan on the floor. The artwork some brain-impaired designer had selected was so riotous and disorganized that a third-grader could have finger-painted it, but what did

I know? I swept past huge, faux plants in containers that resembled giant, military-green hand grenades, and dropped into the remaining chair at our table.

"Made it," I smiled. "Sorry I'm late, girls." Callie fidgeted with her silverware, her complexion pale under the chronic tan. Her bouncy demeanor had bounced right out the door, probably lying dead at Graham's feet. "So he caught you outside, too?" I asked her.

She shook her head. "Sorry. What?"

"Graham."

Her brows drew together. "You saw him?"

"I think he staked us out. He's such a loser. Where's my wine?"

Sherry pointed. "That one. Got us a bottle of 2018 Silverado Cab."

"Oooh. Fancy." I took the empty wine glass in front of me and filled it halfway. Took a sip. "Yum."

Sherry leaned in. "What's up with Graham?"

I glanced at Callie, who nodded her approval to share. "He had an affair. I took pictures. She divorced him. He was mad. End of story."

"I remember that. Early on, with Tom. And he continues to have this strong of an effect on you, Callie?" Sherry asked.

Callie started fanning herself with her menu. "It doesn't last long."

My eyebrows shot up. "What do you mean? Is he hanging around? Are you guys talking?"

"He does the talking. I…try to stay out of his way."

Sherry sat quiet, her fingers running up and down the stem of her wine glass.

"Callie…" I began.

"I know. I know! But what can I do? We have a restraining order, which he ignores. The cops came out once when I called, but he was sweet and charming, as usual. They never do anything."

"Do you need Marlowe?"

She chuckled. "I'm venting. I don't need a watchdog just because he's a jerk. He wouldn't really do anything."

Sherry glanced at me. I got her meaning. Most tormented wives or ex-wives believe their man would 'never do anything'. That was the problem.

We shelved Graham and talked about mundane, safe stuff. Weather. Outfits. Dogs. Cats. The best place to get a pedicure. But sooner or later, it circled back to me. My stuff outweighed everyone's stuff combined, and I couldn't wait until my life settled into a boring, predictable pattern. One that culminated in a steady stream of paid invoices for Watchdog Investigations.

I swallowed a mouthful of cracker and cheese. "Okay, if I bring up local news?"

"You bet," Callie said, her cheerfulness creeping back. "How are the investigations going?"

"Peter Hayes' prints were discovered in my attic and on Tom's old filing cabinets." I didn't mention Dylan's prints because...well, he's dead. What's the point?

"Pete set all the fires?"

"Looks that way, but Pete's telling another story."

"What about Hazel's place?"

"Investigation is ongoing." I sipped my wine. "Have I told you how much I hate that word now? Ongoing?" I looked at Callie.

"The Dylan Palmer scandal is the main story right now. I saw some of the funeral on the news. Lots of cops, but not many attendees. It didn't look like he was very popular."

"Sad," Sherry said. She lifted her glass. "To a wasted life." We clinked.

To Dylan Palmer's decrepit resume, I added post-mortem...*blackmailer.*

I thought about Tom. What else had Dylan convinced him to do? I'd scrape through the 'B' files one by one. Soon.

Only one person knew specifics. My father. The one that might need a little attention to *his* side of the story before anyone else ended up dead. I also wanted to figure out if Pete and Dylan were all buddy-buddy and why. The voice I'd heard in the driveway when I surveilled Hazel's place had been a woman. Pete had been talking about getting info out of Hazel about me to a *woman.*

I felt the rut between my eyebrows dig in and stay there. This was supposed to be recreation time. I could do the crime-solving at the office.

The mood at our table had taken a dive, so I thought I'd give them something new to think about. I cleared my throat. "I'm making plans to meet my father."

By the shock on their faces, I could tell they weren't crazy about the idea.

But they weren't rolling around in dreary thoughts of arsonists and dead politicians anymore, either.

Chapter Thirty-Seven

Hazel puttered around her new apartment, putting up artwork and admiring the furniture she'd rented. It sure beat the ancient, hidebound antiques she'd had in her house. She wasn't one bit sad that much of it had burned.

Her first-floor unit had huge windows and lots of light and sound-insulated ceilings and walls. Her new bird chirped his heart out, as if he knew about Hazel's loss and wanted to console her. She'd bought two this time, a male and a female, and looked forward to tiny hatchlings. Although she wasn't sure what she'd do with the babies, she'd have endless replacements in case something happened. A knock sounded on her door.

Olivia peeked around a large bouquet of flowers. "I got you a housewarming present."

Hazel laughed. "Come on in."

"I'm not breaching the client-therapist thing, am I?"

Hazel rolled her eyes. "These are strange times."

The two women moved the plant with its gladiolas and sunflowers and roses inside. Set it on the kitchen counter.

"I got you something as different from the Foofoo flowers as I could find."

"I see that."

"If I have to look at another daisy or daffodil, I'll throw up. I think Pete has to be the flower Nazi. He's ruined my love for those flowers."

Hazel's face fell. "Ohhh. Were those favorites before the bouquets started showing up?"

"Yeah." Olivia's eyelids lowered. "Wait. What if...what if they're from someone who knew that? Maybe it wasn't Pete."

Hazel chuckled. "Do you ever turn it off?"

Olivia ignored her and sat in a chair. "Wow. These are nice."

"You like them? I'm thinking of ditching my remaining stuff. I like the cleaner look."

"How's it going, anyway? What about your house?"

"I'm good." She pointed to the birdcage that held her new canaries. "Harold and Maude."

Olivia laughed. "Love the names. They're adorable, Hazel."

"I hope they have babies. I would like that." She poured coffee for Olivia. Her hands shook, and some of it splashed onto the coffee table. Hazel didn't seem to notice.

"The house has to be rebuilt from the ground up. The brick frame is okay, but anything else is a challenge. They estimate twelve months before I can move back in." She touched her hair. "If I move back in."

Olivia's eyebrows rose. "That's new."

"I enjoy the condo." She spread her arms. "Three bedrooms on one level. A manageable eighteen-hundred square feet. By the way, Tasha's been by a few times and we've gotten to know each other. She's a darling girl."

'Darling' is not a word I'd use for her, but I'll go with it."

She fluttered her hand. "You know what I mean. She's on top of things, and I like that I get updates on the investigation. Just like she does for you."

Olivia cocked her head. "You moving a little slow today?"

She chuckled. "Not any slower than usual."

"Okay. Are you sure about taking a long break from counseling?"

"Positive."

"Funny," Olivia said. "You've never been okay with it before."

Hazel stared at Olivia an ultra-long time.

Olivia frowned. "Are you okay?"

Hazel blurted out, "Tasha thinks the same person set the fires on both our homes. It's a mission."

Olivia choked on her coffee. "How would she know that? A mission to what?"

Hazel reached for her mug, missed, then tried again. "Why, you don't know? On a mission to destroy *you,* dear."

"She said that?"

She nodded. "She is quite convinced."

"Wh-what about the other fires? It can't all be about me."

"A distraction. Red herrings. Those little fires? Tasha says the person is deranged. Maybe bi-polar. Perhaps...desperate."

Olivia muttered under her breath. "She cannot *know* that. And she shouldn't be sharing her opinions with you."

"Profiling? Isn't that a thing investigators do?"

"Yeah, but they usually don't splash their opinions all over the general population."

Hazel started ticking off possibilities on her fingers as if she'd been coached. "Jealousy. Envy. Revenge. Tom's leftovers, maybe? Tasha thought of lots of reasons. When a person struggles with any type of mania, they really have no sense of logic."

"This doesn't sound like you, Hazel." Olivia squinted. "Your eyes look funny."

"I didn't mean to upset you, dear." She winced, her hand dropping to her stomach. "I must be catching something."

"Since when did you start calling me 'dear' in every other sentence?"

"Oh. I didn't realize."

"Where do you keep your prescriptions? Have you changed anything?"

"Bathroom. Down the hall, to the left."

Olivia jogged into the bathroom, swept the cabinets. Returned to the living area. "No prescriptions that should be doing anything like this."

She swiped Hazel's coffee mug, stuck her nose in and took a sniff. Her lips parted in surprise. "What's in this coffee?"

Hazel stood and drew herself up to her full five-feet-nothing, losing her balance. She groped for the back of her chair to steady herself.

Olivia strode to the kitchen, stood over the sink, poured a bit of coffee into her hand. It was milky, almost opaque. It didn't feel like cream. Or taste like creamer. She returned to the living area.

"Why should it matter what I put in my coffee?"

Olivia opened cabinet after cabinet. She stuck her head inside the fridge and found a small, amber-colored bottle on the third shelf. Unlabeled. Olivia took it out, and sniffed it. She held out the bottle. "What's this?"

"It helps with stress. Tasha made it. I do feel much better. She told me to add it to my coffee or juice, just a smidge."

Olivia grunted. "I think it helps with more than stress, Hazel." She lifted the bottle. "I don't think you should use any more of this, okay? I'm going to check out what it is."

Olivia left before Hazel had a chance to protest.

Chapter Thirty-Eight

I screamed into Watchdog Investigation's parking lot and erupted from my vehicle. I paused two seconds before entering the office to appreciate that the company had finally hung our sign. The sign made Watchdog Investigations official. I wondered when the heck the insanity surrounding me would take a break so I could enjoy interviewing potential clients and putting money in the bank. I shook the bottle I'd taken from Hazel's house. It got foamy. What was in this stuff?

Sherry's hands paused over her keyboard when I walked in. My expression must've broadcast my utter disgust.

"What?" she asked.

I held out the bottle. "Call the lab and put a rush on this. I need to know what it is."

"Sure," she said, picking up her landline. "New lead on the fire investigation?"

I scowled. "Let's just say I've stepped all over the guidelines between therapist and patient relationships in Maryland. Has Tasha been by? I suspect she's medicating Hazel. The question is why."

She shook her head. Held up her index finger as she listened to the lab. Yes, they could put a rush on it. For a fee.

"We'll pay the fee," I told her.

She leaned back in her chair and tented her fingers. Her movement was so similar to Tom's that I felt a pang of regret in my chest. I missed him. Tom would've handled these situations with his usual finesse and good grace. He'd be calm and patient about it, too. I wish I shared more of his character traits. As it was, I was a maniac running around yelling at people, which only made them clam up. I *knew* that. But when I stumbled across the unthinkable, I wanted answers. Social graces flew out the window.

A text chirped its arrival. "Lab says they'll have results in a few days if we drop it off now. You must have a buddy there."

I grinned. "I have buddies everywhere."

After I'd dropped the bottle at the lab, I grabbed a quick lunch with Lilly at the Y and ran by the house to check on Riot and feed him. I tried to work in a little exercise break by walking down my lane to my office. The walk took around ten minutes, depending. It was a nice walk with the birds in the trees and the occasional fawn poking out of the woods with a doe. On a whim, I turned into the woods and walked through the undeveloped part of my lot to the backside of my office.

Halfway there, I heard Marlowe barking his fool head off. My ears perked up. Sherry's voice. Loud.

I picked up my pace through the trees, slapping aside branches, sidestepping the vines and bushes. Marlowe's barking stopped briefly. More shouting. One male. One female. Marlowe started up again. I jogged as fast as possible through the undergrowth, and made it into the clearing at the back of the building. I groped my side. No weapon, but there was one in the safe inside. I crept to the back window.

"They follow me!" a male voice yelled.

I crab-walked to a window. Looked inside. Muffled a yelp with my hands. *Pete.*

Sherry held her arms out in a placating way, trying to diffuse.

I crept to the next window.

I rose an inch at a time, praying that Pete wouldn't see me. His back was to me. With one hand, he pointed at Sherry, with the other…? Did he have a weapon?

Think.

I chewed on a fingernail and edged to the other side of the window for a better angle.

"I needed the money! They set me up." I ratcheted my body to one side of the window, trying to get a better view.

"*Crap,*" I whispered. The full reality of what was happening washed over me. I stopped breathing. Pete had a gun.

"You gotta do something," Pete said. "This is all a misunderstanding. I don't know what to do."

I backed away from the window. Closed my eyes to focus. *Think, Olivia, think!* Pete knew he was the primary suspect in the fire investigation. That he'd overstepped his bail conditions by showing up at Hazel's fire. What else did he know? What would motivate him to do this? And why wasn't he in a holding cell?"

I punched in 9-1-1. Whispered 'active shooter' and the address.

I planted my ear against the pane of glass to hear better.

Sherry's scream rang out.

I vaulted over the landscaping and raced to the back door. Crept inside, tripping over Marlowe on the floor of my office. I bent down. His heartbeat was strong, but he'd been hurt. He whined. I locked him in the bedroom.

My hands shook so hard it took three tries to get the breakroom-safe combination right. Pete continued peppering Sherry with demands. The safe popped open. I retrieved my weapon and stole into the hallway.

Sherry's voice was strong and calm. Sweat had plastered Pete's shirt to his back. I stood in her direct line of sight behind Pete, holding my firearm tight against my waist with both hands. She gave no indication that she'd seen me.

Good girl, Sherry.

The first responders' sirens burbled in the distance. I edged closer. Pete was crying and pleading. His arm shook, and the weapon he was holding dropped from Sherry's chest to her knees. He wiped sweat out of his eyes, then raised the gun and stiffened his arm. He turned his head two inches and saw me standing behind him.

With a gun pointed at the center of his chest.

"Drop the weapon! Now!" I yelled.

The blare of sirens grew louder.

My arms were as steady as steel beams.

Pete threw down his firearm and shot his arms into the air. "Please. I had to talk to somebody. The cops are convinced it was all me. It *wasn't.* I'm not going down like this."

Keeping my weapon trained on him, I locked eyes with Sherry. She was okay.

Uniforms stole by the windows. I decided to wait them out and grab the opportunity to talk to Pete while he was vulnerable. I kicked his gun away. Tilted my head toward the back bedroom. Sherry sprinted down the hallway. Marlowe's soft barks told me he was coming around.

"What is it you're concerned about, Pete?"

He moaned. Rocked his body back and forth. "Why did I do it? Why?"

"Do what, Pete?"

He eyed me. "I needed the money. He paid me a lot of money to set a few little fires." His lips curved upward. "They were so...beautiful." Aiming a vicious scowl at me. "You wouldn't understand! The wonderful beauty of it, the power of it. A fire is a living, breathing thing. She responds to a gentle touch." He stared at his hands in wonder, moving them as if they could take flight. The creep factor was off the chain. "They remind me of you, Olivia."

My heart pegged way above a reasonable heart rate for a human. "Tell me why, Pete."

"Surging, thriving, flames of joy. I set them up in a way that they'd burn a few hours, then run out of oxygen. My work was ingenious. Short-lived, pristine works of art, that's what she and I agreed on." He locked eyes with me. "Fire purifies whatever it touches. They are holy, elemental, organisms. Did you know that?" His eyes bored into mine. "Similar to your experience when you arose from your ordeal a new woman." He frowned. "I thought you'd appreciate the symbolism in the flowers, but you never even noticed."

I had a lump in my throat. The sirens outside softened. The soft crawl of tires on pavement reached my ears. *There must be an army out there.* "Who?" I asked. Pete had alternated between 'he' and 'she.' "*Who* told you to create your works of art? Was that your intention, Pete? Purification?"

I glanced up for a nanosecond, as if Tom's wisdom would drop from the ceiling. My gun arm drooped with fatigue. For the love of God, Tom…how do I talk sense into a firebug?

In seconds, someone would give the command to enter. Pete's focus would be history. I made a quick decision. Slow and gentle, I put my weapon on the floor. A blood vessel in Pete's temple throbbed.

"Can I put my hands down?" he asked.

I nodded. Moved closer to him as he rubbed his arms and stared out the window. He winced at the gathering array of cops. His chiseled features quivered with the sack of misery he must be carrying. Regret creased his face.

"I'm sorry I missed your art, Pete."

"No one understands."

"My home would've been destroyed."

He dropped his head. "I know."

"That's a crime, Pete. You don't want to take the blame by yourself, do you?"

"They won't commit to a deal. I told them I'd give them a couple of names." He grimaced. "Doesn't matter, they want to close the case. They're trying to make me say that I worked alone. That's not how it happened! None of it was my idea." He looked away. "The fires were supposed to look accidental. Guess I'm not as good as I thought I was."

"I'll talk to the police about what you said, Pete. But…tell me. Did you set the early fires, too? The ones before my house?"

Pete was quiet. His glossy, black hair dropped over an eyebrow. I could see his mind clicking along, his jaw working. "Do you realize that most firefighters have pyrophilia? A love of fire?" He chuckled sadly. "That's why I volunteer. I love fire. Respect it. I never thought that I'd…cross the line." He glared at me. "I never meant those fires to get out of control. They were just small tokens to attract attention."

Behind my back, I messaged the takedown squad. Five fingers for five minutes. One of the heads bobbed in agreement outside the window.

"I left a message, you know," he said. "In your attic." He smiled in a creepy, suggestive way. "I snuck in at night, after the crews shut down for the day.

They didn't even lock the doors." He shrugged. "It was easy." Pete reminded me of the actor that played Heathcliff in the first movie version of Wuthering Heights, including the tortured soul and warped life view. Why was it that the best-looking guys on the planet were the ones with destructive issues? Every. Single. Time.

His eyes, anxious, searched mine. "I had such regard for you, Olivia. Your journey, your new life…then someone reached out. I couldn't control myself. I…I was getting a handle on it. I thought I could set a couple and walk away, but…." He shook his head. "Tasha was furious with me."

My eyebrows shot up. Tasha? What did she have to do with any of this?

Pete looked at me with sorrowful eyes. "Tell Hazel I'm sorry. I really like her, and I did *not* set the fire in her house."

"She almost burned to death. Is that how you show people you care?"

"I didn't set that fire!" he insisted. "That's what I'm trying to tell you. I don't know who did. I'm telling the truth." He stared out the window. "You never even joined my Facebook group, did you? Weren't you flattered at all?"

"That's beside the point, Pete."

"I was paid a ton of money to do something I loved. Who can resist that?" Pete's eyes grew wet. "I was trying, though." After a brief pause, he looked at me, resigned. Crossed his arms. "You're the one person I thought would understand. Destruction is the start of something new, something good. Like what happened to you. The accident. You got a fresh start. You're famous now, you can do whatever you want." In a small voice, he added, "They were beautiful. Did you see them?" Pete's eyes glazed.

The words fogged my brain. I struggled to focus. The guy was whacked, and I was *done.*

"It wasn't an accident, Pete. I was assaulted. I almost died. *It was not a good thing!"* By the end of this declaration, it took an insane amount of self-control not to launch the contents of my stomach right in his face. I rose from the floor, gave the waiting uniforms the side-eye and a nod.

"Take him! Now!" The command rattled the windows. The ground shook with the pounding of shoes, front and back. Pete shrank into a terrified huddle on the floor. Cops scrambled inside, threw Pete flat on his stomach, cuffed him, read him his rights, jerked him outside, and pushed him inside a patrol car. Crisis averted. Criminal secured.

I could have a meltdown now.

On quaking legs, I dropped into one of the chairs in my office.

Sherry patted me on the back. "Sit. I'll get coffee."

My fingertips grew cold. My vision quavered around the edges. "Good idea," I whispered.

Marlowe walked into the room, tail waving like a flag. I threw my arms around him.

Chapter Thirty-Nine

A week later

"For cryin' out loud, Olivia, what's going on up there?"

Hunter's voice cracked with concern, but underneath, I detected anger. Sergeant Hunter Faraday was hovering on the edge of a lecture. I smiled.

"It's fine. Pete's in custody."

"So they pinning the fires on him?"

"Trying to, but he told me he had help. That he was paid. I believe him."

Questions kept piling up. I don't think Pete worked alone, and I was having a hard time keeping out of the cops' business. I hadn't been able to get hold of Tasha, either. I think after the debacle with Pete at my office, I was somehow a persona non grata to her.

I ran my hands through my hair. Though I valiantly tried to staunch the curls, they had defeated the stress of the blond dye job and sprang to life no matter how much I flat-ironed them. With a sigh, I listened to Hunter rant. I put him on speaker and turned the camera around to look at myself. The platinum bob had grown out. I made a mental note to set up an appointment to get my roots done. When Hunter took a breath, I dove in.

"I think Dylan Palmer's involved. That was right around the same time his wife was leaving, remember? Maybe someone else discovered his secret life, too. But there's a fair chance Dylan would've hired someone with Pete's issues...by that, I mean vulnerable and in love with fire...to create a diversion.

Dylan was messed up enough to look for these kinds of opportunities." I lifted one shoulder. "Maybe he was a firebug, too. I'm a lowly PI, what do I know?"

Hunter laughed. "A lot more than most."

"You finished being mad?"

"I guess."

He was quiet.

"Hey. It was unavoidable. I only want nice, easy assignments. This stuff landed on me like a train wreck. All I'm looking for is boring stuff like tracking down Medicare fraud. Finding out who stole someone's pony. Whatever pays the bills. Not this."

A blip of silence shimmered between us.

"Did Hazel find a place to stay while her house is being restored?"

I brought Hunter up to date on Hazel, adding the mystery of Tasha's mystery concoction in the cabinet. "I don't know what was in that juice of hers," I muttered, "but Hazel had a tough couple of days getting it out of her system. Could be an allergy. The lab is working on it."

"You believe it was an old family recipe? Like she told Hazel?"

"Maybe." I let the word hang. I didn't tell him that Tasha rested on the tippy-top of my question piles for the moment.

"This is what I know. Dylan Palmer's prints were found on Tom's old file cabinets in my office."

"What would Dylan want with Tom's files?"

Wups.

My brain scrambled to solid ground. What had I told him? Hadn't I told him about the TS file? No. Why? I couldn't remember. I cursed my lingering, stupid, deficits from the TBI.

"I didn't tell you?"

"Tell me what? About Tom's files? Or Dylan?"

So no, I *hadn't* told him.

Would it kill me to keep him in the dark? Did he have to know every detail of my life? If I ejected details about the TS file, I'd have to bring up my dad and the impending meet-up. And my grandad and Tom and the dark underbelly of my mother's past. Simple answer. No.

"I'm looking into it."

He went quiet a few seconds. "It's okay if you don't want to tell me," he said.

I smiled. He knew me too well.

"What else do you have?" he asked.

"Organized fire starter vs. disorganized. Pete's a wrap, but he wants a deal."

"The fires could've been planned that way. I've seen it before. Why don't they give him a deal?"

Hm.

"Motive?"

"Hunter, it's like a spider's web. Since I worked with Tom, I inherited some of his more, uh, cautious clients. Plus, this 'Friends of Olivia' gang is busting it to unearth certain deep, dark secrets of my life that I'm convinced should stay in the ground."

"I'll get a flight."

"You don't need this right now. I've got it. It's okay," I assured him. It wasn't, but he didn't need to know that. He had his own stuff going on.

After a beat, he agreed.

"Any thoughts yet on if you'll keep your Sergeant status?"

He chuckled. "After watching this pandemonium you're inflicting on yourself, I think I might consider staying on the admin side. We'll see."

"It's not *all* self-inflicted," I responded. Yet I knew much of it was. Hazel kept telling me I needed boundaries.

We ended the call on an upbeat note. Him upbeat, and me feeling pretty good about getting through the conversation without dumping my question piles on him. That was a boundary, right?

My visit to Pierre should clear up at least one of the mysteries on my horizon. Mom had kept me in the dark about what happened with my father on purpose—and as close as I was to Mom, I'd begun to doubt her veracity. Was she more interested in protecting me…or herself? Or Tom?

I heard Hunter's voice in the back of my mind. *You just never know about people.*

I was quite certain, however, that some events in the past should stay buried. Maybe with a proper funeral, but buried nonetheless. The more I discovered my past life, the less I wanted to know. Sometimes I wondered if the therapy I'd put up with over the past three years had been worth it. When I boiled it down to basics, digging around in my past had yielded emotional pain and nightmares. Agonizing questions. Fear.

Most of *my* memories didn't need raking up, no matter what Hazel said. More like scraping them up into a pile, loading them in a trash bag, and dropping them at the dump. I'd gotten a do-over. Maybe I should focus more on the present and quit looking over my shoulder at what could've been...but wasn't. What good did it do?

My cell rang. A South Dakota area code. I jerked to attention. "Olivia."

"Ms. Callahan? I have some great news. We located Mr. Pellegra."

I jotted down an address, stared at it. "Thank you," I mumbled into the phone. I tapped the pad with my pen.

Okay. Finding Sonny would be the last foray into the past. After *that*, full steam ahead into my future.

The rest of the afternoon passed in a flurry of airline reservations and researching all the 'B' files. Beyond any doubt, the 'B' stood for Blackmailer. These were records of Tom's coerced investigations for Dylan. Some nasty stuff, much of it redacted. I called and begged the PD for more patrols around my property, and before I left the office, I called a locksmith and set up an appointment for new locks on my office building. Next, I set up an appointment with my security company to discuss enhanced security measures.

By the time I pulled into my garage, it was dark outside. The garage lights flicked on with the opening of the door, blinding in their glorious, safety-inspired brightness. I pulled in, powered the car off, my gaze riveted to the pegboard wall. Monty had populated it with tools arranged in perfect precision. Labeled baby food jars that held various types of screws. A set of small drawers that held every gadget known to man. I halfway expected Monty to step out of the vapor of my memories into reality, for his ghost lingered in this garage. Jaw clenched, I got out of the car, gripped the portable set of drawers with both hands, wrenched it off the work table, and slammed it to the floor. It hit the concrete with a satisfying crack of wood and commingling of tools. I smiled. The baby food jars went next. Thick shards of glass flew under my car, into a dark corner of the garage, across my feet. I put both hands in the air and yelled, "WooHoo!" like a lunatic in a TikTok video. I pictured deep, angry ruts in Monty's forehead, deeper ones around his downturned lips.

The shelving he'd put together clung to the wall beside the worktable. He'd been so proud of that shelving, my daughters had told me. I glowered at the shelves, dug my fingertips behind them, and pulled with all my might. After an exceptional effort that included much grunting, I stopped when I felt my shoulders coming out of their sockets. I rubbed my shoulders and glared at the shelves. I'd get rid of them one way or the other.

Anything Monty touched or loved…in time, I'd erase it all.

Breathing hard, I strode through the garage, the covered breezeway, and into the kitchen, down the hall, out onto the porch. Looked around at the hard work we'd put into this home—the landscaping, the refinished, red screen door, the beadboard walls. The kitchen cabinets he'd put up. The fire had nibbled just one corner of my house, and I wondered if it would've been better if the fire had consumed the whole thing like a tasty barbeque. If my entire home had gone up in flames, would it have been a catalyst to move on? To put the past behind me instead of clinging to it?

Chapter Forty

"Mom!" Lilly tossed her sun-bleached, red curls off her face. The lifeguarding had caused her freckles to spread across her cheeks, her nose, her forehead. She wore a yellow sundress, white sandals, and an angry countenance. "Why are you choosing *now* to leave? I need help packing…and…and lots of other stuff! You can't run off and leave me at Miss Callie's again!"

"Honey," I said, trying to be patient. I knew she'd be upset about my flying off to South Dakota, but it was only three days. "I'll be back in plenty of time to take you to Richmond. You don't have to be there until the twentieth, right?"

She rolled her eyes so hard it was a wonder her scalp didn't peel off. "That's the last day to move in. There's orientation, and freshman parties, and…I have to get a feel for the campus, Mom… and I'll miss the initiation if you're not back on time. For that newcomer club? Remember? This is important, Mom." She stormed out of the kitchen.

Had I ever been that determined? That sure of myself? Instead of disapproval, I experienced a deep satisfaction that she felt comfortable expressing such feelings. How I wished I'd stood up for myself at her age. Or any age, for that matter. Going to college meant a lot to her, and she was driving her own stake in the sand. I understood.

However…my father-hunting trip was going to take *three days.*

I followed her out onto the porch. She sat in her typical spot, the porch swing suspended by chains from the ceiling to the right of the front door at one end of the porch. She'd become such a beauty it took my breath away.

I couldn't wait to see Serena. Since she'd had a summer job in Richmond this year, we hadn't had a proper visit in a long while. I looked forward to gathering my chicks, my mom, and Gray if he wasn't working; and enjoying a meal together in Richmond. Laughing together. The flow of normal conversation. Discussions about college classes, sororities, Serena's boyfriend.

The brand-new cushions on my wicker loveseat made a pleasant whooshing sound when I sat. I spread my arms across the back of the loveseat and looked at Lilly.

"We can go down earlier."

She sandwiched her arms across her chest. "I want a definite date, Mom."

I sighed.

"See? You always do this. I can't trust you."

I got up and sat beside her on the swing. She jerked her face away. I put my arm around her. "Honey. You can trust me. I'll *be* here."

A tear straggled down one cheek. "It's been hard with Mr. Stark gone and you're on your own now. You're busy with the fire investigations and...and everything else. I hardly ever see you. And I'm tired of being at Miss Callie's whenever you think something bad's going to happen."

I brushed a glossy curl out of her eyes. "I'm sorry, Lilly. It will get easier." I stopped short of putting an 'I promise' at the end of that statement, because I couldn't. Soon, Lilly would have Serena, Hunter, and my mother to lean on if she had a problem. Until my life settled down, they were a much better fortress for her than I was. As I rocked the porch swing back and forth, I realized that the calendar was creeping closer to my forty-fourth birthday on November 10. In a couple of weeks, it would be official. I'd be an empty nester.

"Oh well." Lilly took a deep breath. "It doesn't matter I'm going to be gone soon, anyway."

The comment hit me like a punch to the jaw. "Don't put it like that. I'm going to miss you."

Again, the eye roll.

"I'll visit." Did she think I cared so little?

She frowned. "You don't go to Richmond much, Mom."

"I will visit, you can count on it."

She drew her knees up to her chest and rested her chin on it. "Okay."

I ruffled her hair. "Come help me fix dinner. Something fun."

She jumped up from the swing, which set it swaying like crazy. "I'll make brownies. The fudgy ones."

I followed her inside. She scooped up a cranky Riot and covered his soft belly with kisses. He made a pitiful mewing sound of protest. Lilly laughed and replaced him on the floor.

I drank her in. This might be the last couple of weeks I'd have a daughter around full-time.

And here I was, boarding a flight to the tiny township of Pierre at seven-thirty in the morning.

I pushed the guilt away. I was determined to close the TS file and with it, that chapter of my life. With all the questions lurking in the file hanging over me, how could I focus on Lilly, Serena, Mom, and Gray in Richmond? I wanted getting Lilly settled in her dorm room for her freshman year at Richmond University to be a joyous, poignant occasion, and I didn't need 'what-ifs' pinging my brain the whole time.

From the air, Pierre looked even smaller than I'd imagined.

My beached-whale, abused luggage trundled down the conveyor. As usual, I'd packed two weeks' worth instead of three days, and from the looks of my luggage, I'd have to buy a new set soon. I glanced around Pierre's airport. It was small and tidy, and well-kept. I'd reserved a car and planned to drive to the Ramkota, a historic hotel that boasted many stays by celebrities in order to enjoy Pierre's famous pheasant hunting.

I walked outside to pick up my rental and gale-force winds knocked the breath out of me.

Clutching my bag, my dignity, and anything else that could get blown away, I struggled to the Hertz kiosk and loaded my stuff in the rental. I'd read about the prairie winds in South Dakota, but this? The windspeed had to be hitting close to sixty miles per hour. I could swear my car rolled along with one side an inch off the ground all the way to the hotel.

The historic Ramkota presented an imposing presence on the banks of the Missouri River. I parked the rental and checked in. After grabbing a quick rest in the room, I took the elevator to the lobby.

I told the front desk associate I was a tourist and asked all kinds of touristy questions. The lobby was deserted, so I took my time. I had little information other than Sonny's last known address, but I figured I'd chat up the desk clerk and see what shook out.

I'd done quite a bit of research on South Dakota and discovered the state held nine Native American reservations. The associate behind the counter had to be full-blooded Native American. I gazed at his glossy, black hair, the aquiline nose, strong, firm jawline, and piercing, dark eyes in awe. I stopped short of blurting that he might rank in the top ten of the most gorgeous men I'd ever had the pleasure of ogling. He told me the best place to enjoy a drink and have a good steak was The Cattleman's Club out on some highway. I told him I'd check it out, and followed up with a question about Sonny Pellegra. The minute the name left my lips, he backed up in surprise.

"You kidding me? Why would you want to know about *that* guy?"

I made a little pouty sound. "Someone asked me to say hello, that's all."

He laughed. "Why?" His nametag read 'Phineas Wolfhunter'.

I fluffed my hair. "He's a close relative of Sonny's who can't travel. I'm doing it as a favor. I was coming out here, anyway, so I said I would."

This lying thing was getting easier all the time.

Phineas shoved in a drawer behind the counter. Glanced around the lobby, pointed at a couple of chairs in the corner, and invited me to follow. We sat. He placed his butt on the edge of his chair, as though preparing to spring up the minute someone entered the room. I gripped the sides of my chair.

"I've lost track of how many times the guy has been in trouble with our local police, miss. I've heard he's holed up on the rez, and that's not a place you want to visit. It'd be best if...you know...forgot about seeing him." His eyes flicked left, then right, until they settled on my face.

I frowned. "Reservation? Do you know which one?"

His eyebrows shot up. "You'd still try to find him after what I told you?"

Phineas threaded his fingers together. He wore several turquoise rings. "That's not a good idea, miss."

"It's Olivia. I'll pay you to take me there."

The dark, ageless eyes hardened. He glanced around the room one more time.

Still deserted.

"I'm off tomorrow." He smiled. "But I warned you."

The huge, dazzling South Dakota sun woke me. I yawned.

The sun blaring through my window seemed bigger and brighter than it had been in Maryland. Way bigger.

I rose, disoriented for a second. Oh, yeah. Pierre. Dad-hunting. Got it.

I took a shower, then checked my emails and texts. Office, check. Lilly was fine, check. Serena saying hi. I stopped cold at the next text. *Tasha.* She wanted to talk.

I just bet she does.

I stepped into jeans, dragged on a sweatshirt, zipped my belt through the loops, and attached my holster. Tucked in my Smith & Wesson with a fond pat. Ran my fingers through my hair. I hadn't had time to get to a stylist, so my dark, auburn roots were on full display. I looked like Madonna in the 90s.

Could I push aside talking to Tasha until I got back?

I waited in silence for the heavens to drop an answer on me.

My heart became this wild, thrashing thing in my chest.

I had my answer.

If I wanted to avoid a heart attack or stroke, I needed to climb one giant mountain at a time. Finding my dad was enough over the next forty-eight hours. Tackling Tasha would push me over the edge. Whatever she had to say would have to wait.

Turns out Phineas was as good as his word. Right on time.

As I rode in his radically lifted Toyota 4Runner, I thought of Hunter's Jeep and wondered if hot guys and big tires were a thing.

South Dakota was a pleasant surprise. As we passed the undulating hills, I felt a peace settle on and around me. One word kept circling through my mind. *Vast.* The South Dakota prairies were a perfect example of the word. I gasped when a pheasant exploded into the air from the side of the road.

"You live around here, you get used to that. You can't see them in the prairie grasses until they get startled." Phineas rambled on, his voice as pleasant as his appearance, educating me about the Native American Scenic Byway through the heart of the Teton Lakota Nation. I was enthralled. Not so much by the goal of my visit, but by the history and tradition of the Lakota people. "It's a way to preserve the culture of the plains," he finished. After that, in what I imagined was typical of the Native American mystique, he clammed up tight.

We arrived at a building fronted by authentic Native American teepees, and my jaw dropped like a kindergartner on a field trip. "Wow. This is amazing," I breathed.

Phineas smiled. "This was where he landed last time, or he might be in a buddy's trailer. Wait here."

I looked around. Miles of flatland, or 'plains' as Phineas had told me, and a couple of trailer parks that had seen better days. In the distance, a four-story building with a giant, blinking sign. 'Goldstar Casino.'

Phineas' modifications to the Toyota made it a foot taller than the average SUV. Due to its height, I'd have to jump to get out, even from the step bars. Five minutes passed. Ten. I drummed my fingers on the dashboard. Fifteen minutes.

Phineas came out of the building and opened my door.

I frowned. "What's going on?"

I took his hand and jumped.

"What always goes on with Sonny." He shrugged. "Drunk or high or in a cell. They were reluctant to agree to a visitor."

I flew 1500 miles to meet a drug addict and chronic criminal?

I set my jaw and followed Phineas inside.

To meet my father.

For the first time.

This was really happening.

The uniformed guards had the same piercing, silent stare as Phineas. I threw him a questioning look. "Bureau of Indian Affairs, Office of Justice," he whispered. "Reservations are governed by Tribal Councils. This 'friend' of yours got himself tossed into one of our Adult Detention Centers." He glanced at my waist. "That gun needs to stay with me, or it may disappear."

We walked outside. I whipped off the belt with my weapon and handed it over. He locked it in the truck.

"Will we have some privacy?"

"The guards will tell you what to do. I'll wait for you in the lobby."

As I surrendered my watch, phone, and purse into the tubs the guards extended, I marveled at the irony. Maybe there *was* a family curse, as Sherry had joked. It sure sounded like I'd married a man just like my father. I filled out a visitor's form, tolerated a pat down. The guard waved me through. A burly man with a pock-marked face and stringy, black hair led me down a corridor to a twenty-foot-square space floored with dingy linoleum, and cinder-block walls painted the color of desert sand. Black and white prints of Native American history hung on the walls. The room held six tables, each surrounded by four chairs. It was airless, depressing, and windowless.

The perfect setting to meet a ghost.

An earthquake started at my feet and spread throughout my body. I breathed a silent prayer and tried to hold it together. My hands balled into fists.

The door opened.

My whole life, I'd imagined this moment. I stared at the thin man in the doorway, holding out his hands so the guard could uncuff him. He turned his head and looked at me with eyes so dark they looked black. Deep grooves ran across his forehead. Permanent ruts excavated the space between his eyebrows. He had short, silver hair. A long goatee dangled from his chin in two ratty braids.

In short, I was ecstatic that I'd taken after my mother.

He plopped into the chair across from me. Networks of broken blood vessels rimmed his eyes. A yellowish cast permeated his skin.

Lifetime drinker with a damaged liver.

"Look. I got no money. If I didn't pay you enough last time, I'm sorry. As you can see, I ain't exactly killin' it in here." The sour odor of his body almost put me on the floor. I stifled a desire to cover my nose.

I subtly pushed my chair back a little. "Who do you think I am?"

His eyes darted left to right. His tongue played with his upper lip. "You ain't that hooker from three weeks ago?"

I dissected the words, respect for my lineage nosediving with each passing moment. The sole guard seemed preoccupied and uninterested in what we were doing. This was as private as it was going to get.

I cleared my throat. "You remember Tom Stark?"

His expression shifted to suspicion. "What the hell do you want?"

"There's this thing that happened. Decades ago. It involved a hospital and a beatdown."

He cursed, his voice soft. His eyes slid to the guard, who paid him no mind, yawned, and crossed his arms. In five seconds, he'd probably be asleep.

"What are you diggin' for? It's been over forty years."

"The truth." My gaze raked his scrawny shoulders, the shaky hands, nails bitten down to the nub until they bled. The yellow-gray complexion underneath four days' worth of salt-and-pepper stubble. The man needed a drink. And a shower. "Are you familiar with the name Dylan Palmer?"

"Tried hard to forget it," he said, with a muffled profanity. "It's a pretty sorry country that won't hear an attempted murder case," he whined. "Nobody'd listen. I heard he's a politician now. Figures."

"Palmer's wife shot him to death a few weeks ago."

His head jerked back. He smiled broadly, revealing a bunch of tobacco-stained teeth. One missing. I looked away. "That for sure?"

"It's for sure."

His laughter sounded like the squawk of a dying rooster. After a couple of sputum-filled coughs, he continued. "Ain't that a hoot." He frowned. "Then why'd you bring up Stark?"

"Tom's passed on. Leukemia," I told him, wondering why I told him because I was positive that he didn't care. "I'm looking into situations that were, uhh, unresolved. This file had deficits, and I'm here to get your side of things. You're the last person involved that's alive, and I want to archive the file." Good for me if he thought I was a cop. Or better yet, an attorney.

He peered at me. "What about the woman? Is she dead, too?"

"Which woman?"

"Sophie. I forget her last name."

I stared at him. "Her last name was the same as yours, wasn't it, Sonny?"

His mouth dropped open in surprise. "Why are you here?"

"Tell me what happened. Then I'll tell you why I'm here."

He flopped back on his chair, made a rude noise. Took his time thinking how to answer.

A snore burst from the guard's parted lips.

"I dated Sophie off and on. Real nice woman. One day I got a wild hair, up and asked her to get married. I could hardly believe it when she accepted." He grimaced. "Next thing I know, she's pregnant. I asked her, real nice, too, to take care of it."

The word 'it' set my teeth on edge. "Go on."

"She gets all crazy, and I can't reason with her. Then her dad gets involved, high and mighty on that throne of his."

I frowned. "What do you mean by that?"

"He had a lot of money and a lot of friends in the right places. I never had a chance. He had a talk with a judge, and before I know it, Sophie and me, we're not married anymore. That was all fine and dandy, but see here…it's my choice too, that kid in her belly, and I don't want nothin' to do with it. She wouldn't listen. We had words."

"Words?"

"Yeah." He stared at me, his face pinched into a dare.

"Then what happened?" By now, I'd managed to get the records unsealed. He'd almost strangled my mother to death. My grandpa must've been terrified for Mom.

"I was railroaded outta town, that's what happened," he muttered. "Damn near died in the hospital. That Palmer guy? He hung out with a crew back then. Called themselves something, I can't remember. They were mean bastards. After three weeks in the hospital with a broken jaw, broken ribs, a skull fracture, and a broken arm, they told me I was lucky." He squawked that dying rooster sound again. "Lucky? I could hardly walk. I got as far away from Maryland as I could." He lifted one of his saggy, pale arms and made a circling motion. "Seein' as no one would listen, that they'd all locked up their arms against me, I had no choice, I had to leave. Damn cops 'lost' the police report I made, they said." He squinted at me and cracked a smile. "You bringin' new charges? Is that what this is about?"

I channeled my inner Hazel. "Do you think there should be?"

Another cackle. "Hell, yeah! Sophie needs to fry. She's the one that started all the trouble. That bitch needs to be sued for accessory to assault or intent to murder or whatever it's called. If she'd gotten rid of the kid, none of this would've happened. Who knows, we might have had a good marriage that lasted fifty years. Never had a chance to know what coulda been." He worked in a tear or two.

My sigh was long and heavy. I'd experienced more than my fair share of dirtbags, but this one took the cake. Maybe two cakes. "Sonny, cut the BS. I know you assaulted Sophie. You almost killed her."

He uncapped the water bottle he'd brought to the table, and took a swig. Wiped his mouth. "No proof of that. None. You here to bring charges against *me*?"

I shook my head. "I think you've paid your dues. As you said, you're not exactly 'killin' it."

"You gotta have a reason," he grumbled.

I struggled to frame the words. "As it turns out, Sophie did have the kid." I waited for his reaction.

Like a slow-motion video, I watched the expressions crawl across his face. The puzzle he couldn't comprehend, the lifted brows and open mouth of astonishment, the fury of full comprehension. "You're Sophie's kid."

He shook an index finger at me. "Let me tell you something'. I never even knew if you was mine! Sophie, she screwed around, you know. For all I know, that's the reason she hopped up and wanted to get married." He stared at the wall, his breath coming in short pants. He jabbed his fists in the air and cursed. "Guard!" The guard startled awake, rubbed his eyes. Sonny glared at me long and hard. "I want nothin' to do with this. And I want nothin' to do with *you.*"

The guard lumbered over to us, cuffed Sonny, and took him away.

I felt like a stray dog that had been kicked to the curb.

My heart slogged along in my chest on life support. What had I expected? A baby shower? A warm embrace? Would it have hurt to give me a smile or a pleasant look at the discovery of a daughter? I stared at the stained ceiling, my thoughts circling the drain. I contemplated my situation. Phineas waiting patiently in the lobby. The dust-devil hatred gusting off Sonny Pellegra. A Tribal Council. Talk about a stranger in a strange land.

A nice, sizzly, defiance rippled up my back. I looked around for a pen or a stick, anything.

Beside the chair on which the guard had taken a nap, lay a straw. I picked it up.

Then I went back to the small, plastic, water bottle that Sonny had left behind, poked the straw inside, lifted the bottle with it, and took meticulous care placing it in my pocket.

Chapter Forty-One

"Sherry! Did you send in that water bottle?"

"Yes. Same day," she called from her desk in reception.

"How long did they say?"

"Ten days. I asked for a rush, though."

I got up from my desk, walked to the breakroom that divided my office from reception. Lilly and I were heading out to Richmond tomorrow, and I wanted loose ends tied up.

What a lovely dream... loose ends all wrapped up.

I walked into reception. "Guess I could've texted the question instead of yelling."

Sherry laughed. "Doesn't matter. It feels more like home when you yell at me."

"That is *not* a nice thing to say."

Sherry lifted her hands in surrender. "Teasing. So...tomorrow, huh?"

I grinned. "Lilly's climbing the walls. I've never seen her like this."

"I remember how I was. No curfews, no accountability. It was fun."

"She'll have accountability," I protested. "Mom, Serena, Hunter...she'll have more of a family unit there than here."

"Uh-huh," Sherry mumbled, studying her email. "You get with Tasha yet?"

I averted my eyes, avoidance-guilt percolating through me. After the revelations of the trip to South Dakota, I couldn't stand another showdown. Another disappointment. Whatever she had on her mind, I wanted my life to settle before another freaking revelation. And a chat with Tasha in my current state of mind could become a confrontation. "After I get back from taking Lilly."

Sherry gazed at me, put her pen down. "What's going on with Tasha?"

"We'll know more when I get lab results back on that homemade mixture she gave Hazel."

"Understood," she said and returned her focus to her laptop.

I fled to my office. Told myself it wasn't a crime to space out stuff. I had the ability to hold off Tasha and let the chips fall where they may. My life should matter, too, shouldn't it? Things like moving my daughter into college? A nice, normal, sweet family event? Shouldn't that matter more than catching up with Tasha?

Yes. Yes, it should.

With this in mind, I called the arson investigator at Baltimore County PD and asked if there were any new developments with the fire investigations. He was surprised at the call.

"Tasha told me she was keeping you updated."

What? No, she hadn't. Not lately. "She…I couldn't reach her. I've been out of town," I fudged.

He bought it and told me Pete was singing like a canary. I smiled at the reference, and tucked it away to share with Hazel sometime. A deal had been reached, he told me.

"What's he singing about?"

"It doesn't matter now, since he's dead and buried, but Dylan Palmer? Were you aware that they knew each other?"

"Suspected," I muttered. "Can you give me the short version? I'm headed out in a few minutes."

I heard the sounds of paper shuffling. "Report says Dylan Palmer paid him to create a distraction. Get people looking the other way. That Dylan was being outed as gay, and having marital problems, and didn't want it to go public until after the election. Said all he needed was a few weeks. Which makes us think that's why the fires were so close together."

"And mine?" I asked through gritted teeth.

More shuffling. "Report talks about Pete pinning the fire at your house on some woman. He wouldn't give a name."

I struggled through crazy insinuations spinning through my head. A woman? Tasha?

"This doesn't make sense. Do you have that Dylan Palmer's prints were found at my office on a filing cabinet?"

"Oh." More shuffling. "Hold on."

"That's been ruled a vendetta against one Sergeant Hunter Faraday. I believe you know him?"

I sighed. "Yes, I know him. What's the motive?"

"Inconclusive."

I frowned. Was someone screwing with this investigation? "Do you have time to take a statement?"

"Well," he hedged. "Guess so. We're ready to close out this case, though. Fire Marshal's office responded yesterday. We believe the suspect we have in custody to be responsible."

I stifled all the rude things I wanted to say. The ineptness was astonishing. Or someone was pulling strings. My mind stalled over one horrifying name.

Monty.

Had Dylan been connected to my ex? Pete had been in prison at the same time Monty was, so…possible?

"I'd appreciate it if you'd take my statement before you close the case. I can be there in thirty minutes."

"Okay," the detective agreed. "I'll be here."

I raced out of the office building and pointed my Discovery toward police headquarters in Towson.

He was expecting me. I paused in front of his desk. "Let's find a room," he said. I followed him down a long hallway to an interrogation room. I'd be videoed. My words stored in perpetuity. I hadn't thought this through.

Too late now. You've cemented your own little piece of hell forever.

I sat in a cold, metal chair across the table from him.

He opened a notebook. Took a pen from his pocket. "Okay. Shoot."

"Friends of Olivia Facebook group. Sometimes known as the 'Foofoos'. I'll start with that."

He put his pen down and crossed his arms. "No mention of that in our reports. What does that have to do with anything?"

I proceeded to fill him in on our research, deleting Hunter's involvement and pointing to the fact that Pete had been the administrator of the group. I told him about the bouquets, the cards. The messy fire scene at my house, set to look like arson; the explainable fire scenes at the others, set to look accidental. My theory that all of it was planned.

At that, he raised his eyebrows. "Our investigator, Tasha, worked in tandem with the Baltimore County Fire Marshal. Our arson unit corroborated her findings. She told us none of these details, Olivia."

I started to hyperventilate.

The investigator's eyes popped, and he ran to get me some water.

Why is it always *water* that is supposed to help people in crisis?

I stumbled out of the interrogation room and asked where I could find some caffeine. A woman that looked like she sucked on lemons all day raised her hand and vaguely pointed. I returned to the interrogation room.

The detective looked relieved when I walked in. He'd put a bottle of water on the table for me. "You okay?"

I nodded, thanked him for the water, sipped at my coffee. "I need you to explain the discrepancy."

He spread his hands. "We have her reports."

"Can I look at them?"

He left, returned with a couple of files. "See for yourself."

I scanned the documents. What she'd put in these reports was *not* what I'd shared with her. My mind ratcheted up. What was I missing? What was going on?

The investigator tapped his fingers on the metal table. "This is concerning, Olivia. We will look into this. Are you sure you're okay?"

I drained my cup. "I'm good," I said. "I had a brain injury three years ago, and sometimes stress is a trigger." I promised myself to stop using this excuse. I wasn't stuck in that time warp anymore.

The investigator squinted. "Shit. You're her."

I sighed.

"You've got blond hair, now. You don't look like, um, no offense, but you look a whole lot better now than you did when you were all over the media."

I smiled. "No offense taken. Don't say anything, okay? I enjoy not being the center of attention." I winked. "Our secret."

He grinned and leaned in. "That asswipe Monty still in prison?"

"Oh, yeah," I said, thinking about dangling threads and Monty and Pete. Had they collaborated on something? With each other? With someone else?

He started straightening the documents, re-inserting them into the file folders. "Sure hope you get your life back the way you want it, Olivia."

"It's a lot better than it used to be, Detective. Thanks."

"Listen. We're going to look into the discrepancies you mentioned. This raises a lot of questions."

No kidding.

I glanced at my phone as I started the car. Lilly had left eight texts. The last two in all caps.

I pressed the accelerator to the floor.

I drove up my winding lane thirty minutes later, and dashed inside. Lilly was dragging a suitcase down the stairs that rivaled mine in its whale-likeness. I helped her tote it to the front door. "There," she said, out of breath. "I have five boxes, too, Mom. Think they'll fit?"

"We'll make them fit." I hugged her.

"Where did you go, anyway?"

"An interview. It couldn't wait."

She nodded. Her mind was anywhere but on my issues. She was already deep inside her dreams of freshman life at the university. I smiled. I would shove my challenges aside and enjoy our trip to Richmond and a good visit with Mom and Serena. My mind stalled. And Hunter? After Lilly went back upstairs, I called Mom.

"How nice to hear from my only daughter," she said, her tone slightly punitive.

"Sorry. Been jammed up. Listen, I have a question. Did you invite Hunter to our big dinner thing?"

"Of course I invited Hunter, silly. He might as well be part of the family."

I closed my eyes and tilted my head back. How would this play out with Hunter there? I needed some serious face time with Mom about my conversation with Sonny.

"Couldn't you have checked with me first? This could get awkward."

"Why? You and Hunter are back together, aren't you?"

My left shoulder started to throb. "Not really. Mom..."

"Oh, never mind. I didn't think about checking with you. He's family, whether you like it or not. Besides, my house, my rules."

I laughed. "That's an oldie but a goodie."

"Let's assume the best and trust God to take care of the rest, okay?"

Another old homily dragged out of the family closet into the full light of day. I sighed. "Okay, Mom ...the awkward part is about you and me, not Hunter. Better get all prayed up, as you put it."

Chapter Forty-Two

Sergeant Hunter Faraday stared at the Richmond PD badge on top of his dresser and sighed.

His captain hadn't granted his request to come back to work. He gritted his teeth and sulked for a while after the stern directive to take three more weeks off. An image of Marlowe flashed through his mind. Maybe he should get a dog. At least then, he'd have something to do every day. He went outside and sat on a patio the size of Olivia's dining room table. He sank into one of the chairs he kept out there and watched the sun inch above the roofs of the community. Although it was a decent view, it didn't hold a candle to Olivia's front porch. The sun continued to climb, basting him with the muggy heat of August in Richmond.

His cell buzzed. He didn't recognize the number. "Faraday."

"Hunter? This is Sherry. From Watchdog Investigations?"

"Hey. So the business up and runnin' now?" He went inside.

"Yeah. We changed the number of the landline. Because of the fallout from Dylan. Listen. I wanted to prepare you."

Hunter frowned. "Okay."

"Has she told you about her dad?"

"She never tells me anything, you know that."

After a beat, she continued. "She found him."

His forehead beetled. "Huh. So the group didn't find him first?"

"I don't think they had anything to do with it. She's holed up in her house, thinking about their meeting. She flew all the way to South Dakota to meet him, and it didn't go well. Something hit her hard. She's planning an intense conversation with her mom. I wanted you to know you might get stuck in more drama than you were counting on while she's in Richmond."

He chuckled. "I'm sure she doesn't want me to know any of this."

Sherry groaned. "Would you stop? I thought you needed to know where her head's at, that's all."

"What happened, anyway? With her dad?"

"It was a train wreck. She was in no mood to answer a lot of questions. She brought back a water bottle from their visit to check his DNA."

Hunter nodded. "Smart. I'd do the same thing after so many years of thinking the man was dead."

"Maybe so." Hunter heard soft bark, then whining. Sherry laughed. "Marlowe says hi. He hears your voice."

Hunter smiled. "I miss him."

"Anyway, that's it. I didn't want you blindsided by family hysterics."

"Does that family ever not have hysterics going on?"

"I'm hoping," Sherry said. "Nice to chat with you, Hunter. Thanks again for all the help over the past couple of weeks. Take care."

He pressed the 'end' button. "Interesting," he whispered to himself.

The fireworks at Sophie and Gray's dining room table should be off the charts. He and Gray could excuse themselves, go into another part of Sophie's condo, drink a couple of bourbons, and enjoy some good cigars while the girls had it out.

Cheered by Sherry's call, he grabbed his keys. He'd take the Jeep in for a detail, then go work out. Whistling a tune, he grabbed his gym bag, locked up, walked to his garage. At least he had something to look forward to now.

Chapter Forty-Three

Hazel smiled as she pulled the cover off the birdcage she'd tucked into her living room in a corner by the window. The plump, yellow birds sleepily opened their eyes. The male began singing. Hazel beamed. "It's going to be a good day, old girl," she whispered to herself.

Her cell buzzed with a call. *Sherry.*

As Sherry explained exactly what was in Tasha's secret mixture, the light vanished from her eyes. The bright-red lips pursed. When the conversation ended, she stared out a window, pondering what she'd learned.

Tiny hands fisted by her sides, she stalked to the kitchen to make a huge pot of coffee. She needed her brain clear and on high alert in order to come up with a plan. "When am I going to quit trusting people?" she demanded, shaking a fist in the air. "This'll help you, she said." She groaned. "Yeah, right." She walked out of the kitchen, through the living room, and locked the deadbolt on the front door with a flourish of her arm.

Ten minutes later, her doorbell rang.

Hazel almost jumped out of her skin.

She peered through the peephole. *Tasha.*

"Hi, Hazel." Tasha waved at the peephole, her voice muted by the door.

In light of what she'd learned from Sherry, she had a feeling her years of counseling would serve her well in the next few minutes. She went to the kitchen and poured herself some coffee. Then she stuffed her cell in her pocket. After that, she opened the door.

Tasha stood on the stoop, hands on hips. "What took you so long?"

"You know how it is when one gets old. Come in, dear."

Hazel closed the door behind Tasha and followed her into the living room.

Tasha looked around the room with an appreciative smile. "Wow. Your artwork is up already. Looks great, Hazel."

Hazel tucked herself into an armchair. She had no desire to exchange small talk with this horrid woman. What she'd learned had left her shaken to the core, and she wondered whether she should've let Tasha inside. "Any news, Tasha?"

She heaved out a dramatic sigh. "These investigations take forever." She slipped off her backpack and reached inside. "Nothing new, sorry to say, but I dropped by to give you another bottle of my secret additive. She wiggled the bottle. The liquid inside got foamy. "It's been a rough few weeks for you. This should help." She extended the bottle.

"I don't need any more of that. It didn't sit right." Hazel cocked her head, interested to hear Tasha's response. Would she try to defend her elixir? Or would she do the wiser thing and let it go? How naïve she'd been to accept a 'homemade' anything from a woman she barely knew. Thank goodness Olivia sent this stuff to the lab. Hazel tried to keep a lid on the steam building up inside her. According to Olivia, she'd been completely out of it on the poison-laced concoction Tasha was holding in her hands. What had the blasted woman meant to accomplish?

A shadow crossed Tasha's face. She tightened her grip on the bottle. "But you said it made you feel so much better. Are you sure?"

"Yes. Thanks." Hazel smiled.

Tasha's jaw tightened. A vein throbbed in her forehead. She leaned down and put the bottle back inside the backpack.

"What's in that, anyway?" Hazel asked. "Is it a family recipe?"

"It…it…" she stuttered and looked away.

A smile played with Hazel's lips. Interesting how a person acts when they're not telling the truth. Hazel switched gears before Tasha got her equilibrium back.

"Did Pete set the fire in my house, Tasha?"

Her eyes darted. "He's our prime suspect. That's all I can say."

Hazel stroked her cheek. This was almost fun. "I've heard the Baltimore County Arson Unit has another lead."

Tasha's jaw dropped. "How?" Her hands clenched. "How could you know before me? I'd be the first to know—"

"Would you?" Hazel interrupted and rose from her chair. "Have you seen my new birds? I got two this time."

"I'd love to see them." Tasha's countenance cleared with the change of topic.

Hazel walked to the corner of the room and introduced Harold and Maude. Tasha made appropriate remarks, then asked, "How do you tell them apart?"

"The male sings. Females are quiet. The male I used to have sang all the time, but he didn't survive." Hazel squinted at Tasha. "Someone squeezed him to death."

Shocked into silence, Tasha took a step or two backward. Her complexion paled. "Someone killed the bird? What kind of monster would've done that?"

Her pulse is speeding up. The lying hussy. Her heart's going a hundred miles an hour.

"You're carrying something heavy. I can tell." Hazel caught her reflection in the living room mirror as she returned to her chair. The shape of her nose had returned to normal, the bruises had lightened. "Wouldn't you like to share what's on your heart, Tasha?"

Tasha shifted her weight from one leg to the other. Pondering. Considering. In the bat of an eyelash, her skin mottled. A tremor worked its way down her arms. She approached Hazel's chair and jabbed a finger in her face. "You don't get it, do you, old woman?"

Hazel planted herself deep, calm and ready for the storm.

"Get what, dear?"

"Pete and I were fine!" she shrieked. "Until you came along. What you had over him is like...beyond crazy to me. Why was he consumed with you? What the hell was that, anyway? You're old enough to be his mother." She cursed and paced the room. "Then I find out he's up to his eyeballs in that Facebook group that is obsessed with Olivia Callahan." She gulped in a breath of air, reached in her bag, and jerked out a framed photo of Hunter and Olivia. "And look! I found it in Pete's apartment. So, in addition to his fixation on you, I find out he's in love with this bitch." The whites of her eyes showed around the iris. "Now that was some good news, let me tell you," she quipped.

Hazel stared at the photo. "Pete must've taken that from Olivia's house, which means he was in her house. Which means he must've set the fire."

Tasha put her palm across her eyes and moaned. "All he's ever talked about is Mercy's Miracle since that book came out. He's obsessed."

Hazel straightened. "Let it out, Tasha. Or you'll never be free."

She slammed the photo to the floor. The glass in the frame shattered. "I'll never be free? What do you think I need to be free from? And you're what, seventy-five freaking years old?" Her laughter bordered on hysteria. "And here I was, providing you the perfect path to freedom."

Hazel glanced at the phone she'd slipped onto the accent table behind the lamp. "I'm sorry you're in such pain. It had to be a shock, finding that picture. The end of your dream of a life together with Pete."

Tasha started to cry. "It's ruined. You ruined it. He was fine, and now he can't stop."

Hazel perked up. "Can't stop what?"

She lifted her tear-stained face. "It's back."

Hazel fought a sense of dread. Her hand lifted to her throat. "What's back?"

"A few months after we started dating, he confessed that he struggled with pyromania. Do you know how many firefighters turn into full-on pyros? More than you'd think. I looked it up. He was getting help, though. He never did anything when we were together, then all those stupid fires everywhere popped up. I didn't want to believe it. It was too awful to think about. But deep down, I knew. We were looking at a future, and then..." she glared. "Is that what happened? You found out about his pyromania? Did you trigger him on purpose?"

Hazel started fanning herself with her hand. She didn't know if her heart could take any more stress.

"What did you do?" Tasha prodded. "Try to make him pay for his sins in some revolting, backward way? Is that what you therapists do for fun? Pete didn't do anything to you. He's always trying to help people."

"Tasha. Think about it. What would've been my motive? I didn't convince Pete to start anything, and I promise you, I had no idea he struggled with pyromania. I didn't even know he was a volunteer firefighter until recently." She studied Tasha. It had seemed unlikely when they'd first met that this woman was capable of murder, but Sherry's phone call had changed all that. The poison that had slowly worked through her system was atropine, the same ingredient in eye drops. A deadly, calculated plan, and she'd missed the psychopathy.

She needed to retire.

Tasha sniffled. "Poor Pete," she said, miserable. She looked at Hazel with liquid, puppy eyes. "He couldn't help himself. What did you do to him?"

Hazel glanced at the phone with the hope that it was still recording. "The fires…he set them all?"

Tasha scraped her palms across her face to wipe away angry tears. "He's a master." Hazel got out of her chair.

"Sit. DOWN."

A chill slithered up Hazel's neck. "I need some water. I'll be right back."

"I'll get it. You sit." She pointed at the chair.

Hazel sat.

While Tasha foraged in the fridge, Hazel checked the phone. It only had twenty percent of life left. She whispered to Siri, praying that Siri would understand her whispered words and make a hands-free call. Hazel almost lost it when Sherry answered on the first ring. She stage-whispered her address and ended the call.

Tasha returned with a glass of water and handed it to Hazel, who put the water on the end table with shaky hands. There was no way she'd drink anything Tasha's hands had touched. Tasha smiled at the untouched glass of water.

"You have to admit, it almost worked. What I used leaves the body in two hours. It would've been a mystery and eventually ruled accidental death.

Now I have to revert to plan B." She shook her head. "I faked the reports. Baltimore PD thinks the probability of arson in your fire investigation is slim, based on what I submitted." She shrugged. "When they find heroin in your system, they'll think you were a closet user or someone staged it. Suicidal, depressed people do crazy things. Take Pete, for example. The arson charge leans toward Pete, and coupled with your inconclusive death, a case could be made that Pete was guilty of taking you with him since he's going down," she said, thinking aloud. "It's not like he doesn't know his way around a syringe."

Tasha clasped her hands to her chest in satisfaction. "Boom. Either way, it works. Pete goes to prison for the arson charges or gets life for murder, and you go to your eternal reward a little early. Kind of poetic, don't you think?" She smiled. "And my hands are squeaky-clean."

Hazel remained frozen in place, her face chalk-white.

"It was you," she whispered. "Did you mean to kill me?"

Tasha laughed. "The plan was for Pete to take the hit for the fire. For all the hell he's put me through." She scowled. "No, it wasn't my 'plan' to kill you. You were supposed to be at work. There was no way to leave the house without you seeing me, so I had to act. Sorry about the broken nose." She sighed. "And the bird. I shouldn't have done that, but I needed to distract you. Get you to settle in one place."

She reached into the backpack, surfacing with nitrile gloves, a loaded hypodermic, a burnt spoon, a slim piece of rubber. "At least you'll go out riding on a cloud," she said, pulling on the gloves.

"Don't do this, Tasha. There's still time—"

"You really are delusional, aren't you?"

Hazel scrambled to her feet, but quick as a snake, Tasha plunged the needle into the crook of Hazel's arm. As her eyes rolled back, Tasha wrapped her upper arm with the strip of rubber, and threw the spoon on the floor beside her. "Welcome to the sad, sad world of heroin addicts, Hazel. Rest in peace."

Chapter Forty-Four

The girls' room was on the fourth floor, and my arms were loaded with boxes, blankets, and anything else I could get in my arms. I thanked God for the elevator.

Callie stood beside me with an armful of Amy's supplies, including assorted stuffed animals. I grinned. "Thought Amy would've left those at home with her childhood."

Callie shook her head. "Not on your life. She's had this collection for years. Can't sleep without them."

"Lilly would've taken Riot if she could've."

"She hates that cat."

"Something changed. Not sure what. But they're a thing now. He even sleeps with her."

"Aww."

We grew quiet. Dropping off our girls was tough, no doubt about it. Callie was having a harder time than me, and I'm sure her recent divorce from Graham played into it. "It'll be okay, Cal."

"I know it will. In time," she whispered.

We struggled to the girls' room underneath the weight, dumped it on their twin beds, and went into the dorm corridor to wait on our daughters.

Lilly emerged carrying two boxes stacked one on the other, and Callie's daughter Amy trailed behind, pulling two pieces of luggage.

"Almost there, Amy." Lilly's voice rang out across the linoleum hallway on the fourth floor of the Laura Robins Court co-ed dormitory that held 300 students in double rooms. "Isn't it beautiful? All those old buildings?"

"Let's get unpacked before we talk about how beautiful anything is, Lilly." Amy tugged her load down the hallway, determined and panting. A male classmate moving into a room two doors down bounced on the balls of his feet toward them.

"Here. I'll get it for you."

The girls grinned at each other and giggled.

As I watched, it struck me that I was going to have to let go of my uncertainty about co-ed dorms. Lilly had earned my trust. She knew right from wrong. She'd been privy to my struggles, and her sister's as well. I had to believe she'd make good choices.

Older sister Serena dashed out of the elevator, hugged Lilly, hugged Amy, then bounded toward me and crushed me to her chest. "You look great, Mom."

Callie walked out of the room. "What about me?" She spread her arms.

"Hi, Miss Callie. You look great, too. You really do," she added, folding her into a hug. "You've lost half of yourself."

"Stress does that," she remarked.

Serena gave me a look. I responded with a tiny shake of my head. *Don't engage.*

Serena, all puffed up with the aura of junior-in-college status, told us that as a member of the Debate Club, she was helping freshmen move in all around campus, but wanted to say hello. After a few minutes, she dashed away. My beautiful, blond, green-eyed daughter had finally chosen a major. Political Science. She'd interned this summer in Richmond's capitol building.

After my experience with Dylan Palmer, I couldn't be more depressed about it.

However, I knew that my strong, blunt, outspoken daughter would excel in a political career…if she could endure getting her feelings bashed in every other week.

Two hours later, we'd crammed boxes and luggage into every corner of the small room. Callie and I lingered until the small talk disintegrated into awkward silence. Callie swiped at her cheeks. We hugged our daughters with vicious devotion and made promises to stay in touch.

After a quick bite of dinner and pep talks about empty-nesting, I waved goodbye to Callie as she headed back to Glyndon, downcast and daughter-less. My cell shimmied in my pocket. I pulled it out. Mom. "You get the girls all tucked in?"

"Yeah."

"How's it feel?"

"Awful."

She laughed. "Give it time. It'll get better. When will you be over? Do you want me to have something ready to eat?"

"Callie and I had dinner here on campus." I cleared my throat. "Hunter wants to have a drink. So I'll be late."

Two-second pause. "Sounds good, honey. Tell him hello. I'll leave the back door open. Your room is all ready. He is coming tomorrow, isn't he?"

"I'll confirm, Mom. One p.m., right?"

We ended the call. I leaned against my car and took a last look at Richmond University's historic, beautiful campus. Redbrick buildings, beautifully landscaped lots with tons of azaleas. This campus would be gorgeous in spring. Thunderclouds bordered the horizon as the sun began its descent. A light sprinkling of rain dotted the sidewalk. My jaw dropped as I watched a rainbow emerge from the clouds in a burst of color. A wink from God, Mom would say. Reassurance that my girls...and my heart...were safe.

Chapter Forty-Five

The hammering in her head caused little rainbow explosions behind her eyes.

She lifted one eyelid. Gentle lighting created halos around blurry objects. Hazel felt an immense relief. Had she died? A soft voice called her name. A warm hand patted her arm. Angels?

"Hazel, honey," the voice said. "You're okay. You're in a hospital. How do you feel?"

Hazel looked into the warm, blue eyes of Sherry. She knew Sherry. Didn't she?

"Do you know my name?"

It took her a second. "Sherry." She swiveled her head, confused. "What happened?"

"Do you remember anything?"

A beat of silence.

"Tasha."

Sherry's nod was solemn. "Anything else?"

Hazel's forehead creased. "Where's my phone? I need my phone."

"It's here. I've got it. The EMTs would've gotten there faster if…" her voice trailed off. "Thank God for Narcan. We almost lost you."

Hazel squinted. "What?"

"I was about to go outside when the phone rang, and I picked up. I wrote down the address I thought I heard, took Marlowe with me and went to check it out." Sherry closed her eyes, wrapped her arms across her chest. "Hazel, you were in a chair in the living room with a needle in your arm and drug paraphernalia scattered on the floor. I freaked out. That fire investigator was there. Tasha." Sherry smiled. "I think I surprised her. She flopped around like a fish trying to explain she'd found you like that, and I wasn't buying it. Yeah, like you injected yourself with H, a woman of good standing in the community and no connections to drugs." Sherry shook her head. "When she came at me, Marlowe went nuts. He took a chunk out of her leg. The police arrested her. They want to talk to you when you can."

Hazel's lower lip trembled.

"I covered up the birds in the cage when I left."

"Thank you," she said.

Marlowe whined and licked Hazel's hand.

She stared at Sherry. "How'd you get him in here?"

"He's a service dog." She put a finger to her lips. "Shhh."

Hazel smiled. "I couldn't call 9-1-1 because Tasha's so well-connected... why would they believe an old lady? She's been a voice on the news for years when fire investigations are going on. No one would've believed she'd done such a thing." She stared at Sherry in wonder. "I believe in miracles, now."

She patted Hazel's hand. "I'm going to put off telling Olivia until she's on her way back. She deserves some undisturbed family time. Is that okay with you?"

Hazel struggled to a sitting position and plumped the pillows. Leaned back and crossed her arms. "Good call."

"Then it's unanimous. We'll be the two musketeers."

Chapter Forty-Six

"How'd it go with the girls?" Hunter grabbed his napkin and placed it in his lap.

Olivia's gaze took in the jazz trio playing, the romantic décor, the intimacy of the restaurant. "I thought you'd like it here," Hunter said, thinking she'd grown more beautiful since that first interview at her home. He'd never forget the way she looked standing in the foyer, shadows from lit candles flickering across her features. Helpless. Vulnerable. And gorgeous. So thin he'd wanted to fatten her up. Had it been love at first sight? After three years, he had to admit that maybe it had been.

"This looks delicious." Olivia picked up her fork. "I'm relieved she has you, Mom and Gray, and her older sister. When I get home, the empty-nest thing will hit me, full force. Right now, I'm numb." She shook her head. "I'm glad I have a couple of days with Mom and Gray."

Hunter held up his draft beer. "And me."

Olivia blushed. Picked up her wine glass and joined the toast. "Of course. Especially you."

After they'd finished, the server whisked the plates away. Olivia folded her hands on the table, threw him a look. "What next?"

"Surprise." He extended his hand. They walked outside to his Jeep. A full moon illuminated the parking lot and the tidy, redbrick buildings along the block.

Olivia watched the landscape slide by as he drove. She had a different air about her tonight. Maybe she'd had enough time and counseling to be at peace, Hunter thought.

Ten minutes later, Olivia paused on the front steps bracketed by two white columns and soaring crepe myrtles and glanced at him. "This is the first time I've been to your place."

Hunter smiled. "After three years, we should commemorate the occasion, don't you think?"

Olivia let the unspoken insinuation hang in the air for what seemed a lifetime.

She stood on tiptoe and kissed him. Feeling like an eighteen-year-old on a first date, he held the door open. Olivia walked inside, trailing a scent that left Hunter weak in the knees.

Olivia followed him around the condo as he gave her the tour, then asked if he'd fix her a drink. They sat on the couch, relaxing into a night devoid of pyromaniacs and homicides. When he reached for her, she folded into his body like she belonged there.

"This is nice," he whispered and moved in for another kiss.

During the kiss, she stiffened. A flush appeared on her neck and spread to her cheeks. She stumbled over her words. "I'm sorry, I can't...I can't...." She stared at something over Hunter's shoulder, started pumping the air with her fists. "Leave me alone...."

"Oh no," Hunter breathed.

One of her fists caught him in the chest. He grabbed her arm.

He tried to hold her, but she wrestled him away. As he watched her descend into the past, he felt helpless. Was his presence a trigger? Did she re-live the assault every time he tried to be intimate with her? He watched in horror as she struggled against the attack in her mind. Hunter grabbed pillows, pushed them around Olivia, desperate to keep her from injuring herself. He concentrated as he held onto her. What had caused this?

Wait.

He groaned.

He'd been the one to convince her to visit her attacker's condo in order to trigger memories of the event. Her attacker had lived in Richmond, too, which was the reason he'd gotten involved with Olivia in the first place. Up until then, they hadn't had enough evidence for a search warrant. He'd never thought about it, but his condo had a similar floor plan...which had been the trigger. Not him, the floor plan.

He cursed his ignorance. This could've been prevented.

"Olivia, you're safe. *Safe.* It's not real. It's a flashback."

She kept thrashing. She'd bitten her lip and drawn blood. He started to call 9-1-1, but hesitated. He'd seen this before. Gray Sturgis, her neurosurgeon, had told him the episodes would pass if he'd wait them out.

He propped her on one side, made her comfortable and far away from any objects that could harm her. He held her loosely in his arms as she fought her invisible enemy.

Fifteen minutes passed. Twenty. She fell asleep, little squeals of protest floating from her lips. Breathing in the familiar scent of her, he thought about the superhuman effort he'd put into this relationship. Did he have what it took to persevere? He smoothed her hair, settled in beside her, and watched her drift to sleep.

Chapter Forty-Seven

I muttered angrily to myself in my car on the way to Mom's. Mostly telling myself what a terrible idea it had been to take it to the next level with Hunter.

Still.

I relived the feel of him. Which had, as anticipated, exceeded my fantasies about Sergeant Hunter Faraday. Until I ruined it, of course.

Did we have the potential for a good relationship? Would my past ever let me be? Could I continue to call and ask for advice without diving into the murk of a messy, complicated romance? One thing I knew…I was *not* ready to get married. Or live with anyone. Or whatever, as evidenced by last night's outcome. I wanted to focus on Watchdog Investigations. Hunter would have to be okay with that. At least until my screwed-up past stopped interrupting the clarion call to a less screwed-up future.

I smacked my hand on the steering wheel in frustration. I could have pivoted. Gotten in my car and driven to Mom's…a much easier and less complicated decision. One that would not have resulted in another damn flashback—and my complete and total humiliation. Hunter had been understanding, but butterflies hit my stomach thinking about it. Nice way to mess up a romantic evening, that's for sure.

Memories of the assault had definitely diminished, but certain triggers brought them back. The images swirled through my mind. I squeezed my eyes shut and tried to shake them away.

His hands took on a life of their own, unbuttoning, unzipping, tugging off my shoes, insistent. Alarms clanged through every dulled sense. Had he put something in the wine?

"No!" I pushed him away, but it was like pushing through wet cement. "No!" The man backed up. His laughter chilled me to the bone. I blinked, but my eyes wouldn't focus. Was this really happening?

The images dissipated. My body relaxed.

What was the saying? About regret? I had enough regret to last a thousand lifetimes.

I jerked my car into Mom's driveway. Sat there with both hands on the wheel, staring straight ahead, willing myself to block out the past. My mind raced. My heartbeat pounded at my temples. *Calm down. It'll be okay.*

But it wasn't okay, and I'd just added a ton of ballast to the simmering cauldron of meltdown stew when I got home. Mom opened the door, a question on her face. "Olivia?"

With a sigh, I forced the thoughts aside and locked them up. Told myself to live in the moment. Or something.

I hoped Mom would forego the obvious teasing about my overnight with Hunter.

I trotted up the short sidewalk to the entrance of her condo. A smile played with her mouth. Her eyes twinkled.

I pushed past her. "Don't even think about it," I tossed over my shoulder as I took my luggage to the room she'd prepared for me. The last thing in the world I wanted to discuss with my mother was last night's debacle.

Her puzzled look followed me down the hall. "For your information, I wasn't going to ask," she called after me.

When Lilly, Amy, and Serena arrived, Mom and I had pretty much shored up preparations. The girls dove in to put pans of food in ovens, set the table, the timers, and start loading the dishwasher. Gray nagged me to step away for a quick exam.

"Promise it'll be quick?"

"No promises."

I followed him into the master bedroom. "What did my last MRI show? It was good, right?" Gray took out a penlight, shone it in each eye. Told me to turn my hands up, then down. "Your brain continues creating new neural pathways in astonishing ways." He shook his head. "I need to schedule another EEG to make sure, but I see no reason we can't do simple annual check-ups from here on in."

As we finished the perfunctory reflex and motor skill stuff, he asked about dizziness, headaches, blurred vision. Nausea. Ringing in my ears.

Nope, nope, and nope. Except for the stress-related headaches, and coffee took care of that. "I rarely have episodes anymore, Gray." *Except for that little blip with Hunter on the couch, and I'm keeping that to myself.*

He offered his fist. I bumped it with my own.

He smiled, crossed his arms. "Still seeing Hazel?"

I shook my head. "Putting that on pause for now. Besides, I *like* the neurological changes. It makes me…."

"Take unwise risks," he finished. "That's what your mother's worried about."

I dismissed the comment with a flip of my wrist. "Gray, I'm proficient with firearms, I've understudied a darn good private investigator, and I have cop friends in Baltimore County that have my back. You know what the real struggle is? Shedding the 'Mercy's Miracle' persona after my book came out." I shook my head. "My fan club is like a cult. I think we've popped the bubble, though, since their founder is under investigation. I'm hoping the group folds. One less distraction."

"We ready to hit the full celebration experience, then?"

"You bet. Ready for the whole crew. Let's enjoy."

We walked together into the hubbub of chatter, delicious aromas, lilting voices. For a little while, my family was back together.

At one p.m. I answered a knock on the door. Hunter thrust a bottle of red wine at me. "Peace offering."

I took the wine without quite meeting his eyes. "Thanks," I murmured. "Mom will appreciate it."

He gave me a gentle hug, tilted my chin up with his finger. "We'll work it out, okay? I figured out my place has a floor plan like Niles Peterson's. That's what threw you back."

My mother swept down the hall, bracelets jangling, her floral scent basting the air. Gray came out of the kitchen and gave him a manly side-hug. Obviously, Hunter was, as Mom put it, 'part of the family.' Whether we worked out or not, I was stuck with him.

I held the bottle up. "Who wants wine?"

Later that afternoon, when everyone was full and sleepy, I tugged Mom away.

We withdrew to the patio. "What is it, honey?"

"Mom, I don't know how to be delicate with this." I cleared my throat. Waited a couple of seconds.

"I found him."

Mom stared at her condo's postage-stamp-sized yard, the manicured hedge dividing her yard from her neighbor's. Her bird feeders.

"Where?"

"South Dakota. On a reservation."

The clouds slid away from the sun. Reflections from the bright tile patio table between us danced across our faces.

"How did you find him?"

I shook my head. "Doesn't matter. He's been in and out of jail for years. You were right not to allow him into our lives. He's a wreck."

"I don't doubt it." She frowned. "Did you tell him?"

I nodded.

"How did he react?"

"Shocked. Horrified. Wanted *nothing* to do with me. It was quite the experience." I bit my bottom lip. "He thought I was a cop or an attorney, and I let him think it. Told him I had a case to close. Mom, he suggested bringing charges against you for attempted murder. I couldn't believe it."

Sophie smiled a sad smile. "I'd hoped to spare you that experience. I'm sorry, honey."

"He said some other stuff, Mom."

She was quiet.

"Tell me about you and Tom."

A vein throbbed in her temple. She fidgeted with her hands. "Did Sonny bring that up?"

"Let's just say...he wasn't subtle about certain...indiscretions."

"He had anger issues. Tom was scared for me."

"I'm sure."

Mom gulped in a breath, and then the words tumbled out. "Tom and I were involved. I figured you assumed as much. You know, I can't remember why I broke it off with him, but I was pretty wild back then. Dependable and responsible men didn't appeal to me." Mom threw a clump of her reddish mane over one shoulder. "Isn't that pathetic?" She sighed.

My thoughts flew to one of the Wine & Whine group discussions—when we'd laughed about the fact that 'boring' was a far better place to be than catastrophe. After our shared experiences with violence or narcissism or nasty divorces, we counted 'boring' as a triumph.

"Sonny was different. Exciting. Ready to take on the world. We fell hard for each other, and I broke it off with Tom and married Sonny five weeks later. Tom begged me not to do it. I laughed at him. The thought of his expression...." She shook her head. "It sickens me, now...how I treated Tom. When Sonny's *real* self showed up, I knew I'd made a mistake. But we'd gotten pregnant by then, and you know the rest. I tried to hang in there, but he was a monster. I'm not surprised he hasn't changed."

An awkward silence fell.

"I'm sorry for digging this all up again, Mom. It can't be easy to think about." After she'd poured out her soul, how do I bring up my next question? I guess I just ask it.

"I hope you understand why I need to ask this, but are you sure that Sonny's my father?"

She smiled sadly. "No way around it, honey. Yes, I'm sure."

"Don't you think if we shared biology, I'd feel something? He disgusted me. I felt pity, yeah...but since the TBI, I have this...intuition times a thousand. I didn't even get a tiny ping from the guy. I see why Grandpa got involved.

His father's heart knew our lives were on the line."

Sophie teared up. "I couldn't hide the bruises anymore. I was afraid I'd end up in the hospital. Tom was desperate to help me. He told me Dad approached him with a plan." She groaned. "They tried to keep me out of it. I put the pieces together after someone told me Sonny had been assaulted. My understanding is that he almost died. After that, he disappeared. Years later, Tom told me the whole story. It was very hard for him. I begged him to go to the police, but he refused. He was afraid all of us would end up in jail. He decided the lesser of two evils was to suck it up. He handled Dylan's dirty work for years." She folded her arms and stared out into the yard. He wouldn't talk about it after that. He had his life, and I had mine." She smiled. "How do you think Dylan ended up in political office? He couldn't have done it without Tom's help."

"Dylan had his day of reckoning, Mom. Hunter and I split our investigation on election day—one of us at Dylan's polling place and one at Scott Waymire's. It had become a war of the titans or something, and we wanted to…I don't know, be there to help if things went sideways."

Sophie squinted. "What happened? I saw headlines, but they didn't register."

"Dylan's wife tore after him across a field, swinging a revolver and screaming out all his sins. It was like…a scene from a movie." I shook my head. "She was all over social media with memes, opinions, polls. I can find some of it if you want to see. It's terrible, and I'm sure he drove her to it, but she shot his ass. Two to the chest."

She gasped. "And you were right in the middle of it."

"Hunter was in the middle of it, Mom. I was there afterward. Anyway, that's not the point. Can you imagine? If Dylan blackmailed Tom his whole life, what do you think he did to his wife? He had a secret life, multiple affairs, and I bet that was just the tip of the iceberg." I stared out into her yard, beyond the hedges to a small lagoon. "Do you believe in karma?"

Mom looked as if she'd aged ten years. "I believe we reap what we sow. Isn't that the same thing?"

We sat in silence.

Chapter Forty-Eight

I ticked off the closures in my head as I drifted down my lovely lane underneath the tree canopy: Pete was in a holding cell awaiting trial. The judge had cautiously withheld bail.

Dylan Palmer wouldn't ruin anyone's life again. His wife had reportedly pled 'not guilty by reason of insanity,' and her lawyer negotiated bail and an ankle bracelet. Good for her, I thought. If anyone deserved mercy, my money would be on her. I made a mental note to burn all the 'B' files and perform a happy dance while they burn on behalf of Tom.

Sherry had not called me with a single crisis during my weekend in Richmond, thank goodness. I'd had enough on my plate with the emotional experience of moving Lilly into the dorm and later, the painful revelations from my mother. Perhaps I can give that crappy piece of my past a proper burial.

My mind whiplashed to the remaining unresolved item: Hunter. I put him on my virtual shelf to think about.

I parked my car and sat there enjoying all the warm feels of being back in my space with relatively uncluttered spaces in my head. Two days away, and a change of scenery had rebooted me.

My cell vibrated. I pressed 'answer' on the car's display. Sherry's voice bubbled out. "Are you back?"

"Just pulled in. Sitting in the car."

"Okay. I'll give you some time. Call me after you're unpacked."

With the teensiest bit of regret, I responded, "You can tell me."

"Hazel is fine. I want to make sure you know that up front."

My stomach fizzed. I put my hand over my eyes.

"Tasha's in custody."

My eyebrows shot up. "For what?"

"Look. You go ahead and get settled. I'll be here."

"Yeah, that's not happening. I'll be there in ten seconds."

I shot down the lane, jerked my vehicle into Watchdog's parking lot, and rocketed from the car. "Tell me."

She threw beagle eyes at me. "I tried to give you some time."

"When did this happen?'

"Hazel and I made a pact…."

"A pact about what?"

Sherry chuckled. "We didn't want to spoil your weekend. Anyway, the important thing is that Pete was Tasha's boyfriend. I could never have guessed that. And also a firebug. A pyro." She waited for me to digest these nuggets.

I thought about the way Pete had studied fire when I'd run across him on-site. The way he scrutinized Tasha when they spoke. Her expression softening as he walked up to us at Hazel's home after the blaze had been controlled. Tasha and Pete bonded over a mutual love of fire, maybe? It made sense.

"So," I began, thinking aloud. "Pete the pyro decides to volunteer on the ground and legitimize his obsession. Tasha, the arson investigator, became interested in Pete because *she* thought he was legit."

Sherry's voice dropped to a whisper. "Hazel told me that Tasha thought she could fix him." She shuddered. "All to say…it's bizarro-world. What do you bet that when they first hooked up, she didn't know?"

I nodded. "She couldn't have. I hope she didn't…the things women do for a hot guy amaze me."

"She was probably so preoccupied with how he looked that she believed everything he told her."

"You think he told her the truth? That he was struggling?"

"She told Hazel, and I quote, 'he was getting a handle on it.' So he told her, and she believed he was getting better. She blamed Hazel for getting him off track." Sherry shrugged. "She had to blame someone, I guess."

My head spun. I ran this puzzle piece through my filter. This factoid fit neatly into a gaping hole in the investigation. She'd been either avoiding Pete, trying to pin the fire on Pete, or working to distance herself from Pete. Either way, she was a linchpin.

Sherry's big, blue eyes twinkled. "Hazel recorded everything Tasha confessed. I may have forgotten to mention that Hazel's in the hospital, but it's cautionary. They're making sure all the drugs are out of her system."

I laid a hand against my breastbone and closed my eyes. "Drugs?"

Sherry prattled on about the fact that Tasha had injected her with heroin. This was old news to her, and she'd adjusted to the shock. I hadn't. But it made sense that if she wouldn't take the mystery sauce poison voluntarily, Tasha would force something.

"I texted you the recording and made some hard copies. The recording is our little secret." She winked. "I know it's inadmissible."

I started to breathe again. "So Hazel's okay?"

"She's *so* proud of herself, Olivia." Sherry laughed.

I tapped my chin. "Pete was getting too close to Hazel, and Tasha was willing to lose her career over it?" I couldn't figure out what I was missing.

"Some things defy explanation," Sherry said.

Marlowe entered reception, stretched, came up to me, and licked my hand. Plopped down beside me. "Hi, buddy," I scratched his head.

I tapped the armrest of the chair with my fingers. "Tasha was front and center at all those fires in the area. Maybe she knew all along? That he was doing it?"

Sherry lifted her hands. "She missed it by a mile. Pete was obsessed with *you*, not Hazel. If he got close to Hazel, he got close to you. Someone must've given him a tip. Or...whatever. I don't think your therapist's identity was some big secret. But what I want to know is...who wanted information about you and why? Did he want to post it in the Foofoo group? I don't get it." She huffed. "Remember when we were at dinner that night? How he looked at you? It was weird. You didn't notice how creepy he was, the way he couldn't tear his eyes off you?"

I stared out the window. "When I tracked him to Hazel's that first time, I heard a woman's voice on the phone. Pete and this woman were talking about something that involved the fires." I snapped my fingers. "He asked her if she knew my place had burned. I'd forgotten about that."

Suddenly, Pete's face floated in front of my eyes. His lips formed the words 'left a message in your attic.' "Oh, no," I whispered.

Sherry and I piled in my car, drove down the lane, and walked upstairs to the attic. I stared at the attic opening in the ceiling. My hands were sweaty.

"Have you been up there since the fire?" Sherry asked.

"Yeah," I said, pulling on the cord. The staircase gave a mighty scream, then descended in foldable sections. I made sure it seated securely and started up. The smell of new wood and insulation wafted from the room.

Riot ambled out to see what was going on.

The lighting I'd had installed in the attic blinded us when I flipped the switch. We divided the space, and I explained that Pete had called it a 'message.' It could be a note or written in blood or staked to the wall with a knife, for all I knew. We crept through our assigned areas. Five minutes later, Sherry muttered, "Come look at this."

I picked my way across boxes, lamps, extra flooring, and rolled-up insulation left over from the fire repairs. Sherry had found a dried-up, fragile bouquet of daffodils and daisies. With shaking fingers, I pulled the envelope out of the bouquet. Dried leaves and petals crumbled to the floor. The card read: 'The beauty of fire reminds me of you. Love, a dedicated Foofoo'. The small envelope held something else. I pulled it out. A necklace? I showed it to Sherry.

She studied it silently. "It's a twin flame necklace. Twin flames are supposed to reflect a rare connection between two soulmates. They represent two halves of the same soul." I held the necklace in my hands, wondering at all the planning, obsession, and pure evil behind this tiny talisman. I started shaking. Sherry took it away from me. "I'll get rid of it, Olivia," she whispered. "He's going away for a long time, honey. And look, there's something else. She pointed at the wall.

Above the flowers, Pete had scrawled the letters A – G – A – T – H – A on the wall. I sounded them out. Agatha. My jaw dropped.

My pulse pounded in my ears. "It's my agent," I croaked. Sherry's eyes rounded into dinner plates. "The voice from the car, Sherry. It was my agent, *Agatha.*"

Chapter Forty-Nine

Four weeks later

Mom had been right about things getting better.

Patting on the last touches of foundation, I took a minute to notice the lack of shadows under my eyes, the recently touched-up roots, the fresh dimension I'd added to my platinum curls. My hair reached to my shoulders now. I liked wearing red lipstick. If I ever went back to my natural auburn, I'd go back to burnt umber and such, but for now, I enjoyed my anonymity as a blonde and my love affair with bright red lips and vibrant colors.

Four weeks had passed since dropping Lilly off at the University of Richmond. My life had settled into a nice rhythm. Marlowe now slept with Riot at night, and I'd even caught Riot trying to give Marlowe a bath. Marlowe got irritated and embarrassed and tried to heave himself under the bed to get away.

It made me happy that I had time to notice moments like that.

I trotted downstairs to get my keys. My phone buzzed with my office number. "Morning."

"Morning," Sherry said. "You have a visitor. Are you on the way?"

"Yep. Who is it?"

Slight pause. "Louise Waymire."

My chin jerked a little. "Be right there."

Louise and I shared cautious pleasantries sitting across from each other in my office.

"Good to see you again, *Marla*."

I winced at the use of the fake name.

I blamed Tom. I'd been victimized. At least, that's what I'd tell a jury.

"How's your cat?" I asked.

"He's good. And yours?"

"Stressed. I got a dog."

Louise laughed. "I saw in the news that your agent was complicit in all those mysterious fires. That must've been hard to hear."

This was the last thing I'd thought she'd bring up. "I…I was shocked, of course."

"Peter Hayes," she blurted. "He was the pyro, right?" She shook her head. "What a story. Maybe they'll make a movie. You can write another book." Her smile was thin.

What was on this woman's mind? Her visit was so random.

"You seem to have a knack for attracting people that take life, uhh…to the extreme," she added.

"Yes…it was hard to hear. Unbelievable."

"Did you ever talk to her about it?" Louise asked. "I wouldn't have. I would've let her rot in prison without a word."

"I did talk to her. I needed to hear her version." I gritted my teeth, thinking about the conversation. "She used the word 'overreach,'" I said, with a touch of sarcasm. "She'd gotten involved with the Friends of Olivia online fan base, and things went downhill from there. She was desperate for another book. I think she'd already made promises to publishers…anyway, desperate people do stupid things." I shrugged. "I terminated the relationship."

"Sounds like a soapy documentary with a lot of unanswered questions. You know, like one of those 'based on true events' series where you never know what really happened?"

My neck tingled. *What did that mean?* I changed the subject. "Congrats on Scott's win, by the way."

"Thanks. We're separated now, but I guess I should take some credit for supporting him even though things got...complicated." She crossed her legs. Her foot jiggled.

Moisture collected on my forehead.

"Condolences on losing your client," she whispered, staring at the Carroll County Times between us on the coffee table. News about Dylan's dramatic death and secret life had been plastered all over the front page for weeks. "Dylan Palmer, I mean."

Why would she bring that up?

"Dylan was Tom's client, not mine. I completed the investigation that he began. I no longer work with politicians."

A beat of silence flickered between us.

"What can I do for you, Louise?"

She lowered her chin an inch at a time, scrutinizing me. "You completed *Tom's* investigation, even after he died. What, because you gave him your word? You abide by a moral code, then?"

"I guess."

She put both feet on the floor. Her nostrils flared.

She had my full attention.

"Were you thinking about that code when you took those photos of me and handed them off to Dylan?"

I registered her clipped tones and watched in fascination as she rose from her chair and jabbed her index finger in my face. Her voice escalated.

"When you *lied* about the purpose of your visit for a story in some mystical publication? Let's see...." Her light-blue eyes grew icy. "Did that morality come into play when I lost my reputation? My marriage? My job?"

The photos that Hunter had taken. They'd come back to bite me. My mom would call this a 'come to Jesus' moment. My voice hushed, I responded, "I was working a case." I ticked off points on my fingers and pushed aside my encroaching panic. "You were in a public place when the photos were taken. I did not take the photos. Watchdog Investigations wasn't in existence when Tom died, and my firm had nothing to do with it. Tom had already set up the meeting with you, and I honored his wishes to comply with what he'd planned." I cleared a lump in my throat. "I'm sorry for the hurt it caused you."

She laughed. "Ah, yes. The man who stumped for my husband with a flyer acting like a door-to-door volunteer for the election even though it wasn't even his district. I didn't make the connection until later that he worked with you. You didn't take the pictures, but you sent someone to do it. Same thing."

At least she hadn't recognized Hunter as a cop.

"And for the record, you kick-started the process, but Scott and I were headed for divorce, anyway."

"I'm sorry to hear that."

We stared at each other.

Louise's jaw clenched. "I was doing good work, you know. I'm poison now. No good to anyone here, thanks to the photos. The rumors. The articles. They'll have to send me somewhere else, but they're not sure about that, either."

Her glare was so vicious I thought I might vaporize on the spot. "I don't know how those photos got out, Louise. I swear."

"I was saving women's lives. Children's lives." She sighed. "As a moronic side note, Dylan and I had become...involved. But you took care of that, too, didn't you? Even if it hadn't worked out, we still..." she turned away, flicked a tear off her cheek. "We still cared deeply for each other."

My shock must've shown in the way my eyes bugged out of their sockets. "He was the affair," I whispered, remembering Hunter's trek to follow Louise and the sexy shots of her with a guy. Had that been Dylan?

Louise's eyes sizzled. "He'd be *alive* if your investigation hadn't made headlines, do you realize that? I think I could've dealt with all the fallout from the photos of me, ill-advised though they were...but Dylan? He lost it. As far as he was concerned, I was a whore, and he never looked back. Then the photos came out of him with a *guy*."

A rock dropped into my stomach. We'd never released those photos to anyone but Dylan. Who got hold of them? How?

I blew out a breath. "He was gay, Louise. He liked men."

Seriously? That's all I could think to say.

"Maybe he was bi," I added in a nod to sensitivity.

Enraged, she drew close enough to scream in my face. "He wasn't gay!"

I thought about bear attacks. Or was it enraged dogs? Something about staying still and not looking them in the eyes.

"There are hundreds of apps to fake that kind of thing." She paced around my office. I heard someone leave through the front door. "Maybe someone set him up." She threw her arms up in the air. "The point is, he was *not* gay."

"They weren't fake. That's pathetic, though. That he'd call you a whore when he was—"

"Shut up!" Her hand dipped into her purse, and pulled out a small-caliber firearm.

A jolt of realization struck. *She hadn't known about Dylan's other affairs until the story broke. Dylan had conned her, too.*

I sprang from my chair, desperate to reach my weapon.

She fired.

I felt a burning in my right shoulder. I tried to run. Marlowe barked from the back bedroom. With considerable regret, I remembered closing him in there. I zigzagged in the way I'd been taught to avoid a shooter, but there wasn't much room in my office to zig or zag.

Another shot. A nip and a burn hit my leg.

I fell, my eyes wide in surprise. I hadn't expected my life to end this way. Shadows hovered at the corners of my eyes.

My old friend Oblivion opened up his arms and sucked me down a long, dark tunnel.

I heard another shot. Then another. My eyelids blinked once, twice, then nothing.

Chapter Fifty

Three days later

Waking up in a hospital without knowing why is not for the faint of heart. And definitely not twice in a lifetime.

At least this time, I wasn't paralyzed.

It took a few seconds, but the memory returned. Fresh and hard-edged and terrifying.

Soft, velvety morning light floated through the room. I checked out all my body parts, fingers pausing on my right shoulder bandage and my upper thigh bandage. I frowned. Another damn healing journey. I was tired of healing. I wanted to start living.

I turned my head right and left, which sent a zing of pain through my shoulder, but no dizziness, ergo, no concussion. A nurse stepped in and told me to rest. I looked up into her face, opened my mouth to speak, and promptly passed out.

The next time I opened my eyes, my mother and Serena, Lilly, and Hunter had gathered in my room at Carroll Hospital Center in Westminster.

Mom approached. "How are you, honey?"

"How long have I been out?"

"Three days."

"What happened to Louise?"

Hunter walked to the other side of the bed. I offered my hand, he took it in his larger, warm one and squeezed. "She's here. Not expected to survive."

I frowned. That didn't make sense. Louise was the one who shot me, not the other way around. I tilted my head toward the window. The sunset was glorious. "The sun looks like it's on fire," I murmured.

"It is," Lilly said, matter-of-fact. "Science."

"What happened? I was sure I was dead. I only found two bandages. I heard more shots. Did she miss?"

Hunter pulled his chair closer to the bed. "Sherry heard what was happening, went out the front door, and ran around through the back. Got the gun from the safe."

I frowned. "*Sherry* shot Louise?"

Mom nodded. "Louise died a few minutes ago. I heard the nurses talking about it."

I closed my eyes.

As if reading my mind, Mom said, "You are not *responsible*."

"This has to stop," I whispered, my mind floating around in la-la land on pain meds. "That stupid book. It made me a...what's the word?" I frowned. "Martyr? Target? I hope that group is disbanded now." I groaned. "Sherry will have a hard time working through this."

"Sherry will be okay," Hunter said, rubbing my arm.

Tension etched itself across Lilly and Serena's faces. "Girls. I'm fine. This is not like three years ago, okay? I'm good. I remember everything. Don't worry."

"Your mom's getting out tomorrow, girls," Mom told them. "I'm staying at her house a while to keep an eye on her, okay?"

Serena put her arm around her younger sister. Lilly's lips trembled. She wiped her cheeks.

My cell buzzed. Hunter answered it. He handed it to me. "Sherry," he whispered.

"Hey."

"Hi there, glad you're awake. How do you feel?"

"Grateful. I...I can't imagine what—"

"I did what I had to do. You'd do the same, Olivia," she interrupted.

"Maybe," I joked. Floating like a seagull in a stiff ocean breeze, I mused, "I'm thinking about fire, Sherry."

"Okay. Why?"

Pete's words ran through my mind. *Fire purges evil so we can start over.* I don't know why this phrase stuck in my head.

"My past. I need to make a funeral pyre. Like the Vikings." My eyelids fluttered. The drugs made me sleepy. "Burn the ships. Burn everything."

"I'm going to repeat that back when the meds are out of your system, and you can explain what that means," she joked. "Well, I have something in my hand that's worth a look back, and then you can light the flaming torches. I got your DNA results, but they're in a sealed envelope, do you want me to—"

I forced my eyelids apart. "Open it." An envelope ripped. Paper unfolded.

She gasped.

"What?" I cried.

She said words, but they didn't register.

I blinked.

"Wait. Say that again." I put the phone on speaker and lay it on the bed.

"You are not a match for Sonny Pellegra."

Mom's hands flew to her mouth.

"*Tom* was your father," she said, her voice soft.

Mom's lips twisted. I thought she was going to faint. "Mom, are you okay?" She nodded, looking a bit green.

I returned to the call. "Then I'm not the product of an alcoholic scumbag abuser?" I threw Mom a look of apology. She smiled.

"No, girl. You are not the product of an alcoholic scumbag abuser."

I thought about Tom's gentle ways, his kindness, the way he'd referred to me as 'gal' in a loving voice. I wonder if he'd suspected. I thought about our two intense years together and the way he'd mentored me with such fervor. Such encouragement. My smile grew wider. I'd known—really known—my dad. I wasn't a throwaway, after all.

I rolled the great news around on my tongue. "Not Sonny. Tom," I whispered. "Thanks, Sherry." With a jolt, I remembered that Sherry must be reeling from her experience. I grabbed the phone, took it off speaker, and cradled it to my ear. "How are you handling the shooting? Are you okay?"

I listened to her spell out all the reasons why she was fine. Rocked by shooting someone, but okay. We promised we'd unpack it later, when I got out of the hospital. I saw no point in telling her that Louise had died. She'd find out in time. We ended the call.

The regret I saw on Mom's face tugged at my heart. "Mom. Did they even have DNA tests in 1980? How could you have known?"

After my visitors left, I lay in bed, reliving Sherry's words. Tom. Not Sonny. Tom. Not Sonny. I focused on the fact that we'd had two solid, devoted years together. I would treasure them forever. His funeral, while tragic, had been a celebration of his life, and I'd felt privileged to be a part it, and now I was learning...that I was part of *him.* His DNA inhabited my body, and furthermore, it blew my mind that I, as his daughter, had inherited his investigation business as my birthright. No wonder I'd chosen private investigation as a career. It had been eerie how Tom read my mind, and now I knew why. I had a heritage I could be proud of and validation of my purpose. I hugged this truth tight against my chest like a favorite pillow.

Hunter quietly rapped on the door and walked in.

"You're back," I said.

"Like a boomerang," he smiled. "I'm headed to Richmond in the morning, but I wanted to check in one more time. So. Good day, huh?" He sat beside me on the bed.

I reached for his hand. "Now it's perfect."

A Note from the Author

I wrote this installment of Olivia Callahan's life as a nod to the woman she is becoming as she finalizes putting the puzzle pieces of her new life together. She clings to the parts of her past that are powerful and good and begins the journey of laying aside the parts that are painful. This is never an easy task, and even more complicated for Olivia since her memory is compromised. She's had to reconstruct her past one step at a time.

As a backdrop to the suspense of this story, questions lurk that are common to us all. Why do we so often hang onto pain from our past that keeps us from becoming all that we can be? Why do we allow ourselves to live with depression or fear about something that may have happened decades ago? I don't know the answer to those questions, but I hope this story is encouragement to let go of a painful past and hold onto a bright and powerful future.

Acknowledgements

A book is a collaboration, and there are many people that poured time into this story. My editor's time and developmental insights made this book better. Thank you, Harriette Sackler of Level Best Books, and thanks also to Shawn Simmons, copyeditor of this manuscript. My family of beta readers, Brian Thiem, Bonnie Miller, and Nina Wachsman, were all instrumental in shaping the story as well. Thank you for your time and pivotal comments. Additional thanks to my husband for putting up with my writing-cave time, my short temper around deadlines, and helping with my events. You are such a trooper, and I couldn't do this without you. I also thank my writer colleagues at Level Best Books for the reviews and blurbs and hand-holding that is sometimes needed! You are all my cheerleaders, as I am yours. I hope we share many publishing milestones together. My gratitude also to Firefighter Matthew Emison of Hilton Head Fire Rescue, for the time he took talking with me about the day-to-day business of firefighting. I found it fascinating. And most of all, thank you to my readers, who make the hard work so worthwhile. I hope *The Torching* ignites your imagination and burns its way into your heart.

About the Author

Kerry Peresta is the author of the Olivia Callahan Suspense series, Level Best Books. She is currently working on the fourth and fifth books in the series and a standalone domestic suspense novel. Kerry spent thirty years in advertising as an account manager, creative director, copywriter, and editor. She began writing full-time in 2009 as a humor columnist for a daily newspaper, and in 2012, became chapter president of the Maryland Writer's Association. After moving to Hilton Head Island, SC in 2015, Kerry joined the Island Writers Network, the Sisters in Crime organization, South Carolina Writers Association, International Thriller Writers, and became a presenter for the Pat Conroy Literary Center. Kerry and her husband enjoy kayaking, road trips, their grandkids, their two cats, Felix and Agnes; and the scenic marshes of the Lowcountry. Find out more about Kerry at kerryperesta.net.

SOCIAL MEDIA HANDLES:

https://www.twitter.com/kerryperesta

https://www.instagram.com/kerry.peresta
https://www.facebook.com/klperesta
https://www.facebook.com/kerryperesta

AUTHOR WEBSITE:
https://www.kerryperesta.net

Also by Kerry Peresta

The Rising, Book Two in the Olivia Callahan Suspense series, published March, 2022

The Deadening, Book One in the Olivia Callahan Suspense series, published February, 2021

The Hunting, women's fiction, published November, 2013

CPSIA information can be obtained
at www.ICGtesting.com
Printed in the USA
BVHW041703090423
662014BV00001B/5

9 781685 123239